CAPTIVE

Jan Prestopnik

Best Wishes!
Jan Prestopnik

CAPTIVE

- a novel -

This book is a work of fiction. Events, names, incidents, and locales are products of the author's imagination or are used fictitiously. Any resemblance to actual events, locales, or persons, living or dead, is entirely coincidental.

CAPTIVE Copyright © 2014 by Jan Prestopnik

*To my father & mother,
David W. & Eloise H. Sponenberg,*

How could I love you more?

> "Silent, and soft, and slow
> Descends the snow."

Longfellow

Prologue

SHE WAS STARTLED AWAKE by the unmistakable crash of broken glass hitting the floor. Terrified, she stole silently from her bed, peered cautiously through the bedroom doorway, and crept into the living room of the cabin.

Slivers of ice and glass from the broken window glinted in the soft light of the lamp she'd left burning. She stood still, her gaze riveted on the big, wet footprints leading away from the window and into the kitchen. The vision of the Grand Marquis assaulted her again; it had hit her car and careened into a snowbank. Again she saw the face of the furious driver, then his tall frame tracking hurriedly away down the snowy road, no glance back, head ducked against the pelting snow.

She closed her eyes in dread and fought the impulse to return to her bedroom and shut the door firmly behind her. She willed herself to forget that she was the only human soul within screaming distance.

Except for the intruder in the kitchen.

The wind roared violently, shaking the rafters.

Breathing unevenly, her hand shaking, she grabbed the iron poker from the fireplace and entered the kitchen.

Chapter 1

LISSA TEA WASN'T PAYING ATTENTION when the silver Grand Marquis sideswiped her on the snow-covered wilderness road. The bitter January wind swirled around her car; the temperature had dropped unexpectedly to zero, even colder if you counted the wind chill factor. And New Yorkers always did count the wind chill. It could make the difference between a crystal, sun-studded winter afternoon and a day in which the wind howled in prolonged screams that turned your blood to ice.

Today was definitely the latter. The radio announcer had informed Lissa, and all who braved the roads on this frosty day, that with the wind chill, temperatures were diving to nearly twenty below. Yet here was Lissa, forcing her car along Rice Road, heading for the mountain cabin that hadn't seen a human face or a warming fire since September.

She peered into the frozen woods with their undisturbed drifts of deep, rippled snow and shivered at the gusts that rocked the little car. Lissa had looked forward to this three-day weekend for months, planning, organizing, shopping for just the right food, packing her warmest clothing and cramming it all into the trunk of her car. Her two former college roommates had been just as excited. It had been too long since she'd seen Pat and Shelly, since they'd exchanged news, laughed together over each other's Facebook pictures, polished off an entire pan of Pat's special-recipe lasagna. In spite of the best of intentions, there'd been no opportunity for a good time together since graduation a year and a half before. All three looked forward to meeting at camp.

"Camp?" Shelly had written when Lissa texted them the invitation. "Like- your family owns a campground?"

"Or are we staying in tents?" Pat's frowning emoticon was disapproving. "Or a hunting camp?"

"No, just camp, like the Adirondack Great Camps," Lissa explained. "Except it's not great; it's small. You know, a little cottage."

"Where?"

"Arrowhead Lake, in the middle of nowhere."

A flurry of surprised, worried and excited emoticons had flooded the group text. Lissa missed her friends and felt eager and happy; the three roommates would finally have some time together again.

When the Grand Marquis hit her, Lissa was so intent on the snow and the cold and her plans that she hadn't really been paying attention. She watched nervously as the big car punched through the snow coming toward her, and she registered shock as it deflected off her front bumper. She reacted instinctively, tightening her hold on the wheel and fighting to control the car.

Numb, she felt herself go into a skid, veered into it until the car righted itself, then pressed the brake, gripping the steering wheel with shaking hands. She breathed deeply to regain her composure and put her car in park with the Grand Marquis inches away. They were probably the only two vehicles for miles around. If something did pass by, it certainly wouldn't hit them; it would be chugging through six or more inches of snow on the road. If her father were here, or her brother. . . . No, she would not think of them, didn't need them.

The Grand Marquis was right beside her, its engine churning and tires spitting up snow. She caught the face of the irate driver, a dark-haired man who glared back at her. He revved his engine and backed up, grinding against the snow, forcing his car through the narrow passage between Lissa and the roadside snowbank. The Marquis managed to plow through the drifts, and through her side mirror Lissa watched it careening south, butchering the drifts, crossing crazily from one side of the unplowed road to the other. She rolled down her window for a better look; snow fell in clumps on her arm. In sick fascination, she saw the Marquis hit an icy patch under the snow and spin wildly for a moment, then right itself and continue on, oblivious to the snow thickening on its wheels and traveling at a speed her stodgy little compact could only dream about.

Inane radio chatter filled her car.

"... *So watch those snowy roads,*" the announcer reminded her genially. *"It's turning into a blizzard out there."*

His co-host glibly replied, *"It sure is, Pete. And we do expect some lines down, too. Seems like a good day to stay in and get the Scrabble board out...."* Both radio personalities cackled like hens.

Lissa glanced down at her hands; they had stopped shaking. She considered whether or not she was able to drive on.

She wished she'd noticed the license plate number of that car. Well, she doubted the hit had done her much damage, and she knew she wasn't interested in seeing the wrath on that man's face again any time soon. She would pretend the accident had never occurred. She leaned back against the fabric upholstery, closed her eyes, and breathed in deeply, listening to the wind bluster. She would not let the minor mishap or the major snowstorm spoil her carefully-wrought plans.

Lissa, a graduate student, had a whole week off; her college roommates, now contributors to the adult working world, were able to join her for a short three days. She had sent her father a cryptic email message, and he had responded in typical fashion. Of course she and her friends could use the camp. Any time. Enjoy.

Lissa frowned as she recalled her first days away from home five-and-a-half years before. The small Pennsylvania college was a haven to which she had eagerly fled, leaving behind the noisy Tea family in their crowded, shabby bungalow in Binghamton.

She had longed to request a single dorm room - privacy, solitude, quiet - but the cost of such luxury was prohibitive. The room she was assigned had obviously been designed for a very cramped two, but would be housing three. It was ten by thirteen feet - she and Shelly and Pat had measured it once - and privacy had been disappointingly nonexistent. The oldest of three brothers and three sisters, Lissa had learned early to cherish whatever stray moments of quiet she could grab for herself. In college, she found they were few and far between. She'd also learned quickly that not only her time and space, but her possessions, too, seemed to belong to everyone.

Pat had started right in borrowing her clothes, her make-up, her CDs; Shelly had followed suit, and Lissa had learned to accept and go along with it or be friendless. She had borrowed back self-consciously at first, made her two best friends in the bargain, and realized what a worthwhile trade-off it was. They had roomed together in unspeakably cluttered and crowded conditions all four years.

She missed their noise and unguarded laughter far more than she had ever missed her family.

Now, in grad school in Albany, she had a neat, tidy campus office of her own and a spacious apartment, too, with little furniture, no clutter, and as much privacy as she could ever want. Yes, loads of privacy. Tons of alone-time. Twenty-four hours a day, seven days a week of solitude. Especially lately. She could thank William for that.

Lissa opened her eyes. She would save it to hash out with Pat and Shelly. They would offer the wisdom of friendship and be on her side. Her breath came more evenly; she felt confident and in control.

She checked her side mirror. The silver car was still grinding through the snow. One day she would own a car like that, big and luxurious, as impressive as it was powerful. She'd have a built-in navigation system, a music system, heated leather seats....

A sickening muffled thud interrupted her thoughts and she looked up to see the silver car angled into the shoulder of Rice Road. It had plowed into a snowbank and stopped against a tree, the passenger side buried and probably crumpled under the weight of the snow.

Lissa leaned back, her heart racing. She had just seen an accident, albeit a minor one. She should go to the Grand Marquis and check on the driver.

The radio announcers' insane jabbering had been replaced by a fanfare of music announcing the local news. *"The town of Gorham was the scene today of a robbery at the Jet Gas Station, resulting in the theft of close to fifteen hundred dollars in this sleepy upstate New York town."* Lissa recalled a family vacation spent in Gorham, packed into a tiny cottage with her five siblings and two parents. They'd rented skis and ice skates and spent a cold, uncompromising three days of forced togetherness that seemed like ten.

"The perpetrator, described as a young Caucasian man, probably in his twenties, escaped on foot with all the cash in the

register, but a witness later spotted him in a light colored, full size sedan. He may have been injured in the-"

Lissa shuddered and impatiently jabbed the radio off. Suddenly, the sweep of wind and pelting of snow sounded very loud and forlorn through the windows of her little vehicle. Tall trees moaned above her. She rolled her window open again, a hairline crack. The moaning was louder, the creaking unmistakable. Quickly, she closed the window. What if one of those trees fell and crushed her car? Could she survive?

Should she get out now?

Nonsense. These trees had been here for a hundred years; they weren't going to fall today.

She glanced at the other car again. She should check out the driver. Every instinct told her to stay in her car and get moving again, but she couldn't just leave an accident scene; the driver could be hurt.

Yet she hesitated, her stomach churning. Rice Road led directly to Gorham, and the Grand Marquis was definitely a full size sedan. She had not liked the look of rage on the driver's face when he had found her vehicle blocking the road. And, anyway, she was weary of helping. She'd had her fill of assisting and helping and taking charge.

There was no movement from the Grand Marquis.

Guilt and fear intermingled as Lissa opened her car door, willing to help if she could. Snow fell from the door and dumped into her car, jabbing icy prickles onto her ankle in its thin sock and low boot. She slumped back inside and closed the door. She'd call the police on her cell first and keep someone on the line. She'd go over and stand at a safe distance to check things out. Then he wouldn't dare try to hurt or abduct her.

God, what if he really was the gas station thief? Suppose he had held up the station with a gun?

She surveyed the icy snowdrifts separating her from the other vehicle, clutched up her cell phone from the front passenger seat, and told herself to punch in 9-1-1 and exit the car, and take one step, then another.

She was saved the trouble.

The Grand Marquis' door opened unexpectedly and the driver exited. His dark jacket was immediately bludgeoned by pelts of snow. He slammed the door, gave the car a furious kick, and began slogging through the drifting snow. It reached halfway to his knees; she couldn't tell if he even wore boots with those jeans. Away he went, head bent against the wind, down the road, and away from Lissa. Away from his car, over a small hill and out of her sight.

Lissa drew in a ragged breath of relief. The silver Marquis squatted several hundred yards away, silent and still, covered in snow and looking like an abandoned Arctic beast. She hadn't seen a passenger; the driver must have been alone, and she felt relieved that there had been no need to go to his rescue after all. He was obviously not hurt. She sat back, suddenly feeling more relaxed. There was nothing she could do for him now that he couldn't do for himself.

She stared at the big car resting in its snowy grave. If this were the getaway car for the robbery in Gorham, the 'light colored, full size sedan' described on the news, she should call the police. She glanced at the thickening snow and knew they'd never be able to get here. And the man had left his car in anger, annoyed that he was delayed on his drive, annoyed at *her*. She stopped those thoughts. He was most likely an innocent man late getting home to his family, and he had merely gone for help with his car- his car, like thousands of other light colored models.

You can't report someone for looking enraged.

Lissa could hear her own teeth chattering. Opening her car had invited in the frigid air, and she hugged herself inside her wool sweater and lightweight cloth coat. Just the thought of emerging from her warm cocoon made her shiver.

She had left Albany right after her last graduate class at noon. She couldn't wait to get off campus, to get away, arrive at the cabin, get things arranged and get the heat turned on and the building comfortable before her guests arrived Saturday morning.

What she needed to do now was get to camp. She had warm clothes in the trunk, along with food and photos and other supplies. It was already three o'clock, and it would be dark in less than two hours. The cabin was just about two miles ahead, and if she concentrated, if she were lucky, perhaps she could coax her car toward Arrowhead Lake and arrive before nightfall. Then she could unload her supplies with daylight lingering.

Her engine was still running. She cranked up the heat

another notch until she felt it pouring onto her feet, put the car in gear and pressed the accelerator gingerly, then harder. She gave a small sigh of relief as the car began to grind forward. Yes, good. Just a careful, steady movement forward. She inched her way sixty yards, a hundred yards, around a bend, and made the gentle turn onto Arrowhead Lake Road with its line of boarded up summer camps. The road was unplowed, of course. A slight uphill loomed ahead, and she prayed that the car would make the crest of the hill. Three hundred yards, five hundred. She passed cold summer cottages and empty driveways evenly coated with snow.

Breathing heavily, Lissa craned her neck and felt the cold prickle her spine. Her back and shoulder muscles ached and her head began to pound as she forced the reluctant wheels farther, just a little farther.

The snow was gathering faster, and her arms throbbed with tension. On a gradual upward slope, Lissa grimaced as the car slowed, bumping gently to the right over icy ruts beneath the surface, hidden scars camouflaged by layered ripples of soft, powdery snow. The ruts took her car, and she yanked the steering wheel back toward the center of the road; the car refused to respond, mocking her efforts. Weary and disgusted, she watched helplessly as the front end of her vehicle plowed smoothly ahead and came to a stop facing north on the side of the road. Her front end passenger side was buried snugly in a three foot roadside snowbank.

She rocked the car gently, then jammed down on the gas pedal, trying to force it. She tried to gun the engine, then coax it, both useless. Her little car was no match for the dense mounds of snow that held it hostage, sucking it gently into a firm white caress.

Lissa sighed in dismay. She was okay, but her car was hopelessly stuck.

Chapter 2

LISSA GLANCED AT HER WATCH. Three-thirty. If she started walking, even if she started right this second, she couldn't make it to camp before dark. The thought of bumbling onward in the thickly falling snow frightened her. The car, buried to its hubcaps, was unlikely to be hit by a snowplow, she reasoned, and some of her groceries would be fine if they froze in the trunk. And would she also survive if she spent the night curled up in her car in a blizzard?

The sky was already darkening to pearl gray, and as soft and lovely as the flakes of snow looked, Lissa felt panic rising in her throat. She twisted around, grabbed her canvas bag of class texts and notes from the back seat, and removed all but the two volumes and notebooks she would need for the reaction paper due in one week. She plucked up her wool hat, scarf, and warm, heavy mittens and put them on. At least she'd had the foresight to pack for a snowstorm; she had listened to the weather and knew snow was expected. But this?

She felt herself frown and blinked back the tears that tried to squeeze from her eyes. Such careful planning! All for nothing. And it had been so long since she'd seen Pat and Shelly. How would they ever get here? She scowled in annoyance, wishing she could control the weather.

Grabbing her snow brush, pulling the key from the ignition, and yanking her cloth coat tight, Lissa exited the car. Her coat whipped around her as an icy blast stung her face. Her low suede boots sank deep into the snow, and she tried to ignore the wet cold slicing through her jeans and sticking them to her ankles and legs. Struggling, she slammed the door and did a cursory check of the area that the Marquis had hit; there was no damage that she could see.

It took only a minute to brush the snow away, insert her key, and open the trunk. She poked through the tightly packed space, found her duffel bag of clothes, her down parka, her wind pants and fur-lined boots. She slammed the trunk shut and scurried back into the car.

The interior was already cooling, and Lissa's teeth began to chatter again as she dressed for the blizzard, tossing her light coat and fancy boots into the back seat. She saw no point in trying to remove the jeans that were already damp, so she cast her mittens aside, wiggled around on the seat, and slipped on wind pants and two pairs of socks. She stuffed the hem of her sweater into the pants, donned a heavy fleece shirt, the jacket and warm boots, then awkwardly tied the jacket's hood firmly under her chin. As she dressed in the shockingly cold clothing, she couldn't help shivering, but her body warmed quickly with the new layers.

Zipping her keys into a pocket, she picked up her phone, exited the car, and jabbed Pat's number. A signal! Intermittent, but viable.

"How's the weather there?" she asked.

"Lissa!" Pat's voice was an interrupted crackle. ". . . just on the phone to Shelly. It's only starting here, but. . . and worse. How is it on. . . ?" Pat's voice disappeared.

"I lost you," Lissa shouted. "Pat, can you hear me?"

"I'm having trouble hearing you," Pat said. "Can you hear me now?"

Lissa maneuvered herself around the car, hoping for a better signal.

". . . snow there?" Pat asked.

"Tons of snow," Lissa said. "Don't try to come." She wondered if Pat could hear the disappointment in her voice.

"I can hear you better now," Pat told her.

"I can't even get my car all the way to camp. I'm leaving it in a snowbank, and I'm going to hike in. Once I get in there, I'll be fine, but the roads are impassable. They haven't even plowed. Don't come."

"And you probably have trunkful of food, don't . . ." Pat's voice crackled.

"Lasagna fixings, the Pinot, you know - all the good stuff you told me to get."

Pat groaned. ". . . missing it. . . listen, kid, have an extra slice of lasagna for me. I'll tell Grandma. . . her honor."

Lissa laughed. "I will. You take care now. Call Shelly for me. I've got to get going or they'll be scraping my body off the road during the spring melt."

"I'll call Shelly. Be careful." Pat said.

So that was that. No Pat, no Shelly. No three days with friends. No special memory to be made this pitiful weekend, after all. No discussion of William Brashue and his unwarranted treatment of her lately. It was ironic. She could have been lonely back at her apartment without driving all this way. She'd end up spending the weekend as usual, figuring out how not to go crazy all by herself. Only this weekend, she had to think about surviving, too.

Lissa punched the disconnect button and tossed the phone into the car, pulled her snowy mittens back on, trudged to her trunk, and unlocked it. There was still room in the canvas bag, and she would need supplies when she reached the cabin. An extra pair of jeans, a sweater, her shoes and warm fleece slippers. A small loaf of Italian bread, a hunk of mozzarella. She stuffed them into the bag and looked longingly at the coffee pot. Too cumbersome. And the cans of soup and diced tomatoes would be too heavy. She could hike back out and get more provisions if she needed them, but for now she would take the things that would get her through tonight and at least part of tomorrow. She forced in romaine lettuce and an onion, knowing they would spoil in the trunk. A steak followed. Then, as an afterthought, she slid a slim bottle of Pinot Grigio down the side of the bag.

That was it; nothing else could possibly fit.

Was it enough? She could be stuck for days.

Well, she would empty some plastic grocery bags, triple their thickness, and refill with a few more essentials. She had carried a dozen gallon bottles of fresh water; there would be none at the camp. But they were heavy. She needed water to cook, to drink, to wash with. She could melt snow, she figured, but what a pain. And weren't there impurities in snow? She'd learned that in some science class. She placed one gallon jug into the plastic bags, followed it with more vegetables, ground beef, a box of crackers, matches, a flashlight, and then a handful of tea bags.

She forced items in, more food, extra socks, filling up cracks and crevices until the second bag was as stuffed as the first.

She had as much as she could hope to carry. She probably had more than enough. She hoped so.

Lissa shivered and lifted the two heavy satchels, then hoisted her sleeping bag in its weatherproof stuff sack onto her back. She remembered her purse, still in the car, grabbed it up and hooked it over her arm, then tossed her cell phone on top of the items in the plastic bag.

Could she carry all this two miles? Should she carry more?

No, she told herself firmly. You'll never get there if you make the trek impossible.

By the time she had gone a half mile, she'd decided the whole thing was impossible anyway. Gusts of wind chilled her to the bone, and the exposed skin on her face felt every prick of pelting snow. She glanced behind her at first, wary of the stranger who had plunged down Rice Road. He had headed away from her, in the opposite direction, but the memory of his angry stare made her nervous. The smooth roadway of unbroken snow before her helped convince Lissa that he was far away by now.

As darkness descended, her pace became slower and slower. It was exhausting to try to lift her legs over the drifts of snow and even worse to drag them through. Making her way through even the shallowest places was torture. She fell several times, coating her clothing with snow that stuck to her, and once she dropped the plastic bag from her numbed hand and watched forlornly as items spilled from it and sank deep into the snow.

Crying out in frustration and stiff with cold, Lissa plunged her mittened hand into the snow. She managed to unearth the cheese and onion, brushed most of the clinging snow off them, replaced them in the bag, and began searching for other items. A carrot surfaced, a package of mushrooms. How long would the snow keep up? Wet, white flakes dotted the gray-violet sky. There was no sign of it stopping.

Sniffling back bitter tears, she stooped to see what else she had lost. The loose tea bags had clumped together, splotched and wet. She picked them up awkwardly in one thickly-mittened hand and dropped them in, along with a good handful of snow.

Tiredly, she straightened up and resumed her endless journey.

The snow gusted around her, but she felt warm from the hard walk, the bending and retrieving. With every brutal step, she could feel the perspiration on her back and arms and the cold in her toes and fingers, which she wiggled consciously to keep them from freezing. Her ankles were wet and clammy, and she regretted leaving on the damp jeans. She'd been foolish to expect them to dry.

The worst part was the impending darkness. Seeing was nearly impossible with the snow stinging her face, and the flashlight lay buried in one of the bags. She was increasingly aware of the cast in the sky turning from teal to purple to nearly black. She guessed it must be nearing four-thirty. When all the light was gone, how would she see the road?

She was more than halfway to the cabin, but still had perhaps three-fourths of a mile to go. She should have stayed in the car with the heat on. She could have been warm there, at least for brief periods. And maybe someone would have come along.

A shudder went through her. Staying in the car would have been crazy. The plows would clear the populated areas long before they plowed Rice Road, and Arrowhead Lake Road might remain snowbound for days. And she wouldn't have dared to leave the heat on; she recalled learning about carbon monoxide poisoning in her high school driver ed. class. Well, maybe that kind of colorless, odorless poison would feel soothing right about now.

She shook herself and took another step, lifted first one foot, then the other. Someone might have found her if only she had stayed with her car.

No, they wouldn't have.

Lift one foot; put it down. Grip the plastic bag tightly. Don't let the sleeping bag fall, and be sure you are holding the canvas bag's strap, even though you can't feel your fingers.

She juggled her bags, trying for a better grip.

Lift one foot, now the other. Again.

Wiggle your fingers. Now your toes.

The snowflakes fell around her as the wind howled through the tall pines and hemlocks. Lissa trudged on, her hands numb and face raw, her body aching, rivulets of sweat pouring down inside her clothing from the powerful exertion of working so hard to cover the two miles.

She peered up at the menacing shapes of trees, the strange, unfamiliar contours that loomed in the darkness around her. If she kept her eyes on the white road, made ghostly in the weak moonlight, she should stumble across her own driveway marker before another half hour had passed.

She set her bags down carefully and removed one mitten, plunging her hand into the canvas bag and then the plastic ones. When she finally felt the flashlight, she worked it up, past the other objects, removing a few and trying to replace them compactly.

She turned on the flashlight and swallowed at the eerie, weak glow that splashed across the snow at her feet. She picked up the two bags and secured them in her fists, clutching the flashlight, too, and aiming it before her.

Lissa breathed in and out heavily, her throat rough with cold and pain. Her nose was running, and she ignored the salt dribbling over her chapped lips. She took a step.

And then another.

Lift. Again. Again.

Chapter 3

NED MARCHESS COULD BARELY MAKE OUT THE ROAD before him, and the pain from the gash in his arm made it hard to think. Down this way were those summer cabins he'd noticed last year, a quiet row of camps on a gently sloping, wooded hillside. He recalled that they were close to the lake and knew the road ran right along the shoreline. So he must be on the Arrowhead Lake Road. In the summer, a mountain vista rose up beyond the scattering of wooden docks that jutted into the water like crooked pickets in a weathered fence. Of course, he couldn't even see the lake in this darkness, and he knew the docks would be dismantled now, eerie mounds beneath the snow.

They were nice little camps, each one on a double or triple lot, each one with plenty of privacy, lots of woods, an expansive waterfront. When he'd spotted them last season, he had been impressed. Wouldn't it be nice to have a place like that? The kind of cottage people like Ned Marchess could only admire from afar.

He wondered if any of those cabins were winterized. He doubted it, but at least he could have shelter from the wind. Tonight their driveways would be filled with snow; it was unlikely any camps had been visited this winter. But someone was in one of them now, of that he was pretty sure. And he intended to be inside, too. Invited or not.

He forced his legs to move, his wet jeans plastered to him, the cold biting through. He'd be lucky if he didn't end up with frostbite or hypothermia or worse. His throat was so cold he could hardly force his breath out. Not exactly dressed for the weather, are you, idiot? Didn't quite expect to be hiking in the dead of night with your arm a bloody mess and your head a hot, aching sponge. Ned mastered the urge to slam at something with his injured right arm; there was no point in making the wound worse.

This was Cassie's doing, and Ned didn't bother to tame the rage that crept up his throat when he thought of her. If he ever saw her again, he had a few choice words; if not, even better. He blamed her for this and for much more. Everything she touched turned black and rotten and festered like a running sore. He realized he was muttering his anger; his throat rasped raw.

Save your energy, dolt.

A fuzz of moonlight was trying to break through the dense cloud cover above, and Ned widened his eyes, banishing thoughts of Cassie, trying to see which way the road went. Straight ahead, it looked like to him. Just keep going, plant one foot in front of the other. That row of buildings had to be somewhere in here. One of them would be occupied. And maybe warm.

Don't lie down in the snow, he told himself. Don't succumb to the need for sleep or the steady ache in your arm. You need shelter. You need medical help. Walk. Hike. You can do this.

Man, he'd give anything for a cigarette.

He bent his head against the wind, glad he'd at least had the sense to stuff a knit hat into his pocket. Icy pellets stung his face and burned his skin.

He trudged forward, angry, pained, and exhausted. And his heart cried out in anguish. How could things have gone so terribly wrong?

Chapter 4

LISSA FUMBLED FOR THE KEY with frozen fingers, unlocked the door, and collapsed onto a painted kitchen chair. Her feet felt numb. Inside, the camp was dark and still and just as cold as it was outside, but at least there was no wind, and there were no icy snowflakes blinding her.

She breathed deeply for a few moments, relishing the heavy rest settling over her and rejoicing in the four solid, silent walls. The hike was over; she had made it. Gratefully, she dropped the heavy bags to the floor. Her supplies. All that stood between her and starvation. She looked longingly at the bag that held her frosty water jug, then dismissed the idea. She wanted to conserve it.

Guided by her flashlight, Lissa hobbled to the small cubby on the living room wall that housed the main circuit breaker. She flicked the switch, and the refrigerator in the kitchen hummed to life. She turned on a tableside lamp; pale gold light flooded the corner. Relieved, she removed the towel holding the refrigerator door open and let it swing shut, then sank onto a chair and took stock of her situation.

The camp was old, one floor, a kitchen, living room, two small bedrooms, and a bathroom, comfortable but modest. The walls and floors were pine, the furniture well-used. Many people had enjoyed camping here at Arrowhead Lake, and the Tea family always managed to crowd in one more.

Two sofas, some overstuffed chairs, a recliner, a squeaky wooden rocker, and a clutter of small tables crowded the living room. No television, no internet, no telephone. If you were going to camp, Uncle Jeff always said, then you were going to *camp*.

The decor was a crowded mix of hand-crafted Adirondack

picture frames and mirrors and the cast-off remnants of everyone's homes. The curtains were white muslin, sewn by Lissa's aunt and mother, and on one wall, Lissa's uncle had hung a large, flat sailing ship. Its sails were real canvas, its spars stiff wire. A taxidermied pheasant stood on the mantel; her father's mounted fish hung on the walls.

Her father and Uncle Jeff had made the decision to renovate and insulate three years before; Lissa never would have invited Pat and Shelly otherwise. The kitchen stove would work; she could use the appliances, the outlets. She could cook, boil water, refrigerate her food. She felt sure she would be fine here for a while.

Once she got the heat going and started a fire in the brick fireplace, it should warm up enough. She turned on the electric baseboard heaters in the bedrooms and set about firing up the stove.

She would need to trek back outdoors to turn the valve on the propane tank. Mustering her energy, she braved the snowdrifts, tramped through the deep snow to the back of the camp, brushed the tank cover clear, lifted it, and turned the valve. Lighting a match to the gas stove back inside, she was rewarded with a soothing hiss as the gas flowed to the pilot. When blue flames began to dance behind the glass, Lissa held her hands before them and felt the numbness begin to subside. She turned the fan to high and its roar filled the room. The noise was music to her chilled ears. Slowly the cabin warmed. Finally, Lissa began to believe she might be comfortable tonight.

She removed her snowy outer clothes, draped them over chairs and on hooks, stood her wet boots by the kitchen door, and dug her fleece slippers from the canvas bag. She hunted up some paper towels and sopped up the puddles made by the melting snow, the wet footprints she had left throughout the living room and kitchen, the dampness where she had sat. She could feel the cold leave her, but not enough, so she walked about the building, massaging her arms.

In the larger bedroom, Lissa spent a few moments looking over the family photographs clustered on the dresser. Everyone was represented - her parents, her five brothers and sisters, Uncle Jeff and Aunt Louise, their kids, daughter-in-law, and pets. The frames were mismatched, mostly old, tarnished, and chipped, frames removed from the Tea households, but good enough for camp.

Lissa picked up the photograph of her parents sunning themselves on the dock. Her mother smiled at the camera, unkempt as usual, a cigarette dangling from her stained fingers. Her father lifted a glass in a mock toast.

It had been two years since her mother's death. Lung cancer had crept up on her, a furtive thief stealing Julia Tea's breath and robbing her children of their caregiver. Lissa felt a hot flush saturating her cheeks as she recalled her last conversation with her mother.

She put the picture down abruptly. She wouldn't think of that now.

The photograph of her sister Katie caught her attention. Seventeen years old now, Katie still acted six. Well, that was hardly Katie's fault, and anyway, Lissa intended to take responsibility for her now that their mother was gone. The crippling arthritis that plagued her father had meant paring back his work hours; less money coming in meant cutting some corners on Katie's care. And besides, now that Lissa realized. . . . She turned her back on the photo. The decision to take Katie had not been easy, but she knew it was the right one. And William would see it, too. He just needed a little time.

A sudden noise made Lissa jump. A thick crest of snow had slid from the pitched roof and crashed into the bushes under the big window that overlooked the lake. She sat on one of the three twin beds jammed into the room and glanced at the two mismatched dressers and the tall bookcase housing a collection of musty, dog-eared dimestore paperbacks. A few plastic laundry baskets held badminton rackets and birdies, cracked beach toys, and board games with broken covers.

Children's artwork covered the walls - finger-paintings from her own childhood, her sister Margie's beaded chain hanging from a light, a giant fungus her brother Steven and cousin Neal had found in the woods and embellished with childish Indian symbols. Lissa glanced around in distaste. If this were her place, she would get rid of all this junk and decorate. But that was not the Tea way. Everyone was welcome; therefore, everyone needed a place to sleep and everyone had the right to bring belongings. Their house in Binghamton had been the same.

No wonder she had fled to a college a state away.

Lissa wandered to the other bedroom, which looked out from the back of the camp to the woods beyond. She preferred the quiet privacy of this smaller nook and decided she would stash her things and sleep here for the duration of her stay. The furniture was worn and threadbare, but there was less of it. The double mattress was a little lumpy, chair cushions sagged, and an old rocker listed slightly, but at least there was space to move around.

She removed her sweaty turtleneck and damp jeans and dressed in several warm, dry layers, then returned to the living room and lit a fire in the fireplace, hanging her clothing to dry and enjoying the heat from the stove and baseboards. The familiar brick fireplace soothed her; she stretched her legs before the flames and felt a welcome tingle tickling her feet in their heavy socks and slippers.

Her family had summered here every July of her childhood - cramped, crowded, noisy Julys. They had bunked in haphazardly, two parents, six kids, sometimes a dog or cat that had wandered into their lives. In August the camp was her Uncle Jeff's, and his family would take over with gusto. Often, one side of the family would invite the other for a barbecue or picnic. It wasn't unusual for all the Teas to camp out together for several days at a stretch, her brothers or cousins sleeping on threadbare couches, the others squeezed into the bedrooms. They sprawled where they could, making up the extra mattresses leaning against one wall in the larger bedroom; sometimes they set up a tent in the yard to accommodate the overflow.

Lissa sighed as she poked the fire. Dusty old magazines and books, deflated beach toys, dressers with sticking drawers, and tattered upholstery - this was her parents' legacy. She recalled her years spent as part of the Tea clan, caring for Katie, always Lissa's own personal charge. Sometimes, she admitted, it had made her feel important. Mostly it had just been a burden.

She forced herself up to tackle a little cleaning, knowing she wouldn't want to use the kitchen until she at least wiped off the counters and the oilcloth-covered table and scrubbed the winter's residue from the stovetop and sink. The cleaning warmed her some, and she retreated into her small, square box of a bedroom to make up her bed. She pressed her face to the one bedroom window and tunneled her hands, but could see only pitch black with a foreground of plummeting snowflakes. The sudden roar of wind around the cabin startled her, and she held her breath, listening to the old building creak. Well, in the morning, her view would look clean and pretty and white with snow. In the morning she could think about getting back to Albany.

She was glad she had brought the sleeping bag. Animals loved to nest inside the camp during the cold Adirondack winters, so the family always folded the blankets and quilts over sturdy wires running the length of the bedrooms a foot or two from the ceiling. Lissa had no desire to climb up and take down blankets. Instead she spread her sleeping bag over the mattress, confident it would be warm enough. She opened the steamer trunk in the corner and removed a pillow and a clean pillowcase.

In the kitchen, Lissa put her meager food supplies away. It was a rule of camp never to leave food out at night, and though she hadn't seen signs of mice or squirrels, they had been known to chew through cereal boxes and nibble their way across every cookie in a cellophane-wrapped package. She stored nearly everything in the refrigerator. "No sense taking a chance," she said to herself, and then jumped a bit at the loudness of her voice in the empty camp.

A cup of tea would have been welcome, but it would mean boiling water from the gallon jug she had lugged from the car, and she was just too tired to bother. She opened the box of crackers and munched a few, then poured herself a small cup of her freezing cold water.

With luck, the storm would abate, the plows would clear the lake roads, she could get her car free, and she would be back at her apartment by Monday evening as planned. Or maybe she'd be able to leave earlier.

The camp was warming up nicely, and Lissa turned the stove fan down. Grimacing, she struggled into her heavy, damp jacket, her plaid tartan scarf, mittens, boots, and hood. There was a tidy little bathroom in the camp, part of the renovation project three summers ago, but the white porcelain toilet and sink, and the narrow, pristine shower were absolutely no good to Lissa without running water.

Gritting her teeth, she picked up her flashlight, exited the camp, and plowed her way to the outhouse fifty yards into the woods. She groaned when she saw the drift of snow blocking the door and scooped the snow up and away until she could force the door open.

By eight o'clock, Lissa had had enough. The howling wind accompanied her to her bedroom, and as she lay in the sleeping bag, dressed in layers of wool and fleece, it struck her how very isolated she was. The string of cabins along the shore were deserted; no one was here now. Except Lissa Tea, of course.

Chapter 5

SHE TRIED TO GET COMFORTABLE, bound up in her confining clothes, listening to the wind screech. She could still see big puffs of snow sliding over the window glass in the gauzy moonlight, falling as thickly as they had hours before. Would the storm never end?

It was incredibly dark in the room. No streetlights shed their pale, protective glow over her, just the watery moonlight, slanting across the pelting snow. No sounds soothed and caressed her into sleep, just the disturbing ebb and flow of the storm as it rumbled around her.

She stared into the darkness and thought of her roommates, how excited they had been after graduation that all three of them had ended up in or near New York State. They had vowed to spend time together, to meet frequently; it hadn't happened. She thought of Pat now, tucked safely into the Utica apartment she shared with another beginning teacher, of Shelly, who had moved back home to live with her parents as she began her fledgling engineering career.

Everybody had somebody. Well, she had, too. She had William. And a huge, bubbling family bursting the seams of their humble Binghamton bungalow and their tiny Adirondack camp. She had been so glad to get away from them. So glad for the chance to cross the state line into Pennsylvania to study music, a subject that made her parents scratch their heads in confusion. Steven had hooted with laughter at the idea that Lissa actually thought she could write songs. And Katie had predicted she would end up a big fat failure if she left.

Lissa sighed, remembering.

A violent gust shook the window.

Funny how any one of them, yes, even Katie, would have been welcome company tonight.

Overweight, overindulged Katie - whiny, self-absorbed, clingy, dependent. Lissa knew she couldn't help any of it and felt a tremor of guilt at the critical thoughts. Leaving for college had been necessary for Lissa and hard on Katie. Occasional phone calls had resulted in a guilt so profound that after a while Lissa stopped calling altogether. She hadn't seen Katie in almost a year, hadn't spoken to her in months. She knew her father was overwhelmed by the burden of Katie's care, and Daniel, as devoted a brother as he was, just couldn't give Katie everything she needed. They were talking about sending her away. . . .

Constricted in her sleeping bag, and suddenly too warm in the layers of clothing, Lissa peeled off her fleece shirt and one sweater and dropped them to the floor. She plumped her pillow and snuggled in again. She was exhausted, so why were her eyes wide open? She had double-checked all the window latches and the lock on the door. She had left a dim light burning in the living room, right outside her closed bedroom door in case she needed to get up in the dark, and had left a light on in the kitchen, too. She was alone and isolated, but she was also intelligent and resourceful. She would be fine. She could wait out the storm.

Wind pummeled the window casing, shaking the glass panes, as icy snow hit the window. Lissa turned her head the other way and stared into the darkness.

The driver of the Grand Marquis had probably managed to hitch a ride once he made it to the highway. It was unlikely that his car was actually the getaway car for a crime. All that was long over. She was sure the angry driver was far, far away.

It certainly was spooky to be sleeping all alone in this little building, though, knowing that for miles around there were no other people. Lissa closed her eyes, forcing herself to think of the paper that needed to be written for her first day back at school. At least she had the whole week.

She had planned to leave camp on Monday, along with Pat and Shelly, but had brought her schoolbooks anyway, intending to get the paper written this evening so she could relax the rest of her week off. Well, she could work on it tomorrow while she watched for the snowplow. She would call the County Highway Department first thing in the morning and find out exactly how long she could expect to be stranded. Would there be a cell signal? They needed to know she was here.

She congratulated herself on stuffing the research materials into her canvas bag. Then a flicker of sheepishness tickled her. Who else would bring schoolwork on a three day vacation with friends she hadn't seen in months? Who else would stuff books in first when packing for her very survival? No one. Just Lissa Tea.

Why was she like that? Why so neurotic about deadlines and lists, proper methods and schedules and rules? Why not hit the books on Wednesday? Or Thursday? It wasn't as if she had anything pressing to do or anyone in particular to do it with. William had been distant since their first discussion of Katie weeks ago.

And now Pat and Shelly weren't even coming. She had looked forward to telling them about William Brashue, the sudden romance that left her breathless and hopeful. Lissa smiled to herself as she thought of him. He was handsome, serious, and smart, and no one called him Bill, which she liked. He had an aura, a dignified presence that had impressed her the minute he took the seat next to her in their shared Aesthetics class. He was an art student, more, an artist, talented and confident.

Countless times it had occurred to her that they might look over the artwork in the student gallery or maybe attend a classmate's recital together, or buddy up to review their assigned class readings, but she had never worked up the courage to ask him.

She had overheard him in the campus center talking over his plans with some brown-haired girl who appeared to be just a friend. William was saying he intended to have his Masters in Fine Arts by May and was busy looking into galleries on the west coast.

"Won't you miss New York?" the girl had asked.

Stupid question, Lissa had thought. Why would anyone want to stay in upstate New York if an opportunity could be had in sunny California? Or anywhere else, for that matter?

Lissa had listened with great interest as William explained his goals. He had a future mapped out and plans to travel to Los Angeles over spring break to investigate those galleries. He intended to work as an artist while he lent his talent to supporting other artists. She admired him.

In fact, she hoped to spend her life with him.

Actually, it had taken several attempts to talk to William before he had finally looked at her, *really* looked at her. It had taken all her nerve, but she had swept aside her natural shyness and approached him after class one Tuesday.

"Interesting class, wasn't it?" she'd said companionably, falling into step beside him.

"Mildly," he answered.

Lissa summoned her bravest voice and made a suggestion she had never made to any man on campus before. "I'm on my way to the student center for a coffee. Want to join me?"

William Brashue glanced over at her before he answered. "No, thanks, I have reserved time in one of the studios."

Lissa nodded brightly. Not for the world would she allow him to see her embarrassment. "All right. See you, then."

Twenty minutes later, he entered the center with two or three other guys, all discussing something - she couldn't hear what - with great seriousness. The young men parted company and she saw William go to the counter and order a coffee. She bent her head over her textbook and hoped he wouldn't look her way. He didn't, and, she realized, maybe he wouldn't have recognized her anyway. He left the student center alone, sipping.

Well, maybe he did have a studio reserved. He could certainly take a five minute break to get coffee, couldn't he?

Her second attempt had been later that same week. She had made up her mind not to extend an invitation, but simply to initiate a friendly conversation. She was determined to get to know him.

"Wasn't that hockey game amazing last night?" she said to him as they left class. He had been at the ice rink with friends; she'd had her eye on him most of the evening from her position behind the ticket counter.

"Sure," he said. "Good game."

She fell into step beside him again, but hadn't even had a chance to reply when he turned abruptly down a side corridor toward the fitness center. She realized then that he was carrying a gym bag; it hadn't been meant as a slight.

Swallowing her embarrassment, she smiled cheerfully at a group of girls who passed her. One of them said hello, and Lissa scurried past. Back in her tiny office, where she organized tutors as a graduate assistant, Lissa sat down and put her hands to her hot cheeks. It was okay; he just hadn't been prepared for her overture of friendship. She was sure the right opportunity would present itself. She was determined to get acquainted with William Brashue; he had all the qualities she wanted in a man, and she had four more months to make him notice her.

She hadn't given up. People who gave up never accomplished the things that mattered. It was one of the traits that set her apart from her brothers and sisters, from her parents. She had wanted to learn music, and she had. She was determined to have an education and a career. It took dedication and purpose to attain those things, and she was willing to work hard. Hours of practice every day didn't faze her, and neither did being rebuffed by William Brashue.

A few weeks later, when he had sat down across from her in a lounge area of the campus library, Lissa couldn't have been more surprised.

"Hi, Lissa," he'd said confidently. "Mind if I sit here?" Without waiting for her to respond, he plopped his stack of books on the table between them and sauntered back into the stacks to retrieve another volume. By the time he returned, Lissa had composed herself and pasted a bright smile on her face.

He'd been thinking about her, he said. He'd been so busy keeping up with his classes and fighting for time in the art studios that he hadn't had a chance to acknowledge how friendly she'd been lately.

His smile was beautiful; he had perfect teeth, and Lissa had to make an effort to concentrate on the words he was saying.

They had talked. He talked. About classes, upcoming campus events, his art. And he had asked her out - finally.

She smiled to herself, remembering. For three months, she thought of little besides William Brashue, planned her days around him, reserved her evenings. And he had been very attentive. For three months, he'd been crazy about her, hadn't he?

Until the subject of Katie had interrupted their world. Katie again. Even now, Katie controlled her.

"She's my sister, and she has to depend on someone," Lissa had said. The bar was noisy - not the best place to have this conversation, she realized belatedly.

"I know, but she sounds hard to deal with." William drained his beer and signaled for another.

Lissa sipped at her glass of wine. "Well, sure, but I have to make up for lost time. There are circumstances. . . ."

William leaned back and crossed his arms over his chest. "And you intend to keep her with you? She'll live with you?"

"Well, yes. We were very close when we were younger, and now my mother isn't there anymore. Daniel doesn't know what to do for her."

"Daniel?"

"I told you, my brother. And it's too much for my dad. He's not in great health, and there are money issues."

William gazed at her, his face serious. "But this is your life, Lissa. You have a career ahead of you, maybe marriage, a family of your own."

She felt herself blushing. "Well, I'd like that. But I can fit her in, too. It's the right thing to do. Don't you see it?" She was begging him to understand.

William shrugged. "I like you, Lissa, but we're young. We want to have fun, explore the world, you know?" The waitress set his second beer on the table. He picked it up, took a swallow and thought for a moment. His voice became low, confidential. "What if someday we decided to take this further, move in together, even get married? I'm not saying that's going to happen," he added quickly, "but just think about it. That would be a lot to ask. It'd be like marrying someone with kids."

He took another gulp of beer and avoided her eyes. "You know, I really don't even have time to finish this," he said. "I shouldn't have ordered it. I should get back and work on that painting for my exhibit."

She could see him visibly distancing himself. He flipped through his wallet, tossed a few bills on the table, and stood up. "Do you mind if we cut this short? Or, no, you stay if you want. Finish your drink." He smiled down at her. "I'll call you."

Within moments, she was sitting alone.

He *had* called, of course, and they were still dating, but something was off. She lacked the nerve to bring up Katie's name again and seemed to be spending more and more evenings alone in her apartment, wondering if William were truly this busy.

A burst of wind against her window startled Lissa and brought her back to her solitude in the isolated cabin. She pulled her sleeping bag more snugly around her neck and wondered how long she would be here by herself and whether they might send a plow a little earlier once they received her call. She hoped so.

She was annoyed at William, she realized. Taking Katie was right, and nothing could shake her resolve in that. But recalling that conversation made her shiver with anticipation, too. He had brought up marriage; it was almost a proposal if you looked at it a certain way. Lissa smiled to herself, longing for the closeness she had shared with William before.

She prided herself on her patience and was used to waiting for what she wanted, so if this break would help, she told herself, William could take as long as he needed to accept Katie as a part of their life together. She didn't want to nag or rush him or. . . . She wished again that Pat and Shelly were here; she needed their opinions.

She lay on her back, staring up into the darkness. How many miles away, she wondered, was the nearest person? How long would it be before she made contact with another human being? In a way, it was strange. For the first time in her life, Lissa felt really and truly alone.

Lonely, even. Maybe even scared to be so alone.

Well, wasn't this need for privacy exactly why she had rushed off to college? And since starting grad school she had lots of it. She lived, worked, and studied alone, practiced the piano alone. She could often hear the music of the couple who lived below her, and in the campus library she was always aware of students and teachers coming and going. There was a constant backdrop of people moving around in Lissa's life, her family, neighbors, casual friends, but she'd usually opted to keep those people at arms' length.

Until William.

She would think of him now, of the kind of man he was and the future they might have. They would marry and raise a family, live in a beautiful home. She would spend her days composing, and he would work in his studio, a little moody, but always cheered when Lissa stopped to see his progress. She would be supportive, would worship his paintings, would accept that he was driven, a gifted artist. And he would applaud her songs.

Another windy gust shrieked around the cabin, and Lissa listened to her heart gallop loudly, then subside again into a steady, rhythmic pacing.

Hours later, sleep came.

Chapter 6

NED SHIVERED inside his leather jacket and hoped he'd find civilization soon. He had taken a wrong turn and realized after an extra hour of walking that he was headed away from the lake rather than along it. He had no idea if he'd even been on a road; it was possible he had followed someone's long, winding private drive or even just an animal's forest trail. Who could see in this light? It had been a relief when he backtracked over his own trail and came upon the smooth expanse of Arrowhead Lake.

He was pretty sure he was on the right track now. He just had to stay alert a little while longer. His knit hat and jeans were soaked with snow, and he could feel cold sweat pouring down inside his shirt, whether from the exertion or a fever he wasn't sure. His gloved hands and his feet inside their rubber boots felt numb, and his right arm screamed in pain.

Thank God for the thick leather jacket. It was ruined but had probably saved him from more serious injury. He could hardly force his legs to keep moving. What was he doing out here in the night, following a ghostly path to an obscure destination? If only he could collapse in the snow and forget.

He was more tired than he'd ever been in his life and wondered how much farther he could go. Well, he had no choice. Following the tire tracks had paid off, and finding the compact car burrowed into the side of the road had been a stroke of good fortune. He was sure the driver was holed up in some camp along in here. It was just a matter of staying patient until he found signs of life, smoke from a fireplace maybe, a light, anything.

He could break into an unoccupied cabin, but how nice it would be to have heat and food and water for his parched, dry throat.

His right arm was throbbing now. He believed the blood flow had finally stopped, but the makeshift bandage he had fashioned irritated his skin; he probably had an infection starting. He needed soap and water and a proper dressing. A pain killer wouldn't be a bad idea either.

When he first saw the light, he refused to hope. It might be a figment of his exhausted imagination or some weird natural thing, like the eyes of a wild animal or a phosphorescent rock. But as he approached closer, his heart gave a leap of joy. A light glowed inside a cabin, a beacon signaling him in from the cold.

And none too soon. His teeth chattered, his face stung with the snow, and his arm was burning with pain. Fat snowflakes rested on his shoulders and eyelashes. As he came closer, he could see several lights glowing. Their soft shimmer revealed disturbed snow near the cabin. Someone was here. The lighted windows looked warm and welcoming.

Ned hoisted himself to the front stoop and banged on the wooden door. There was no response, and he pounded again and again. He would break in if he had to. He needed to get a better look at the injury before he gave up the ghost altogether, and walking any farther in the blizzard was not an option.

Frustrated, he forced his shaking legs around to the back of the building and, for a full minute, stood staring at a low window. What would he use to break the glass?

His mind fogged over, and he leaned against the cabin, suddenly unable to make the slightest effort.

Break the glass, he told himself. You need to break the glass and get in there, and lie down and let someone help you.

His eyes closed against his will as he raised his left fist, smashed it through the brittle window glass, and listened to it shatter on the floor inside.

Chapter 7

THE SOUND OF POUNDING penetrated Lissa's sleep. Katie was calling for her, crashing a stick against the frame of her wheelchair, demanding that Lissa pay attention.

Lissa suddenly sat bolt upright. This sound was not Katie. Terrified, Lissa listened for the pounding sound again. All was quiet. She sucked in her breath, perfectly still, focusing on the silence. The sour taste of panic crept up her throat.

She jumped at the sudden explosion of breaking glass just a few feet away, right outside her bedroom door, then more glass tinkling as it fell to the floor.

Her first thought was that a tree branch had been blown through the window. How on earth would she repair such a thing? When she heard the heavy fall and something moving, a far more frightening thought struck her and she pushed it away. An animal then, she told herself, seeking shelter from the storm. A fox? A bear? It must have come through the jagged window; it would be bloody and injured. . . .

Lissa forced her thoughts away from the accident on Rice Road.

Terrified, she stole silently from her bed, peered cautiously through the bedroom doorway, and crept into the living room of the cabin.

Slivers of glass from the broken window glinted in the soft light of the lamp she'd left burning; the curtains whipped around in the wind. She stood still, her gaze riveted on the big, wet footprints leading away from the window and into the kitchen. The vision of the Grand Marquis assaulted her again, the face of the furious driver, his tall frame tracking hurriedly away down the snowy road, no glance back, head ducked against the pelting snow.

But he had been going away from her, not toward Arrowhead Lake. Lissa forced calm, even breaths and willed herself to forget that she was the only human soul for miles around.

Except for the intruder in the kitchen.

She closed her eyes and wished she could go back to her bedroom and shut the door firmly behind her.

The wind roared violently, shaking the rafters. Breathing unevenly, her hand shaking, she grabbed the iron poker from the fireplace and entered the kitchen.

A young man slumped on one of the chairs pushed away from the center table. His head listed sideways, his eyes squeezed shut in pain, teeth gritted together. His face was ruddy from the cold and his nose dripped. She noted the snow coating his brown leather jacket. The knit hat he had worn and his stiff, frozen gloves were tossed on the kitchen table, where melting snow crystals made little puddles on the worn oilcloth.

With his left hand, he clutched his right arm. Lissa stared in horror at the icy red stain congealed on his jacket sleeve. She gasped aloud in fear and gripped the poker more tightly.

His head snapped up; his eyes flew open. She saw his startled glance take in the poker, her rumpled clothing, her hair tied in a messy knot on top of her head. She knew she must look terrified.

"I broke a window," he started.

"Don't move," she rasped. "If you do, I swear I'll kill you with this."

He stayed perfectly still in the chair, slouched backward, staring. When he lifted his left hand off his bleeding arm, she staggered forward a step.

He gestured to the injury. "I need help."

Lissa's thoughts were spinning wildly. Was this the man from the Grand Marquis? He could be. She remembered the dark hair and jacket and the face of that man, but his look had been snarling, venomous. If this was the same man, calmer, tired, and hurt, she needed to be smart and do everything she could not to antagonize him.

She glanced at his arm. The frozen blood was warming up in the heated room and a drop fell, glistening and slick, to the vinyl tiled floor.

Had he been holding his right arm that way when he ran

from his car? She couldn't remember. He had been moving as fast as possible through the snow, she knew, but as if he were hurt? Maybe the pain hadn't set in yet. Maybe he was injured later, maybe cut by glass when he broke her window. That couldn't be. The wound looked icy; the congealed blood looked frozen.

"Can you help me?" He remained unmoving in the chair.

She still clutched the poker, not sure of her next move. "How did you hurt your arm?" she asked finally.

"It was an accident."

"What kind of accident?" She held the poker firmly, a spear ready to strike. The Gorham thief might have been injured, according to the news report. Or maybe the impact when his car hit the tree. . . .

His eyes fixed on hers. "I fell against an air conditioner."

She glanced out the window. Steady snow sheeted past the glass, illuminated from the inside light.

He gave a shallow laugh as his eyes followed her glance. "Yeah, I see the irony." He shuddered and shifted slightly in the chair. She gripped the poker more firmly.

"I won't hurt you," he said. "That isn't why I'm here. Can you help me with my arm, please? Could I wash it off? I need to bandage it up better."

"What do you mean, you fell against an air conditioner?"

"I was carrying it and I fell against it. Look, I'm bleeding on your floor here. Can we have the inquisition later?" His glance fell on the gallon jug on the table. "Could I have some water?"

Lissa drew herself up to her full five feet three inches. Her water? She thought of the eleven extra gallons nestled in her car trunk. "This is my home you've broken into," she said. "I call the shots." She hoped her voice sounded more confident than she felt.

"Right," he muttered. "I'll just continue to bleed. Let me know if I go into shock."

She cringed slightly.

He began to massage his right arm. "Do you at least have an aspirin or something you could give me?"

She hesitated. Her pocketbook was behind him on the counter next to the stove, and she always carried a small supply of aspirin and ibuprofen. Lately, she had found she was prone to headaches. It was the stress of her classes, she knew. That and her recent decision to take responsibility for Katie. And William, maybe. It was many things.

"Don't move," she ordered him. "I'll get it."

Exhaling a frightened breath, she stepped around him, near enough that he could have reached out and grabbed her if he'd wanted to. Quickly, she picked up her purse and scurried with it back to the other side of the room. She leaned the fireplace poker carefully against the cabinet next to her, well out of his reach, pulled out a metal pillbox, and dropped two aspirin into her shaking hand. She glanced at the plastic gallon jug of water on the table, hesitated, then picked it up.

"Listen," he said, "I know my entrance was a little unconventional. I was banging on your door for ten minutes before I broke the window."

She poured two inches of water into a juice glass and stepped close enough to hand it to him, then put the two aspirin on the table before him and stepped back.

Greedily, he downed the pills and the water. "Thank you. I wouldn't mind another couple aspirin if you can spare it. Or something stronger. This is pretty painful."

"I have ibuprofen."

"Could I have that?"

"I don't know." The words twisted out of her. Should she even be helping this man? The congealed blood thawing on his jacket looked nasty. Maybe someone at the gas station had stabbed him or there had been gunfire. It might be a bullet wound. How could she possibly know?

Lissa wished, not for the first time, that she had left the radio on and heard the rest of the news item about that robbery. How foolish she had been to turn it off midway. This man could be a killer. She couldn't take her eyes from the bloody stain on his sleeve.

The wind howled, louder and closer now, through the jagged living room window. She shivered.

"Do you think you can mix them?" he asked quietly.

Lissa jumped.

"I didn't mean to startle you," he said. "Aspirin and ibuprofen. I never take them together. Can you mix them?"

"I don't know," she said. Her voice shook.

"I guess I'll take my chances," he said.

She placed two ibuprofen on the table before him and poured another inch of water into the glass.

He reached for the glass, swallowed the pills, and thanked her again. "You don't have a cigarette, do you?" he asked.

Lissa recoiled. "No, I don't."

"It's going to keep getting colder in here with that window broken," he said. "I wanted to break just enough glass to work the latch, but I couldn't get a grip on it. I'll fix it if you have some boards to cover it and some nails and a hammer."

"I have them," she said, but she didn't move. She could hear the wind whipping through the living room. Should she let him fix the hole and keep guard over him with the poker? Could she safely leave him here while she repaired the window herself?

"Well, get them," he said. The words came out thickly.

The wind blustered in from the living room; Lissa caught an icy blast on her ankle. She had to make a decision. "I'll take care of the window," she said. "You stay here." Should she tie him up? How? Lissa glanced around for rope, wire, ribbon, anything.

"I can help you," he said, and she watched in horror as he lumbered to his feet.

"No!" she screamed and grabbed the poker. She swung wildly, and he caught the iron shaft in his left hand, looking at her in shock.

His grip was strong, and Lissa realized that any thought she might have had of fighting this man was a delusion. If it came to that, he would win. There was no question.

She backed away and he stared at her. "I didn't come here to hurt you," he said roughly.

"Then put the poker down." She said the words through clenched teeth and felt tears stinging behind her eyelids.

His eyes never left her face, but he gently placed the poker against the wall, away from her and also away from the chair he had been sitting in. He turned from her and started toward the living room, taller, bigger than he had appeared sitting. "Where are the nails and hammer?"

Panic seized Lissa. She couldn't stop the sob that traveled up her throat and escaped through her lips.

He turned around, and she saw his mouth go slack as he fumbled for the chair. He collapsed heavily, and his breath seemed labored.

"Did you really get this from an air conditioner?" she said, suddenly strengthened by his weakness.

He glanced up at her and then his eyes closed. "Yes."

"I'm not sure if I believe that."

"Believe what you want." He said the words slowly. His left arm grasped his right; his mouth was twisted in pain. "Just help me."

Lissa watched in shock as his body slackened. His left arm fell loosely at his side, and his head lolled over onto his shoulder. His mouth opened slightly; his eyes remained closed.

Had he fainted? She crept closer. He could be faking, but if he wanted to grab her, he could have done so before now. He'd had the poker in his hands; he could have killed her if he'd chosen to. She stifled a sob of fear and took another step closer. Reaching out a trembling hand, she shook his shoulder. There was no response.

"Can you hear me?" she asked. It came out a whisper. Then louder, "Can you hear me?" He remained slumped awkwardly in the chair, sprawled backward, left arm hanging, the right demanding her attention with its now liquid stain of thick, red blood. A drip of blood fell from his arm, landed on the soft cotton of her sock and soaked through to her foot.

It mobilized her. She whimpered and ran to her bedroom, flinging off her sock and jamming both feet into her warm slippers. She yanked open the drawer where her father and Uncle Jeff kept the household tools, grabbed a hammer and a fistful of nails, and scurried to the living room.

What could she use to cover the window?

Her glance landed on a blown-up photograph of Arrowhead Lake her cousin Neal had taken years before. The family had liked it so much that Uncle Jeff had enlarged it to poster size, framed it, and mounted it on thin plywood. It would do. She would apologize to Neal and have another copy made. She felt behind the poster for the nail and hanging wire. She hoped she'd be around to apologize to Neal.

She yanked the picture off the wall, set it down, grabbed the broom from the closet, and hurriedly swept the glass shards into a pile and shoved them out of the way behind the bathroom door. As the wind shrieked and blew her hair, she fitted the poster over the window opening. The floor beneath her was dotted with puddles and tufts of snow, and she worked carefully around a few glass splinters that still shimmered. Finally, she hammered one nail and then another into the wooden frame, anchoring the picture until the opening was covered.

A sudden sound from the kitchen startled her, and she froze. Only the piercing wind assaulted her ears. She crept toward the kitchen doorway. The stranger was still in the chair, his head at an awkward angle, the empty juice glass on the table before him. Nothing seemed disturbed.

Lissa shook herself and returned to her task. Frightened tears ran over her face. She listened for sounds from the kitchen and stopped her work once more to peer in at the intruder. He still sat slumped, motionless. His feet in their rubber boots rested on the wet floor just as they had minutes ago.

She was relieved to finish the repair. The picture covered the jagged opening, but cold still seeped through cracks around the perimeter. Lissa grabbed up handfuls of tattered towels and stuffed them in. It would have to do. Someone else could do a better job later. This summer, they'd all come up and everyone would have a good laugh, hearing about Lissa's great adventure during the January blizzard. Katie would take her hand and tell her she had missed her, and she'd tell Katie she had missed her, too, and she was so sorry. . . .

Exhausted, Lissa leaned against the window frame. She needed to take care of the problems here and now, never mind the problems back home in Binghamton.

If she had been too tired to make tea before, she changed her mind now. She returned to the kitchen and began boiling water, keeping a wary eye on her uninvited guest. The man had not moved, and his breath was slow, raspy. Lissa wished she'd studied nursing. Her degrees in marketing and music composition seemed even more useless than usual. What could she do for him? Develop him a sound marketing strategy? Play him a concerto?

His gasps of pain filled the little kitchen. He needed medical help, and he needed it soon.

Hesitantly, she shook the stranger's shoulder again, but there was no response. She glanced around the kitchen, spotted her purse, and took it into her bedroom. Her money was there, her wallet, her credit cards and keys, all as it should be. Grateful for that small favor at least, she buried the pocketbook in the back of a dresser drawer underneath a pile of someone's summer clothes.

Her cell phone. She would get it from the kitchen and call for help. She should have done that in the first place, as soon as the Grand Marquis had hit her, and certainly as soon as she had connected it to the robbery. What a fool she was. She prayed there was a good signal here at camp.

In the kitchen, she glanced around, expecting her phone to be lying in plain sight. Where had she put it earlier, when she had stumbled into the kitchen, cold and shivering? She didn't recall unpacking it, so maybe it was still in one of the bags. She took a cursory look, already knowing she had unpacked every item. She knew she hadn't taken the phone to her bedroom or the living room.

Had she put it in the refrigerator with all the food? In her exhaustion, she might have. She gazed at the refrigerator, then at the man slouched near it. Cautiously, she opened the refrigerator door; her cell phone was not there.

She looked around again and her glance came back to the intruder. But when could he have taken it? She was sure she would have seen any move he made. Maybe he had picked it up before she'd even found him. While she had repaired the window? Not likely. He had looked too exhausted, in too much pain, to be stealing things like cell phones, especially when he had ignored her purse, which had been within his easy reach.

It was then that she spotted the tea bags. They had fallen from the plastic bag in a clump. She had retrieved them from the snow and later spread them on the table to dry. There they still were, a damp, shriveling testimony to the fate of her phone. She had tossed it into the top of the plastic bag, and it had fallen into the snow along with the groceries and matches and other items. And it was still there, she was almost sure, somewhere along the Arrowhead Lake Road, buried under a foot of snow and absolutely useless to her or to anyone else.

Lissa groaned and sank distractedly onto a chair, burying her face in her hands. Her cell phone was her last hope of contact with the outside world. She would not be calling the police; she would not be calling the highway department. And here she sat, across the kitchen table from a man who might be anyone, whose past might hide anything.

Growing up in her crowded house on Keltic Avenue, she had always felt trapped. All those noisy brothers and sisters had driven her crazy, her parents had never understood her, and she had rejoiced when she finally was set free to pursue her college dream. But being trapped on Keltic Avenue, she saw now, was a pleasure compared to being trapped at Arrowhead Lake.

Should she leave the camp? Run away? Take her chances on meeting up with someone, anyone, who might help her before she died of cold and exhaustion? Leave him slumped there, wounded and unconscious, and hope someone found him before infection took over? Well, she would send help back. If she made it out herself.

She stared at the unwelcome stranger. She wanted to do the right thing. She had made a huge mess of her relationships at home by leaving suddenly and without a backward glance. Her brother Daniel had long ago lost patience with her, and Katie, she knew, was sad and confused and hiding it under belligerence. And her mother, her mother. . . . Lissa recalled the shocked hurt in her mother's eyes, brown eyes that turned down at the outer corners. Bewildered eyes that wondered how it could be that a daughter would speak in such hurtful tones. . . .

The man across from her moved slightly in pain. Lissa knew she couldn't just abandon an injured man. She had restitution to pay, sins to atone for.

And last night's two mile trek through the blizzard had taught her a little about her own stamina. She would never make it back to the highway. And with no phone to call for help. . . . She let the tears resume, hot and frightened, and thought of the house on Keltic Avenue, with its stuffed shelves and overflowing closets, its clutter of clothes and toys and junk and people and pets.

How very warm and appealing it suddenly seemed.

Chapter 8

IT WAS ONE-THIRTY in the morning, and he had been unconscious for a good half hour or more. Lissa sat and stared at him, wondering how long a person could safely stay in a faint. She had never fainted, but she had seen it once or twice. In church one summer, a teenage girl had fainted, and a crowd of people had gathered around, all offering suggestions, until one woman had stuck a vial of smelling salts under the girl's nose and she had come to abruptly. Well, here at camp, in fact anywhere in her existence, Lissa didn't have smelling salts.

She recalled a college choir rehearsal, another member who had felt faint. The director had made her sit with her head between her knees. Did she dare do that to this hulking man? The thought of it made her cringe.

If this were the man who had glared at her from the Grand Marquis, where had he gone when he left his car? She'd seen him go off in the other direction, away from Arrowhead Lake, so how had he ended up here? There had been six hours between her arrival at the camp and his. What was he doing all that time? Robbing another gas station? Doing something that resulted in this bloody injury to his arm?

He looked like the same man; the build seemed right, the hair and jacket were dark.

Big deal. Lots of men had dark hair.

She stared at his face; he was decent looking, with nice, even features. She couldn't be sure if it was the same face; it looked so pale and slack right now. And he hadn't said or done anything so far to make her think he was a thief - or worse.

The injury bothered her. Had there been an altercation during the robbery? Maybe he had injured someone as badly as he had been injured. Maybe he had even. . . .

She jumped up from her chair and removed the pan of boiling water from its burner. Just the thought of braving the blizzard to collect snow exhausted her; she would not allow even one precious drop of her water to boil away.

And she would not allow these thoughts to consume her.

She set a mug for herself and filled it with hot water, then congratulated herself; she had heated exactly one mug's worth. If she decided to give him tea, she would boil more later.

"Can you hear me?" She shook his shoulder gently, as she had before. "I'm not sure it's safe for you to be out like this. Wake up."

He didn't stir.

"I'm making tea. Wake up."

His silence terrified her. Carefully avoiding the blood on his arm, she placed her hand inside his jacket pocket, searching for a weapon, identification, anything that might help her know how to proceed. The pocket was empty. She felt inside the other pocket. That was surprisingly empty, too.

Praying that he would remain unconscious, she checked the pocket of his flannel shirt and the front pockets of his jeans, then pulled him toward her. He was heavy and she gasped as his full weight fell onto her shoulder. She reached for the back pockets of his pants. A comb, some loose change, and that was all. No wallet, no keys, none of the usual items men carried. And no cell phone.

He hadn't taken it then. It was buried under mounds of snow a mile or two down the road.

Breathing hard, she released him and he fell back against the chair. She stared at him. Who was he? This was certainly more than just some guy, injured by his air conditioner, who happened to stumble across her isolated cabin one January night with his arm torn open.

Would he die here if she ignored his wound and the fact that he had passed out nearly forty minutes ago?

As gently as possible, she bent his right arm just enough to remove the damaged and bloody right jacket sleeve. He gasped in pain and his eyes opened briefly, then his head rolled back. Lissa forced herself to continue. With the jacket out of the way, she could see that he had already removed his arm from the right sleeve of his shirt. His blood-soaked white tee shirt was twisted into a makeshift bandage, wrapped around his upper arm and fastened in a crude knot. Blood was oozing through the cloth layers, and gingerly, holding her breath, Lissa unwound it and stripped it off. She gagged as she exposed the raw wound and backed away from the still-oozing, bloody smear. Had she started it bleeding again by moving his arm?

She retrieved a handful of clean dish towels from the living room chest and a cake of soap from the bathroom, then found a large mixing bowl in the kitchen cupboard.

Pulling a chair close to his, she poured water into the bowl, then dipped one of the rough towels into it. She realized how cold it would feel and, sighing in disappointment, emptied her mug of hot water into the bowl as well. She worried about touching her hands to his wound and delayed long enough to search for rubber gloves. When she spotted a pair tossed under the kitchen sink, she murmured in shaken relief.

As she dipped the cloth into the water and cleaned gently around the injury, she wondered idly if maybe she should have become a nurse or a doctor. She had certainly nursed Katie through enough mishaps.

Why did Katie keep popping into her mind this weekend? She barely spared her a thought at school, but the past two days it seemed Katie was at the surface of her thoughts, beckoning Lissa with her silly, lop-sided smile. Lissa shook her head clear of those images. She had made her decision about Katie. There was no need to obsess about it.

The skin around the wound was cleaning up well, but the gash continued to bleed. Lissa dreaded getting any closer to the actual injury. The towel was stained with blood, and she dropped it into a garbage bag and started again with a fresh one. She dampened the towel, rubbed it with soap, and moistened it again, then gritted her teeth and probed the open wound with it.

Her patient jerked his arm, but she held on firmly, dabbed again with the towel, and removed more of the congealed blood.

"Oh, man."

She looked quickly at his face and found his eyes on her, his mouth clamped shut, and a look of intense pain on his face.

"I'm sorry. I'm trying to clean it," she said.

"Keep going," he muttered. He turned his face away. She

continued her dabbing and wiping.

She could feel tears forming. What if this were *her* arm? What if she had to depend on some uneducated stranger to fix her up? "I'm sorry," she said again. "I don't really know what I'm doing. If we had the Internet here. . . ."

"Is there more water?" She heard him mumble the words quietly, rose from her chair and filled his juice glass, handing it to him. Then another idea struck her. She dug the corkscrew out of a drawer and pried the cork from the Pinot Grigio bottle. She took his already empty glass from him and filled it with wine, then handed it back.

"Maybe it will help," she said.

He took the glass gratefully. "Maybe you need some, too. Your hands are shaking."

She laughed self-consciously. "Oh, I don't know if that's a very good idea." She continued to clean the wound, and silence loomed between them.

"How did you get this?" she asked.

He was quiet for a moment, then said, "I already told you how."

"It's not a bullet wound, is it? Because if it's a bullet wound. . . ."

He barked a laugh. "No."

She held his arm firmly to the table top. He was weak and dependent on her for help, and it gave her the courage to question him. "Were you stabbed by someone?"

"No, it's just a jab from some sheet metal, nothing serious."

"It looks pretty serious," she said. "You fainted from the pain."

"I fainted from getting up too fast."

"Well don't faint again," she said uncertainly. She wasn't sure which was worse, having him conscious - or not.

. . .

He stared at her blonde head bent over his arm. Her hair was tied up in a knot and stray tendrils escaped in messy profusion.

"Medusa," he mused. "Feared by mortal man."

She looked up briefly, then went back to work.

The truth was that he felt faint and weak right now, and it was soothing to have this young girl nursing him, in spite of the sudden quick stabs that made him wince as she cleaned his open skin. He watched her as she tried to cleanse a stubborn particle of blood and matter, and he grimaced, watching her brow furrow in concentration. Rubber gloves. She was smart and fastidious. He wondered what else she was.

"I'm sorry," she said. "I know it hurts. I can tell."

After a moment he said, "Only when you dig around in it."

She stopped working suddenly, and her face flushed.

"No, keep going. Thank you for trying to help me."

She sat back and dropped the blood-stained cloth into the bowl of pink-tinged water. "You're welcome."

He looked at her pretty, serious face. She reached for his right arm again and held it firmly to the tabletop, and he watched in surprise as she picked up the wine bottle and splashed a generous portion of Pinot Grigio over his injury.

"Ow, oh. . . okay, that's interesting." He sucked air in through his teeth.

"Well, maybe it will disinfect it somehow. I don't really know what I'm doing."

"I don't suppose you're a med student or anything?"

"No, I wish I were." She gestured to the bottle of wine. "I saw that in a movie once."

"Do you have any hard liquor?" he muttered. "For my arm, I mean." Then he glanced her way again. "Or don't you stock that?"

"I don't drink it," she said. "There's none here." She dabbed at the wine running over his raw flesh. "Your arm could be broken or something, you know. How would I be able to tell?"

"It's not broken. Look, I can bend it." Slowly, grimacing, he flexed his right arm, making a loose fist. Pain crossed his face, and more blood oozed from the slash in his skin. "Okay, no more of that. Do you have something to bandage it with?" He saw her hesitation and the way her glance darted toward the bathroom door. "Listen," he said, "I'm not going anywhere, and I'm not going to hurt you. If you can get some bandages, I'd be glad. I'll just sit here and hold this cloth to it."

Chapter 9

LISSA STOOD UP STIFFLY and went into the bathroom, exhaling heavily as she caught a glimpse of herself in the medicine cabinet mirror. *Medusa* was right. She looked frightful, her long, light hair bundled on top of her head. There were smudges under her eyes, and her clothes were rumpled. She smoothed her hair with one hand as she opened the medicine chest.

It was right to help him, she knew. And it was her penance for ignoring the driver of the Grand Marquis, whether this were he or not. Let it be right to help him, she prayed vaguely. Don't let him hurt me.

But how could she possibly know if she were doing the right things for him? Maybe she was just making his injury worse.

She found a package of gauze bandages and some medical tape in the medicine chest, then spotted a bottle of hydrogen peroxide on an open shelf.

He was still in the chair when she returned. "See? Still here," he said. "Try to relax."

His casual talk emboldened her. And anyway, didn't they say you should befriend your hostage-taker, let him see you as a person? Then he'd be less likely to hurt you, right? "This isn't a particularly relaxing situation," she said lightly. "A guy broke into my camp, bled on my floor, then fainted in my kitchen. It doesn't happen every day."

He chuckled under his breath, a wheezing sound, and nodded.

"I found hydrogen peroxide," she said.

"Good, it's a disinfectant. Go ahead and add it to the mix."

"Unfortunately, it's been here awhile. It's probably frozen

and thawed a few times, so maybe it's no good anyway." She poured some over the wound. "I wish I had some kind of antibiotic ointment." She had placed the box of gauze on the table, and now she gestured to it. "Do you want me to bandage it? Or would you rather...?"

"I only have one hand; you have two."

She blotted gently at the glossy, uneven moisture around the wound, then pulled several pieces of gauze from the box and folded them neatly to fit the area.

He stopped her before she taped them in place. "Wait a minute. What if I bend my arm like this, and we make a sling somehow. Then I won't be tearing the bandage off and making it bleed every time I move my arm."

"Okay."

He bent his arm at the elbow, and she taped the bandage and started from the room to get a sheet from the bedroom trunk. Suddenly she stopped and turned back, staring at him, made brave by his pain and vulnerability. She took a deep breath and plunged in. "Why are you here? What really happened to you?"

"What? I don't get a sling unless I make a confession? I've been walking for hours in the storm. I was looking for a place-"

She interrupted him. "Who are you?"

If his eyes could have looked through her, they would have at that moment. She backed away, surprised at the deliberateness in his gaze. "Ned," he said softly. "My name is Ned. What's yours?"

. . .

She fled to the bedroom and sat stiffly on her bed until her breath began to come easier. That look he had given her. Not the violent look she had seen from the safe confines of her car, but a different look. Deep and penetrating. In some ways, a far more frightening look.

She returned with a bed sheet, yellowed with age, and sat across the table from him, ripping the sheet in half, then ripping it again, until she had a manageable piece to use for a sling. She folded it over to make several strong layers, then offered it to him.

He lifted his right arm and placed his bent elbow against the faded fabric, then smoothed the longer edges up toward his neck. "Can you tie it?" he asked her.

She stepped cautiously behind him and stood perfectly still. She ordered her hands to tie the sling. All she had to do was pull the edges behind his neck, move his longish hair out of the way, and tie the sheet. It was not hard.

She was glad the stranger couldn't see the flush she knew was staining her cheeks. She'd had so few relationships with men before William, a few awkward dates. It felt uncomfortable, intimate somehow, to touch this man's neck.

"I can't do this myself," he said gruffly. "Would you mind tying it, please?" He bent his head forward a little so she could snug the sling ends against his neck.

"I have to move your hair aside," she said.

"Right. Do that. If you get lice, I'll mail you some spray later."

Blushing furiously and grateful he couldn't see her, she gently touched his hair, moving it off his neck. She picked up the ends of the sheet and tied a single knot. "Is that too tight?"

He twisted his head and neck a little, getting the kinks out, and suggested, "A little tighter, maybe."

She tightened the sling and knotted it.

"Thanks," he said. Then he spoke to the air in front of him. "Why are you still standing behind me?" He twisted his head to look at her, grimacing at the pain that shot up his arm to his shoulder. "It would be easier to talk to you if you were over there."

"Who says we're talking?" Was that the way to go? Friendly conversation. Banter. Whatever it took to stay alive.

"You," he answered. "You said you wanted me to tell you how I happened to drop in."

She emerged from behind him. "Okay, tell me."

"My car got stuck in the snow. I needed help. I came here." He gestured ambiguously with one hand. "It's not much of a story."

Lissa stared at him. She could feel the tension rising in her. She suspected it was much more of a story than he wanted her to think. "It's three o'clock in the morning," she said finally. "If you need sleep you can stay. Tomorrow, you can leave. You should see a doctor."

"Well, I'll definitely stay, but as for leaving, there's not much chance of that." He glanced at the dark kitchen window. The gusts had died down a bit, but snow still fell steadily. "I bet there's over two feet out there by now."

Lissa looked, too. Yes, two feet and counting. And she was held captive in her own camp by the weather and a man who could be anyone, was no one.

She glanced at Ned and found him looking at her. He smiled disarmingly, pulled the wine bottle to him, and lifted up the mug she had planned to use for her tea. "Is this yours?"

"It was. I was intending to have some tea."

He poured wine into the mug. "Have this instead. It will steady your nerves."

"There's nothing wrong with my nerves," Lissa said in annoyance.

"Oh, are you always this on edge?" He pushed the mug toward her.

"On edge?" she said incredulously. "Look at the circumstances! And just today a gas station was. . . ." She stopped herself. Why was she blathering on like this? "Why don't you carry a wallet?" she asked him.

"What?" He glared at her. "How would you know that? Did you. . . ."

"I'm not used to people breaking in. I want to know who you are. Why don't you have keys?"

"Are you kidding?"

"No, I think it's odd."

He turned his face aside and she wondered if she had gone too far. His eyes came back to lock onto hers. "I have no idea. Maybe they're out in the snow somewhere. Why don't you go hunt for them if you want proof."

"You lost your wallet *and* your keys?" she asked.

He leaned back and smiled a little crookedly. She waited for a sarcastic reply, but there was none.

"Did you just happen to choose this building?" she said. She picked up the mug and sipped at the wine.

Ned hesitated, then the grin returned. "No, I saw your lights. You had the whole place glowing like a Christmas tree," he guffawed. "What an invitation if someone did want to hurt you."

"Why were you on this road? There's no one-" Lissa stopped

abruptly. Not a great idea to announce that she was, at the moment, the lone inhabitant of Arrowhead Lake Road.

"I know there's no one else around," he finished for her. "My car plowed into a snowbank. I knew there were camps down this way, so I figured I'd get inside one to get out of the storm. When I saw the little compact stuck in the bank, I figured someone walked to one of these camps. There's no place else you could go. I looked for signs of life and saw your many welcoming lights. It's your car, right?"

Lissa's face took on a look of complete indignation. "You know it's mine," she said in disgust.

"What's that mean? How would I know?"

"You own the Grand Marquis, right?"

He didn't need to answer. His surprised look was answer enough.

"You don't have to look so shocked," she said. "I was there, remember? You hit my car. You drove like a madman."

"I never drive like a madman."

"There's no damage to speak of. I'm going to forget it happened. Where were you between then and the time you got here?"

The fight had gone out of him, and Lissa turned her back, a daringly brave gesture. She poured more water into the saucepan and turned on the burner. She sipped her wine, and then turned back to her unwelcome guest. "When you hit my car and then rammed yours into a snowbank, where did you go? I came here. You showed up hours later."

"I was walking," he said weakly. "I didn't. . . ." He stopped and stared at her.

"For six hours?"

The question hung in the air between them.

"I'm really tired," he said at last. "Can I lie down somewhere?"

"Those questions shouldn't be that hard to answer," she said. "You must know where you were."

He said nothing.

"Fine," she said, "you can stay here, and I'll even share my food with you in the morning, but I expect you to leave after that. I'm not afraid of you, but I don't want you here."

Ned was staring at her, his mouth a straight line. He

gestured out the window. "That might not be possible."

This time it was Lissa's turn not to answer.

She scooped up the remnants of the ruined sheet and stalked from the kitchen, folding the sheet scraps and stowing them on top of the dresser in her room. She was surprised that she no longer felt particularly frightened of Ned, whoever he was. She chastised herself, though, for her brazen accusations. He could be dangerous, and her frivolous remarks could make him angry. And that was not a smart move.

She pulled sheets from the trunk and took them to the extra bedroom, where she quickly made up one of the lumpy beds. She pushed the family photographs aside and climbed onto the dresser, pulled several warm blankets and a quilt from the wires suspended across the top of the room, and spread them on the bed, then systematically emptied the dresser drawers and the small bedside tabletop of anything that Ned could use to hurt her. These she deposited in her own room. She went back and stacked up the family pictures, carrying them to her room as well. Criminal or not, she would give him a prisoner's cell.

Her glance fell on the top photo - her unkempt mother, her dangling cigarette, the very thing that had killed her. Ned, if that was even his name, had asked for a cigarette; it was practically the first thing he'd said. Disgust filled her. Yes, he would be on his way in the morning, storm or no storm. Righteously, she found clothes for him and piled them on the bed. She assumed he might like to change out of his wet, bloody ones.

Back in the kitchen, she placed her empty mug in the dishpan in the sink, turned off the boiling water, took two clean mugs from the cupboard, and wiped them out with a clean cloth. "I'm going to make you tea," she said. "I think it would be a lot better for you than a cigarette."

"No, thank you, but I'd like to lie down." The paleness had come back into his face. His breathing seemed labored, and she realized that he was in great pain. She felt contrite.

"Can you make it?" she asked.

He stood up shakily and clutched the tabletop; the oilcloth skidded slightly to one side. "I think so." He leaned back against the wall. "You want to just show me?"

She took him to the extra bedroom and pointed out the change of clothes she had found for him. "Before you change, though, the outhouse is behind the camp and up the hill."

He groaned. "I can't do that."

Lissa shrugged. "Suit yourself. There's a flashlight by the kitchen door or a chamber pot over there. Take your pick." He glanced at the corner where a chipped white porcelain pot stood, an antique now, with a spray of plastic flowers springing from it.

Lissa closed the door and returned to the kitchen. It would serve him right to suffer all night. If he wasn't a gas station thief, he sure acted like one. And he was, at best, a trespasser, uninvited and unwelcome.

She could hear him moving slowly around in the bedroom and an occasional whimper of pain as he maneuvered his injured arm to accommodate the dry clothing. Lissa poured boiling water into her mug and steeped her tea bag, then drank thirstily. The gallon was more than half gone. She would have to go out in the morning, gather snow, and boil it to sterilize it. She didn't look forward to the task, and she could blame the stranger in the extra bedroom.

She finished her tea and turned off lights; she could feel her face flush as she decided to leave the kitchen light burning. How dare he accuse her of inviting intruders by leaving so many lit.

In her room, she rued the fact that the bedroom doors were not equipped with locks. She dragged her dresser across the floor and jammed it in front of the door, pulled the plug on the dresser lamp, carried it across the room, replugged it, and left it on. If Ned the Thief wanted to kill her in the night, at least she'd give herself a sporting chance.

Noises from the other bedroom drew her attention, and Lissa was surprised when she heard him exit his room. She held a fearful breath, then heard him go into the kitchen. Moments later, the outer door opened and closed. What was he doing? Was he leaving? Surely he was too worn out to be that stupid. Suddenly she stifled a laugh; he must be on his way to the outhouse. It occurred to her to get up and bar the kitchen door. She could secure all the locks and drag furniture in front of the windows. Yes, and then he'd find a way to crash through and break things and she'd have a bigger mess to clean up. And maybe it would infuriate him as much as he'd been infuriated before. She wasn't entirely convinced he wouldn't murder her.

She lay in her bed with the dresser lamp burning, staring at the window, looking out on the deep, black forest.

When she heard him return, she glanced at her watch and saw that it was after four a.m. By the time she woke up, if she survived until morning, she wouldn't need the lights she'd left on. Quickly, she emerged from her sleeping bag, flicked off the light, and stumbled back to bed, looking forward to daylight.

. . .

He lay in the dark wondering if he'd sleep at all. He needed to be a lot smarter, but the pain was so much worse than he was letting on; it was a miracle he could even talk to her. A few aspirin was definitely not going to do the trick with this.

It was in his own best interests to get her to like him, believe him, so why was he avoiding her questions? And his stupid sarcastic remarks. Head lice? Really?

Way to gain her trust.

She was so righteous, though. He couldn't help noticing the snobby little tilt to her nose, her superior tone.

Ned groaned and tried to turn over, sending shooting pains up his arm. She'd gone through his pockets. She might look like a fragile little thing, but for God's sake, she'd gone through his pockets! And where was his wallet? He groaned again. All that money.

Sleep, he told himself. You need to be on top of this tomorrow. Quit thinking that if you allow sleep you might never wake up. Not that that would be such a loss to the world. He twisted in the uncomfortable little bed, and felt his eyes begin to close. Sleep. Let it come. Sleep.

Chapter 10

LISSA TEA HAD KNOWN since the age of ten that she would make something of herself.

The family always celebrated birthdays the same way - a cake, a pile of presents, the family gathered in noisy confusion. There were usually a few squabbles, settled amicably by her father while her mother bustled back and forth, grabbing up a fistful of forks and spoons from the silverware drawer or hunting an elusive book of matches from somewhere in the dining room hutch.

On Lissa's tenth birthday, things had been delayed, but essentially no different. Her father had taken little Katie on an outing to buy ice cream. Lissa hoped for chocolate marshmallow or black cherry, her favorites, anything but rum raisin. If you ate rum raisin, you might as well not have ice cream at all. They'd been gone too long - everything took longer with Katie - and Mother was fussing about it.

"When are we going to have my cake, Mama?" Lissa asked. The cake stood on the kitchen counter, its yellow icing dripping deliciously down the sides, ten candles standing crookedly on top. Her mother had spelled out her name with green sprinkles. Daniel and Steven were clamoring for milk and attention. Lissa got the milk carton from the refrigerator and poured them each a glass to hush them.

"As soon as Dad gets back," her mother said. "Steven, get off that stool. We don't need any calamities around here today."

Steven climbed down, clutching his glass, hurling drops of milk to the floor and countertop. Lissa wiped it up with the rag from the sink.

The rag smelled like sour food. She dropped it back into the sink and sniffed her fingers, wrinkling up her nose. She went into the bathroom and washed her hands with soap.

When she returned, there was a faint gray smudge on her cake. Lissa leaned into the counter, peering at the cake. When she saw the ash on her mother's cigarette, she knew. "There's cigarette in my cake," she said.

Her mother glanced at the cake and deftly scooped the offending smudge with her finger, licking it off and smiling at Lissa. "It won't hurt anything. Don't tell Daddy."

When her father and Katie returned, her mother cut the birthday cake, serving a generous wedge to each of them. Lissa watched without speaking. She wanted to be served from the clean part of the cake. Her mother had swirled the frosting back into place, and Steven was served that section. He didn't know, and he didn't care.

Lissa was relieved.

"What kind of ice cream are we having?" Daniel asked.

Katie chortled, strapped snugly into a high chair. She was four and the chair was too small for her. "Oh, Lissy will be surprised!"

Two kinds as it turned out- mint chip and chocolate swirl, two good kinds. Lissa couldn't help smiling when she saw her parents exchange a grin. "Thanks," said her mother, "for taking Katie along to help."

"Not a problem," her father said. "She was my assistant." He made a funny face at Katie, who laughed. "Unless I was hers." He turned back to his wife. "If we could have someone full time it sure would help, but we do okay, don't we?" He leaned over to ruffle Katie's already tangled hair.

"With Lissa's help, we do," said her mother. "Don't we, Lis?"

They did. Her mother held down a part-time job as a contractor's receptionist and, to accommodate Katie, had arranged to work late afternoons, Saturday mornings, and two evenings a week at the office. At those times, Lissa cheerfully stayed with Katie.

The other children had after-school daycare, but Mrs. Jericho had drawn the line at caring for a handicapped child. "She's so easy, though," Lissa's mother had argued, but Mrs. Jericho could not be persuaded, so it fell to Lissa.

And Lissa was a willing helper. She had few friends anyway,

and if some little girl did happen to call, Lissa usually tried to invite the child over. Sometimes they came, sometimes not. They knew that if they did, they would share their time with Katie as well as Lissa. That was simply the way it was. Lissa never complained and never minded.

Until the phone rang three days after her tenth birthday. She had just come in from school; her mother had flown out the back door; her father wasn't expected for three more hours. Katie was napping peacefully in her high-sided bed; Lissa was in charge.

She picked up the telephone on the second ring.

It was Janet. "Can you come over to my house? Jenna and Maureen are here. We're going to do a chemistry experiment with the set I got for Christmas."

"Can you bring it here?" Lissa asked. "I have to stay with my sister."

The voice became muffled, and Lissa could hear the discussion as if through water, distorted and fuzzy. Janet came back on the line. "No, my mom says we can't come when your mother's not home. Can you come here?"

"I guess not," Lissa said.

She wandered the house for a while, looked in on Katie, and wondered what the experiment was about. She had played with Janet and Jenna several times, but never with Maureen. She suspected Maureen might be nice; they had shared an art table in school once or twice.

Katie gurgled in her sleep, content in her dreams. Lissa held the high side bars of the bed, gazing at her little sister, and wondered for the first time in her life what her mother would do if Lissa weren't there to help her. What must it be like to stop off at another girl's house after school? To walk with a gang to the ice cream stand or actually get invited to one of the bowling parties that seemed to be popular for birthdays that year.

When she grew up, Lissa decided, she would make sure she could *afford someone full time*, her mother's words, if she ever had a child like Katie. It took money, she knew that. And her father, a factory supervisor, didn't make enough, even with her mother's help.

She recalled vividly the day newborn Katie had arrived at their cramped Keltic Avenue house, sweet-smelling and wrapped in blankets from her three week stay in the hospital. Lissa had been impressed with her tiny size and wanted to hold her right away. Her mother had made her sit on the overstuffed sofa and hold her arms in front of her, a cradle for baby Katie to rest on. Lissa did exactly as she was told, extended her arms, and sucked in a deep breath. She wouldn't do anything to lose this privilege.

It never occurred to her that the silence in the house that day was unusual, that the younger children - Daniel, Margie, and Steven - had all been shipped out to neighbors, that she alone, the oldest, had been chosen to greet the special infant just home from the hospital.

"You have to support her head, Lis," her mother said, sitting down next to her and teaching her to hold the baby securely, to gaze into Katie's bleary eyes, to coo at her to make her feel content. "Here, like this." Mother jostled Lissa around on the couch some, pulled Lissa's arms up and around the tiny body, and then stood up herself, pleased with Lissa's natural gentleness and quick understanding.

Lissa gazed deeply into her baby sister's eyes. The little pupils did not focus; the baby's head lolled slightly to the side.

"She doesn't like to look at me," Lissa complained.

"She will," mother insisted. "Of course she will." She lit a cigarette and blew the smoke out impatiently, making gray clouds, careful not to blow the smoke toward her daughters. "I'm going to quit these things," she said vaguely.

Lissa stared at Katie's sweet face, rocking her gently.

She was not aware when the rest of the tribe returned. By dinnertime, the house was noisy and congested as always, and the new baby had been placed in her crib in Lissa and Margie's room, where she slept and cried alternately.

The next day, Lissa had asked to hold the baby, and her mother had said yes. Margie and Daniel, next in age, had not been permitted to do so. They were too little and too rough. They might do some damage. Babies had to be treated very carefully.

Lissa held and rocked her little sister, petted and coaxed her, learned to feed, change, burp, and play with the undemanding, darling little girl who was to become her constant companion.

For the next eight or nine years, the pudgy, giggling toddler and the thin, serious big sister were rarely apart except for the hours Lissa spent in school. The moment Lissa returned home to Keltic Avenue, there would be Katie, lying in her crib or sitting on the floor or, later, strapped into her wheelchair, waiting.

"Hey, Katie, my matey," Lissa would say, tickling her sister under the chin or making a funny face so Katie would laugh.

"Missy Lissy," Katie would respond, and they'd spread dolls and doll clothes on the floor or build a dream house out of blocks. Lissa never really noticed that she herself spread the clothes and built the houses. She was six years older; it made sense that she'd be better at things than Katie. Katie would sit by and watch and chortle, and Lissa loved having a built-in audience, an admirer at her beck and call, any time, every day.

Lissa had craved the responsibility, too. She loved to hear her mother brag to friends, "Lissa is a savior to me. I don't know what I'd do without her. Katie just loves being with Lissa."

Hearing those words was enough motivation for Lissa - her chance to shine, her opportunity to be more than just one of the Tea kids. So the more her parents praised her, the more she insisted on taking over responsibility for Katie. Even after years passed, and she understood that her sister was unlike other children, she kept to her task. Her mother depended on her. Katie loved Lissa best, and that was as it should be.

When Lissa was ten, the subtle change began; she wondered now and then how her life might be different without Katie. At eleven, she stifled a few resentful feelings as she missed out on a boy-girl party at Janet's house and realized she would have to forego membership in a school art club just starting up; the meetings were held after school. Well, that didn't matter, she rationalized. She could draw on her own at home; she always had. Katie needed her.

Janet started piano lessons when the girls turned twelve, and Lissa begged her mother to enroll her as well.

"Sweetie, I'd love to give you the lessons," her mother said, "but we just can't, Lissa. We can't afford it right now."

They could never afford it, and Lissa allowed that dream to evaporate along with the boy-girl parties, the art club, and Saturday swimming lessons.

It wasn't until Lissa registered for high school that the real trouble began. The special education program in the district was housed in the high school Lissa attended. She and Katie would ride the specially-equipped bus together, go into the building together, then go their separate ways. Lissa buried the guilty relief that surfaced some days when she finally walked away from her sister.

"But Lissee. . . ," Katie would call after her. Katie's special aide might try to coax quiet from her, but often, even as the aide whisked Katie away down the corridor, Lissa could hear her demanding cries. She would find herself hurrying away, hoping the clump of girls giggling in the corner or the boys standing around with bookbags slung over their shoulders would somehow not equate her with the *Lissee. . .* of the plaintive wail.

At night she would tell Katie, "You can't call after me when we're at school. Once we're in the building, you have to go to your room quietly and I have to go to mine."

To no avail. If her aide were late or not paying attention, Katie would try to follow her big sister, ramming through the corridors in her steel chair, once even barging into Lissa's homeroom. Her face flushed and heart pounding, Lissa escorted her back to her own wing. Other kids seemed to stop talking and stare after her as she walked stiffly beside her sister's chair, while Katie's flustered aide ran to meet them.

Lissa talked to her mother, who sympathized and called the school to intervene: Lissa must be allowed to exit the bus first. She must be well out of sight before Katie emerged. The aide *must* pay better attention. Her mother's interference helped, but often Katie's unhappy cries still followed Lissa through the crowded hallways, announcing to all that the Tea sisters had arrived.

In January of her freshman year, Lissa discovered that she could take a class in piano, and told her parents that she intended to sign up. The class was free, and she could practice at school during her study hall.

"That's fine, Lis," they said, "as long as you keep up your other grades."

She did, and she spent all her free time in the practice room at school, progressing quickly through the beginning and intermediate level books. By senior year she was playing difficult pieces and had decided to study music in college.

"College?" her father said. "Do you think you need to?"

"Yes, Dad, I definitely need to," Lissa replied confidently.

"It's expensive, honey, and, you know, your mom and I do fine without it."

An unconvinced stare was Lissa's only reply.

He buried his head inside the newspaper.

Lissa at eighteen was one of the mob of Teas attending the high school. Daniel was sixteen, Margie fourteen, Steven thirteen. Katie was twelve. Only little Sammy spent his days at the elementary school two miles away. Only Sammy was truly his own man. The whole gang of older Teas would pour off the bus and scurry ahead, then Katie would roll down her special ramp, bumping her way through the throng of students. "Bye, Lissy!" she would shout, and Lissa, wanting to appear the loving sister, would give Katie a cursory wave, grit her teeth, and storm off to homeroom.

Was it any wonder she was so anxious to get away? Her father seemed to understand it eventually, although the idea of studying music baffled him. "What kind of job are you going to get?" he kept asking.

"I'll perform," she insisted.

He wasn't convinced.

"I'll write songs for other people to perform," she tried.

Her mother was bewildered and worried by the entire concept. Lissa and Katie had always been so close. What would happen to their special friendship if Lissa went away to school? And why so far away? Couldn't she find a school closer to home? What was the sudden need for independence all about?

Lissa knew it was hardly sudden. Her mother must be blind indeed if she hadn't seen her oldest daughter's anxiety building all this time.

She had to get away, to become educated and independent and successful. She wanted to study music, but she couldn't be sure it was a skill that would earn her money. Enough money that if she ever had a child like Katie she would be able to hire the best kind of help.

"Business, that's what you want to study," her father insisted.

He helped her fill out the application forms, wrote a grudging check for the non-refundable deposit, and bragged to everyone he knew when the scholarship notification arrived in the mail. His daughter would be the best marketing analyst in New York when she came back home to Binghamton.

Her mother remained puzzled - What would happen to Katie?

Lissa could hardly wait to pack her bags and be on her way. To college in Pennsylvania. To become a new Lissa Tea.

Within two days she had set up an appointment with a counselor who showed her the option of a double major, arranged her audition, and helped her choose the courses that would earn her two degrees. Marketing had been the compromise that got her here. Music was the passion that would get her through.

And her roommates, Pat and Shelly, had become real friends who had given, Lissa knew, far more than they had gained from their friendship with her.

If only Shelly and Pat were here right now. It would help to talk to them, to hash out this new problem with William and discuss her decision to take over Katie's care.

She could just hear the exchange of jokes, smell the delicious scent of Pat's lasagna bubbling in the oven, imagine the caustic comments about each other's clothes, jobs, and whatever current guys each of them might be dating - or hoping to.

What would they have said about William Brashue? She knew, of course. Shelly would say he sounded pretty nice and then give her all kinds of crazy advice. Pat would be far more brash: He's blowing you off now? What a jerk!

Lissa grimaced to herself and turned awkwardly in her sleeping bag. The cabin bedroom was chilly, and her toes felt cold. She missed her friends. She wondered if, in some way, she even missed Katie a little. Not that she and Katie would ever share the kind of friendship she had with Shelly and Pat. But she had been close to her little sister, knew her inside out. And still felt guilty about the way she had gone off to college five years ago. After all, it was hardly Katie's fault that Lissa had outgrown her.

Well, she was remedying that.

Lissa punched her pillow and tried to get comfortable.

If all went well, in another year she would be on her own. She would land a job in marketing and make good money, and in her private time, she would compose serious music, maybe sell her work to vocalists, even see her name on a CD or two. She would be earning money of her own, taking care of Katie and making a name for herself. Eventually, she'd drop the marketing if the music was successful enough. She would be going places. With

William, she hoped.

What time was it? Four-thirty, she was guessing. Maybe closer to five.

There were no sounds from the other bedroom, so Ned the gas station thief, or whoever he was, must be sleeping.

What, she wondered, would her roommates think if they could know how she'd spent the night. What if they could see Ned resting in the next room? She knew their reactions. Gorgeous, Pat would say, really hot. Shelly, of course, would be horrified.

Her legs felt cramped inside the sleeping bag, tensed from the cold and her fear of what might be. She stretched and made herself breathe deeply. I need sleep, she thought. If I don't sleep, I won't be in any shape to handle whatever comes tomorrow.

Tomorrow would bring more of the same, she thought dully. She was trapped, snowbound, with no chance of escaping from Ned or the storm. Lissa squeezed her eyes shut and begged sleep to embrace her.

Chapter 11

WHEN LISSA AWOKE, she knew immediately that something was different: Ned's presence. She looked at her watch. Nine forty-five. Snow fell steadily outside her window. Well, she had made it. She had lived to tell the story. So far.

Her eyes felt gritty and her body ached. She blamed the unfamiliar mattress and pillow, but knew the culprit was her own jittery fears. Maybe she should have thrown the stranger out to find his own way in the blinding snow. Well, she hadn't. No decent person would have. It would have been cruel, and she couldn't afford to chalk up any more sins on her soul. She would give him breakfast and then expect him to be on his way. It was his turn to do the decent thing and leave her secure and alone, the way she liked it.

She dressed hurriedly in jeans and a turtleneck, pulled on her fleecy sweater, caught sight of the dried blood caked on the cuff, and quickly took it off again. She would try to wash it out later. For now, she had one other sweater and it would have to do. It wasn't as warm, but she would stoke the fire and turn up the stove. She pulled on warm socks and glanced at her fleece slippers. She would forego those for now; somehow it seemed inappropriate to wear bedroom slippers with a strange man sharing the cabin. She laced up her leather shoes, straightened her sleeping bag, hauled the dresser away from her door, and went into the living room to start the fire.

Through his doorway she could see him asleep in his room. That open door surprised her; there was something vulnerable about sleeping in a strange house with the door open. Obviously he trusted her far more than she trusted him.

Well, why would she trust him? He still hadn't answered her

questions, after all. What was he doing here in the middle of the night? How had he really injured his arm? And who was he, anyway? Why no identification? No wallet? If his car had gone off the road, where, at least, were his car keys?

She could leave the camp. She might not have an opportunity this good again. She could slog down the lake road and be miles away and, with his injured arm, maybe he would never catch up with her. She considered it seriously, but where would she go? With the snow still falling steadily, running seemed pointless.

She gulped back a cry of frustration. She was snowbound. Stuck. An unwilling prisoner.

She watched him sleep for a moment. He lay on his stomach, and his arm in its sling poked up from his body, looking distorted and painful. He moved slightly, and she could see the effort it took him to move the arm. His face looked innocent, awakening her sympathies; it was hard to equate it with that hard, angry face staring out at her from the Grand Marquis. He wasn't a professional man, she was sure. His hair was a little too long and curled over his neck, making him look young and uncared for. She had noticed how rough his hands were, the scars and cuts still healing. So, what did he do for a living? Maybe crime was his living.

She stopped herself. He truthfully hadn't said one thing to make her suspicious. It was that stupid news bulletin. She wished she hadn't heard it.

He stirred again and startled Lissa by muttering, "Give it back. . . .'s mine."

Lissa stared at him, still and afraid. Was he awake or asleep?

"Not jail," he said clearly, then muttered several unintelligible syllables. Then, ". . .'s mine, my medal." His fist clenched tightly.

Frightened, Lissa backed away.

By now, she had half convinced herself that the Gorham gas station thief had been apprehended and that this man was someone else.

Jail, she chastised herself. Did she need to have it spelled out for her?

Well, maybe he wasn't the Gorham thief. Maybe he was a different criminal, one who had not robbed a gas station but had done something else. Maybe he had attacked someone, murdered an entire family on some desolate mountain road, maybe he was wanted in four states. . . .

Lissa shook off her thoughts impatiently and busied herself crumpling up newspapers, cramming them into the fireplace between sticks of kindling. She got the fire going and placed in the two logs lying on the hearth. That would burn for a while but she'd have to bring in more wood.

Her outer clothing had dried during the night, so she donned her parka and wind pants, pulled on her boots, and grabbed the kitchen door key just in case he tried anything funny like locking her out. She stole a last look at his bedroom. To her surprise, the door was now closed. She could hear the creak of the old bed as he moved.

Picking up his ruined leather jacket, she felt for any inside pockets she might have missed the night before. Yes, there was one, and it wasn't empty. Her hand came away with a fistful of bills. With one eye on his door, she counted twenty-eight dollars. There was nothing more in the pocket. Was it robbery money? It wasn't fifteen hundred, but perhaps he had hidden the rest. It was odd, placed in an inside pocket with no wallet, no identification. Her fears mounted again, and she hastily replaced the money.

Stop, she told herself. It's not a gun or a bloody knife. It's twenty-eight dollars. Lots of people carry twenty-eight dollars. Go out. Use the outhouse. Brush your teeth with snow. Get firewood. Don't make more of things than they are.

She opened the kitchen door and stepped into a gray winter wonderland. Snow still pelted down in big, fat, puffy flakes. It was hard work getting up the hill to the outhouse and hard getting back down again to the woodshed. Snowshoes would have made a world of difference, but she had none.

She glanced back at the camp. She knew Ned was stirring, but really, how long would it take him to dress, discover her missing, follow and overtake her – with his arm in a sling, bleeding, fainting. . . . There was a good chance she could outdistance him.

Could she leave her purse and money behind? She would. She needed to be pro-active; hadn't she always been proud of her level head?

Lissa passed the woodshed and camp, made her way to

Arrowhead Lake Road and continued on, slogging through the snow, lifting herself over the deep drifts. Sweat poured from her limbs, and exhaustion overtook her quickly.

She glanced back and saw her camp still in view, cheery smoke pouring from the chimney. A lump formed in her throat. What was she doing? Where was she going? She would never make it to her car, let alone to any town where she might find help. She was better off inside with heat and food, using her wits to survive. Slowly, painfully, she forced her aching legs to carry her back to the woodshed.

It took her longer than she had expected to get the wood. The wind swirled her hair into snarls, and she wished she had stuck the ends up under her hat. The snow near the shed door looked disturbed, and her face prickled with cold as she dug the new snow away from the door and forced it open, wondering what animals lurked near the cabin in the dark of night. The air inside was still. Lissa breathed deeply, glad to be away from the wind.

As little girls, she and Margie used to play in here, hiding from their brothers in the slat-sided dog pen their father had built for a beagle who'd adopted them one summer. The pen's top was counter height, a workshop bench for her father and Uncle Jeff, but the pen underneath was plenty big for two little girls to curl up in. She and Margie would crawl in through the outside dog door and sit in the matted straw, smelling the dog smell and stifling giggles. Huddled together, straw sticking to their clothes and hair, they'd peek between the slats and hear the ruckus around them, teasing the boys who knew they were close by but never seemed able to find them.

Lissa smiled at the memory and tried the door under the workbench, expecting to find it sealed with years of grime and dirt. But it opened easily, and Lissa peeked in. She recognized the pile of moth-eaten blankets, straw clinging to them, and saw the clutter lying along the sides. She was surprised that the old straw looked matted, as if an animal had been there recently. The dog door at the back was open, and a sift of new snow lay inside the hole. The space smelled stale, of frozen sweat and heat.

She shuddered with distaste. The door creaked as she forced it shut again and twisted the handle to keep it from swinging open. If something was making its bed in her woodshed, it was large. She looked around, feeling prickles on her skin inside her warm clothing.

The wood was stacked against one wall, and there was plenty. Her brothers or her father and Uncle Jeff must have spent time last summer chopping and stacking, and Lissa felt grateful. Grabbing as much wood as she could carry, she returned to the camp.

With any luck, Ned would never know she'd attempted to leave.

Chapter 12

WHEN SHE PULLED OPEN the kitchen door, she was surprised to see him at the table, sitting in the same chair he had the night before, holding a paperback book he had plucked from the shelves in his room. She frowned when she saw the clothes he wore - the men's cast off jeans, a little big, that she had placed on his bed, and his own flannel. The shirt was draped over his bare arm in its homemade sling; the ripped, bloodstained sleeve hung empty and loose.

She dumped the wood on the floor and twisted out of her jacket and boots. "You'll catch your death," she said shortly.

"Thanks, Mom," he replied.

"I'm not kidding. It's not going to warm up in here that much," she said. "You need more clothes than that. What's wrong with the shirt I left you?"

He shrugged. "Well, it was very thoughtful, but it's a pullover. Or was I supposed to rise to the challenge?" He gestured to his arm. The sling was askew and the knot had frayed. The whole contraption hung noticeably looser on his arm.

"Oh. Right," she said. "I'll find something else." She jammed her feet into her shoes and tied them, then picked up a couple of logs to carry to the living room.

"I can carry that," he said.

"No, I have it."

He rose anyway, picked up the rest of the wood, balanced it in his arms, and followed her. She set her wood down on the hearth and watched him as he knelt before the fireplace and, one-handed, positioned another log on the flames.

"I don't need your help," she said. "I'm used to being very independent. I'd rather do it myself."

He shrugged. "In this life we can't always have everything we want."

"Obviously," she muttered. She gritted her teeth, watching him poke at the fire. "I'll see if I can find a shirt."

"That would be swell. I was wondering if you might have a toothbrush around that I could use, too."

She escaped to her bedroom and picked through a pile of comfortable emergency clothing - discarded sweatshirts and terry cloth robes, old swimsuits and printed tee shirts. She held up a gold chamois shirt that must have belonged to her Uncle Jeff. It seemed about the right size and looked soft and warm. She took a deep breath and returned to the living room. "Try this one," she said as she handed it to him. "Before you put it on, I want to ask you. . . ." He stood waiting. "Did you try to open the shed door last night?"

"The shed. . . ."

"The snow is disturbed."

Ned plucked at the soft chamois of the shirt he held and looked down, thinking. "Yeah, I might have done that. I mistook it for the privy."

"Okay," Lissa said. She turned to the fire, staring at the flames, and felt fear prickle her neck. It was a logical mistake. In the dark, at camp, one outbuilding could look like another. Why did she have the feeling that he had made it up?

In the bathroom, she found a cup of old toothbrushes laced through with cobwebs. She had no idea whose was whose and doubted whether anyone would ever use them again. She congratulated herself on the extra toothbrush she always carried in her pocketbook, and wished she had brought the toothpaste that was locked in her car. She had brushed her teeth with achingly cold snow, and could still feel the fresh tingle in her mouth. She selected a brush for Ned and shrugged. It was up to him whether or not to use it.

Lissa went to the kitchen and scrounged through all her food, wondering how she could make it last. One onion, six bagels, mozzarella cheese, tea bags, a box of crackers, a small loaf of Italian bread, three carrots, wilted romaine lettuce, a few mushrooms, a pound of ground beef, and less than half a gallon of water.

She sat at the table, her chin in her hands, and tried to think creatively. Ned came in, sat down across from her, picked up his paperback book, then tented it on the table. He spotted the used toothbrush and picked it up. He was wearing the gold chamois shirt; he had managed to fit his injured arm inside the roomy sleeve and that inside the sagging sling.

"Thanks for the shirt," he said. "I'm sorry to be a bother."

"Do you want me to tighten that?" Lissa asked.

"If you wouldn't mind."

She stood behind him and pulled up gently on the sling. "Put your arm where it feels most comfortable," she said. Her fingers felt under the long hair on his collar, untied the knot, and retied it.

He reached back with his left hand and touched her fingers. She immediately stepped back. "You caught some hair in it," he said, fumbling to loosen it, then twisted his neck around to see her better. "Gosh, did I touch you by mistake? Maybe there's some disinfectant in the bathroom."

Lissa stared at him. "I'm sorry," she stammered, "I didn't mean. . . ."

"Forget it." He turned around again. She remained frozen behind him. "Anyway, it feels better. Thanks."

Lissa stepped to the kitchen window and looked out with longing. "I wish this snow would stop," she said.

"No such luck. I think we're stuck here. What did you think you were doing out there?"

"What?" Lissa felt her face flushing. Had he been *spying* on her?

"You were pretty far down the road. Did you think you were leaving?"

"Well, yes. Going for help," she added quickly.

"You wouldn't have made it."

"I made it last night," she said firmly.

He guffawed. "Last night your destination was a heated building. What was it today? A car stuck in a snowbank?" He picked up the paperback, but instead of reading it, gazed at Lissa. He was quiet for a moment before he said, "Look, I appreciate the bed and the shelter. But I'd also appreciate it if you wouldn't treat me like I'm some kind of leper or a convicted felon. I told you last night that I don't intend to hurt you. I don't have any choice but to stay. And you don't either."

Lissa shrugged helplessly and nodded. Discouraged, she sat across the table from him and waited until he spoke again.

"I'm sorry to ask, but do you have any more aspirin or something? This is hurting quite a bit."

"I'll get it," she said. She retrieved her pill case from the bedroom, handed over the entire case, and poured him water. "You know better than I do what you want." She sighed in resignation and sat back down.

He swallowed two pills and handed the case back.

"You can hold onto it," she told him. "There aren't many left. Just take them when you want them. Do you want me to change the bandage?"

"It's all right, thanks."

Lissa didn't answer, but got up and found a frying pan in the cabinet under the sink. She wiped out the pan, peeled the wrapper from the ground beef and turned the heat on low. The meat began to sizzle quietly.

The sound of slow chopping caught her attention. She turned and nearly dropped the fork she was holding. Ned held a carrot on a plate with his right hand. His left hand wielded a long-bladed kitchen knife. The knife came down, crookedly slicing another strip of carrot. She gasped involuntarily and he glanced at her.

"Put it down," she said coldly.

"Put it. . . . You mean put the knife down?"

"Yes, that's exactly what I mean."

He dropped the knife onto the oilcloth-covered table top. One carrot sat split in half, a few slices cut into uneven short lengths. "Would you rather I didn't help?"

"Just sit there and stop doing things." Her nerves were raw. Every sound he uttered, every move he made was setting her on edge. "Please. I'll do this myself."

He sat silently in the same chair he had occupied before. He always chose the same chair, Lissa thought dully, as if he had branded it the night before with his blood. The meat began smoking in the pan, and Lissa moved the pieces around with the fork.

"Is this your name? Lissa Tea?" he asked her.

She whirled around. He was looking through the books she had brought. There was her name scrawled across her notebooks and on the flyleaf of her Aesthetics textbook. She was furious. "Who gave you permission to look at those?"

He looked as if he'd been struck. "Well, they were just sitting here. I didn't know your name was a deep, dark secret."

"You have no right to go sifting through my things," she said hotly. She scooped up the books and deposited them on a corner of the countertop.

"And you had no right to go sifting through my pockets," he retorted.

She turned to face him, could feel her face flushing hot. "Well, this is *my* camp, not yours."

"And they were *my* pants, not yours."

Furious, she turned back to the hamburger and began stabbing at it with the fork, prying the uncooked clumps apart so the heat could reach them.

"So is that your name?"

She refused to answer.

"Lissa?" There was belligerence in his voice.

She slammed the panful of cooked hamburger onto a cold burner and tore open the box of crackers. "This is breakfast. Enjoy yourself." She dumped a handful of crackers onto a plate and left the kitchen. His bed was unmade, she noticed as she passed the bedroom door. The blankets and quilt she had given him trailed carelessly down the side of the bed and onto the floor. It irked her that he hadn't picked up after himself; people should make an effort to be neat. First her mother's sloppy housekeeping for eighteen years, now this moron making a mess of her weekend.

She went to the living room, and sank onto the couch before the fire, wishing Pat and Shelly were here to share her anger, her frustration, and her fear.

She heard him in the kitchen, the sounds of the frying pan being centered on the burner, a chair being pushed in.

He came into the room. "I'm sorry," he said behind her. "I know it's a pain having me here." His voice sounded tired, as if the apology had been an effort. He walked to the window and stood there, watching the unrelenting snowflakes fall to the white ground and mix in.

"It would be nice if you could at least make your bed," she said tersely.

He looked at her dumbly. "Why? Are we expecting guests?"

"It's what civilized people do." She turned her head away, watching the flames.

"Do you have a plan for the food?" he said finally. "Do you want me to try to make something out of it?"

She shrugged, uncaring. "Whatever."

He went into his room and she could hear him tugging and grunting, pulling furniture out from the wall, then shoving it back again. A frisson of guilt spiked in Lissa, then died away.

Soon she heard him in the kitchen, chopping and cooking. She realized she was hungry when the smell of frying onions wafted into the living room, but she refused to give him the satisfaction of returning to the kitchen. As it turned out, it didn't matter; he brought her a plate. On it were eight crackers. On each rested a melted slab of mozzarella, crumbled beef, and a mound of cooked onions. A little pile of roughly cut carrot sticks sat beside them. Lissa took the plate wordlessly and ate a cracker. He watched her and seemed to be waiting for a verdict.

"It's very good," she said contritely. "Thank you."

"You're welcome," he said.

She forced herself to speak politely. "There's more food in my car. Also some buried in the snow someplace. I brought all I could carry when my car went into the snowbank, then I dropped half of it." She found herself devouring the crackers, her first meal since lunch the day before. The food tasted delicious. "Did you have some?"

He nodded.

She finished the last crumb and put the plate aside. "Are you left handed?" she asked him.

"No."

"But you cut the vegetables and cheese with your left hand?"

He grinned at her. "That's why it took awhile."

She had nothing more to say to him. The polite words had seemed a mammoth effort.

Silently, they put the leftovers away together and placed the greasy dishes into the dishpan. "We're going to have to start melting snow," Lissa said finally. "We'll have to boil it if we're going to drink it."

"You don't really have to boil it," Ned offered. "It'll be clean enough."

"I'd rather boil it," She insisted, "just to be safe."

Ned shrugged. "Okay. I'll get some." He put on his jacket and boots, hat and gloves, and found two big plastic bowls in the cabinets. Lissa watched him through the window as he trudged off the stoop a little way, looking for a place where the snow might be purer. He carried both bowls under his left arm, dropped them into the snow, and filled them to brimming. With one hand, he packed the snow down and added more. He stopped occasionally, winded, but returned only when the bowls were full.

"Start these," he said, hauling them in one at a time, "and I'll get more. There seems to be plenty. Start with about an inch of water from the jug in each pan."

Did they really need this much snow? Lissa started to protest, but he was already outdoors, tamping the snow into two more buckets and dragging them in. He stomped snow off his boots outside the kitchen door, breathing heavily. She took the buckets from him, transferred the snow to two cast iron pots and set them on the two remaining stove burners.

"Not that way," he said. He shrugged out of his jacket, removed the big pots from the stove and rummaged for saucepans, placing them on the burners. "If you do it this way, it'll melt faster." He poured a dash of water from the jug into each pan, then his left hand scooped up fistfuls of snow and dropped them into the saucepans one by one. As the snow melted, he stirred and added more.

"Okay," she said. "I get it. Go sit down or something. Your pants are soaked. Your dry ones are in the living room."

"I'm happy to help."

She spoke through clenched teeth. "You're injured. I'd rather you didn't faint today."

. . .

The snow melted down to just over six cups. She added a few handfuls of cold snow and plunged the greasy dishes in, washing and rinsing them. Ned dried them awkwardly. She tossed the dishwater outside.

"I'm tired, and I have a paper to write," she said. "I'm sorry I can't entertain you all afternoon. You'll have to think of something to do for yourself."

"Okay. Fortunately, I know how to read."

"All right, I'm sorry," Lissa said. "Listen, I'm not myself."

"Hmm," he retorted. "You seem very much yourself."

"How would you know?" she muttered.

"At least, the self I've met so far."

She glanced at his face, caught the hint of an amused smile, and squelched the little guilty flicker inside her. Why was she being so abrupt with him? It was not only rude, but foolish. She would try to be more civil. "How is your arm?" she said. "Is it feeling any better?"

He smiled at her, a truce. "Some. I don't think there's an infection. I think the wine did the trick."

"Well, all right then." Lissa gathered her books and barricaded herself into her bedroom. She would much have preferred to work by the fire, but that was impossible with him lounging in the living room. She sat down on the bed and opened a book. The tears that came unbidden to her eyes surprised her as they ran silently down her cheeks and fell onto the open page in front of her.

What was wrong with her? He didn't seem dangerous; he seemed like a guy who had needed a good Samaritan and had come across her. Here was an opportunity to help someone else, and she was acting like a shrew and making the worst of the situation instead of striving to make the best of it.

She wiped her tears on her sleeve, lay down on the bed, and pulled her sleeping bag over her. Exhausted, she was asleep in four minutes.

Chapter 13

NED WAS FEELING more and more relaxed, rocking slowly in the creaky wooden rocker he had angled toward the fire. He munched a handful of crackers and gazed at the low-burning flames as the minutes ticked by and the snow continued falling outside. The Robert Frost collection sat open, upside down on the painted coffee table. A glance at his watch showed two o'clock. There hadn't been any sounds from her room for almost an hour, and he wondered if she was really writing in there or if she might be asleep, or maybe plotting some grand scheme of escape.

She was terrified of him.

Leaving Gorham had been a mistake. He had known that all along, but his father's lessons were embedded too deep. So he'd shot out of there, ignoring the chaos at the gas station. And now he had a wounded arm to show for it and a car that was buried down the road. Things were in a worse mess than they had been in a long time.

Why did he stay in Gorham anyway? His business was failing, and he could hardly pay his bills. And people were starting to look at him funny whenever they saw him.

Right, like he had any choice about leaving Gorham.

He sucked in a rattled breath. If it could keep on snowing for the rest of his life, he'd be glad just to stay right here and boil snow and carry wood. It was little enough to pay for the privilege of avoiding it all.

He heard a sudden sound and jolted, then settled back; it was the fire, popping and crackling. He didn't need to be so on edge. The snow was getting deeper by the hour, and it was very unlikely he'd be seeing any familiar faces around here in the next day or two. His nerves were taut and every sound was spooking him.

He was safe; he was fine. He needed to relax. He also knew how impossible that was.

Another noise.

He realized the scratching was within the wall and breathed easier. There was a mouse in the camp. He listened again and heard it once more, a quick, quiet tapping, the sound of tiny claws scrabbling behind the wood panels.

The mouse popped out from a crack near the fireplace and jumped to the mantel, where it trembled, whiskers quivering, underneath the proud tail feathers of a stuffed pheasant. What did her family do about mice, he wondered. Set traps? Kill them? Capture them and let them go? Ned stared at the small black eyes examining him. Helping this one escape into the woods might sound like the humane thing to do, but not today, not in this weather. Two of a kind they were, captives of the storm. He wondered how Lissa Tea would feel about sharing the camp with yet another intruder.

He got up and went to the fireplace, softly crumbling a cracker into a tidy mound in his palm. "Hey, little one," he said in a soft, crooning voice. "Here's dinner." The mouse sat still, afraid, its jet black eyes staring back. Ned let the crumbs fall into a pile on the mantelpiece. The mouse stood still.

"Well, go on, then," Ned said quietly. "I'm not going to stop you from going about your business." He watched the mouse pop back into its hole and disappear. He could hear its movement in the wall for several more minutes, then nothing.

"We usually trap them and let them go in the woods."

Lissa's voice behind him surprised him, and he twisted his head to look at her. She wore the same bulky sweater she'd had on earlier and held a hairbrush while she unknotted the elastic that had become tangled in her hair. Her features showed the softness of sleep, and her clothes were rumpled. He took in her smooth complexion and slim, schoolgirlish shape.

"Did you get some rest?" he asked.

"I told you I was writing a paper."

He sat down in the rocker and looked at the fire.

Lissa sighed. "All right," she admitted, "I intended to write the paper, but I fell asleep. You'll probably recall that I was up all night." She pulled the hairbrush through her tangled hair. "I have a mousetrap in the other room."

"Do you want to set it?"

"It's not the kind that kills them. It just traps them and then we let them go behind the camp. We have a rule that they have to be set free beyond the boulders; it tricks us into thinking they won't come back."

"It would freeze," he said. "And I'm not volunteering to find the boulders anyway."

She came around the couch and sat down on it, opposite him, tilting her head. "With the amount of food we have, you decided to feed him?"

Ned laughed. "It's one cracker. He may be back for it."

"I hope not. So you intend to let him run loose in here?"

"Unless you object. It's your camp."

A peach flush stained her cheeks. "Well, I do object," she said stiffly, "but I don't want him to freeze to death either."

"Then let him have the run of the place."

Lissa hesitated, then said, "I don't particularly like mice."

"Then scream when you see him. It'll scare him back into the walls."

"And what's your best suggestion for at night? I don't want to find him in my sleeping bag."

Ned shrugged. "He'd probably burrow down to the bottom, so you won't even know unless you kick him."

She closed her eyes briefly, tugged the brush through her long hair, and glanced at Ned. "Great. My weekend just gets better and better."

"This is a nice little cabin, Lissa," he said, looking around. Out of the corner of his eye he saw her flush at the use of her name. "That's your name, right?"

She hesitated. "It's Melissa," she said finally, "but no one has ever called me that."

Something in her expression made him ask, "Do you want people to call you that?"

She shrugged. "Sometimes, maybe. It's more dignified. Lissa sounds like such a little girl."

"Well, then, Melissa, how do you happen to be staying in this camp all alone? Do you own it?" It was obvious she was juggling her need for privacy, her fear of him, with a decision to be courteous, working hard at being polite. "It's a great place," he added.

"Thank you. It's been in my family for years. It belongs to my father and his brother."

"So you come here every year?"

"I used to. Not lately." She ventured a wary smile at him and put the brush down. "Now it's my turn to ask questions."

Chapter 14

SHE WATCHED A SHADOW creep over his eyes and saw a flicker of nervousness in them before he spoke.

"Ask away," he said.

"Who are you really?"

"I told you the truth. Ned. Last name Marchess."

"From. . . ?"

"What do you mean, from?"

"I mean, what town, what city? You didn't just happen to be walking along the lake road. Where did you come from?"

He laughed uneasily. "A little town not that far from here."

"Gorham?" He stared at her. "Where a gas station was robbed yesterday?" she persisted.

"What do you know about that, Lissa?"

"What do *you* know about that, Ned?"

"Not as much as you think I do," he said. "I know it was robbed. I know some money was stolen. Did you hear it on the news?"

A silence stretched between them.

Finally, Lissa broke it. "I don't believe you came here to hurt me," she said, "but you have to appreciate my position. I need to know more than you've told me, for my own peace of mind. How involved were you?"

"Why do you assume I was involved with that?"

"Stop answering me with more questions." She forced herself to unclench her teeth. "Please," she repeated, "how involved were you?"

He didn't answer directly. "Look, I needed help," he said. "My car got stuck in the snow. I was out there, no-one around, so I couldn't get to a hospital. I needed to find a place where I could at least get warm. Finding you was even better. You took care of me and let me stay here. You've been great. I wish you wouldn't be afraid of me, Lissa."

She sighed and turned away. His evasions were far from subtle, yet she believed him. She had cleaned his wound, bandaged him up, fed him, given him a bed for the night. And now she was sitting and chatting with him as if his past didn't matter. As if she would willingly help him keep his secret. For he was the thief; she was sure of it. She glanced at the poetry volume on the table and back at Ned's clear, dark brown eyes. She would never cover for someone like him. Would she? She shifted on the couch. "And you still say you hurt your arm by running into an air conditioner."

He looked away, not answering.

"Is the Grand Marquis yours?"

"What difference does it make?" he asked.

"You have no car keys. No wallet. Where are they?"

"They may still be in my car," he said. "I don't know."

"How can you not know if you left your keys in your car?" She didn't bother to hide her agitation.

He shrugged. "It must sound odd to you."

"And your money? Credit cards? Where are they?"

"I guess I lost them."

"That doesn't make sense. Lost them how?"

"I don't know how."

"All right," she said finally. If he wouldn't tell her, there was nothing she could do without inviting that angry look she'd seen the day before. Maybe the less she knew, the better. If she knew, maybe she'd become some sort of accessory. Accessory? She was a hostage. She sighed audibly.

The fire crackled and Ned got up to throw another log on. He stood and leaned back against the fireplace mantel. "What's the paper about?" he asked congenially.

She gazed at him for a long moment. There were two sides to him, one that frightened her and one that was almost appealing. She could choose to converse with him and let the afternoon pass in a friendly fashion, or she could keep her guard up. Maybe she could do both. "Aesthetics," she said. "That's the philosophy of art."

"I know what it is," he said.

She lowered her head. "I'm sorry. That was condescending of me."

"Where do you go to school?"

"I'm in a graduate program at a small school in Albany."

"Studying what, art?"

"Music composition. I had a double major in college. I got degrees in music and business." His questions made her nervous, but she couldn't see how to evade them. Anyway, what difference did it make if he knew all about her? She was sure he didn't intend to harm her, and any information she gave him was just so much small talk. She had no secrets. She was smart and educated; she was sure she had progressed far beyond whatever this man could hope to achieve. If necessary, she could probably outwit him.

"Business and songwriting? That's a unique combination. I can see how you could use one to enhance the other. Smart."

Unique? Smart? Where were the jeers and laughter, the hoots and mocking jokes? "It's unusual," she admitted. "Marketing was to please everybody else. The music is for me."

"Composing, though. So you'd rather write the songs than sing or play them?" he asked.

"I'm not that great a performer," Lissa said honestly. "I didn't start taking lessons until I was in high school. Piano lessons, I mean."

He was thoughtful for a moment. He picked up the iron poker Lissa had brandished toward him just a few hours before and stabbed the fire with it. Hot sparks flew up. "You must have caught on fast to be studying it in graduate school."

"I guess so. I would have liked to start earlier, but there wasn't enough money." She had struggled with some of the theory classes; many of the students had seemed light years ahead of her. Still did, in fact. Maybe music lessons in the primary grades would have helped. She shrugged. She would never know. "Too many mouths to feed," she said vaguely.

"Brothers and sisters, you mean? You have a big family?"

"Too big," she laughed and was surprised to discover it was an honest laugh. "Six kids. Everybody fighting over space and food and everything. I felt like a captive growing up, like some kind of prisoner in my own house." She stopped suddenly and sucked in a breath.

He gazed into her eyes and shrugged. "I'm not keeping you prisoner, Lissa. Go ahead and yell your head off for help if you're scared of me. Or make a quick run for it like you did this morning."

She answered him through gritted teeth. "And what good would that do?"

He laughed, surprising her. "None, so why not relax a little and make the best of it. I needed you," he said reasonably. "You helped me out, it's snowing, we can't leave. Accept it."

"I do accept it," she muttered. "I'm still here, aren't I? Not dead in some snowbank."

"Five brothers or five sisters? Or a combination?" It was so easy for him to swing back into the conversation. She sat rigidly, pressing her hands between her knees, wishing the snow would halt suddenly, the sun would beat down and melt it in a rush of heat, and she would flee far from Ned Marchess.

"Three brothers, two sisters," she said at last. "I'm the oldest. What about you?"

"I have one brother."

"That's all?"

"That's enough." He waved a decisive hand. "I don't want to talk about him. He frustrates me."

"I can sympathize," Lissa offered. "I have a sister who's learning disabled. We were pretty close when I lived at home. But it got to be so. . . well, frustrating is exactly the word. She had a lot of trouble in school. I almost dreaded seeing her there." Almost? It was a white lie.

"You went to the same school?"

"Well, yes." She hesitated. It was one thing to tell him her course of study, where she went to college. But his questions were threatening to dip into areas that Lissa didn't like to think about. How much of herself should she reveal to this stranger? "It was the same building," she answered, "but her class was in a separate section. I. . . I used to go down to visit her during my lunch break."

Sometimes, at first. And Katie would cling and cry as soon as Lissa had to leave. Needy, demanding Katie had begun to feel more and more like an encumbrance, an embarrassment to Lissa, just as their mother, with her sloppy clothes and messy habits was an embarrassment.

Ned was looking at her, smiling slightly.

She brought herself back to the conversation and said with effort, "Having Katie for a sister was exhausting. I haven't seen her in a while."

"Your choice or hers? Or just circumstances?"

"Mine," she said righteously. She was sick of the inquisition. If any questioning was happening, she'd get some answers of her own. "What about your brother? What does he do that bothers you? Is he younger than you?"

"Quite a bit younger. He's nineteen; I'm thirty-two."

"And there are just the two of you?"

"Just the two of us." Lissa was very aware that Ned Marchess was looking her over. He peered into her eyes, then turned his gaze back to the fire. "I'm guessing you're in your early twenties," he said at last. "Twenty-two, maybe. Am I right?"

"Twenty-three."

"And you've already graduated from college."

"I did it at the typical age. Did you go to college?"

He seemed to be concentrating on the fire and didn't answer at first. "I'd have liked to. There wasn't money for that, but I do okay. I own a business."

"What kind?"

He craned his neck and grinned back at her, and his eyes crinkled. "Household appliances. Stoves, washing machines, air conditioners."

"Oh!" She tried to cover her flustered reaction. "What do you do with them? Sell them? Repair them?"

"Both. Now and then I get cut if I'm not careful."

She ignored the comment. "Then your business must be right around here. You were coming back from Gorham, or somewhere up north, when you hit me, and you ended up trying to find an inhabited camp, and. . . ." No, it didn't make sense. If he lived around here he would have walked toward home, not here. "How did you say the air conditioner happened to injure you?"

"I didn't say, Lissa."

. . .

Ned turned back to the fire and poked it briefly. A shower of hot sparks burst above the logs and settled on the grate. He leaned the poker against the brick and sat again, leaning into the chair cushion, stretching his long legs before the fire. His feet were clad only in the socks he had hung over a chair to dry the night before. He wiggled his toes, getting comfortable, and breathed in deeply. His sling rested against his chest; his left arm lay relaxed beside him. He was grateful that the throbbing in his right arm had abated some. He closed his eyes.

And Conor immediately appeared. And Cassie.

Ned opened his eyes again, banishing the picture.

How could he explain to this girl that he needed to stay in her camp, needed her food and heat and some time to sort out what he must do next? And that he must keep her here? He couldn't have stumbled upon a more perfect place to consider his options; peace and quiet were rare commodities in his life lately. But she still saw him as some kind of monster. Well, he needed to convince her otherwise. The very desolation that provided him a chance to think was the thing that was scaring her to death.

He felt his hand scrabbling toward his shirt pocket. Cigarettes. He thought he'd kicked that habit three years ago and was glad there weren't any to be had. He didn't want to start up again; it was just stress making him think he did. He glanced at Lissa. "Looking for cigarettes," he explained. "I don't really smoke. I quit." But he would have smoked one the night before when he'd gasped out his request as if it were his last wish. And that look she'd given him! Judgmental. Superior.

He looked at her briefly again and found her guileless gray eyes staring at him. He had noticed those eyes the night before, while he drifted in and out of consciousness, watching her clean and bandage his arm.

"My friend Jim smoked. Bad habit I picked up from him," he said. "I started working for this guy Jim Polinski when I wasn't even out of high school. Part time job, after school, summers. I didn't know much but I found it interesting."

Lissa was listening politely, sitting erect, proper and in control. He wondered if it was his presence that brought out that rigid demeanor. Nah, she was probably always like this. He stretched out and smiled at her, settling in to tell the story of his life. Well, some of it. He hoped his easy, untroubled posture might erase the agitated look from her face.

"I bought my business from Jim," he continued. "He's a great guy. He started thinking about retiring three years ago and asked me if I was interested. Told me to start saving. When he retired last year, I gave him the down payment I'd saved. Now I send a payment every month. I have nine years left, then I'll own it free and clear."

And he had nearly lost that chance. He and Jim had hit it off immediately; Ned had tried hard to be an ideal hire, honest and polite, fair to the customers. Jim had liked the way Ned could trouble-shoot problems, had been pleased with his willingness to work long hours when things got unexpectedly busy. After high school, Ned considered himself lucky to have a job waiting and had eventually managed to put some money aside to buy a little house not too far from the shop. It was a fixer-upper, a handyman's special, but it suited him. He hadn't done much to it yet, but he would.

When Cassie Sillington's cat was found dead, it had affected Ned, of course. Everything about Conor affected Ned. Conor was still in high school. The event had thrown the Marchess family into a trauma, and Ned could have predicted his father's instructions to quietly hush up the incident.

"Family matters are private," Gus Marchess had said.

Ned and Conor had gone to him, Ned holding his younger brother's shoulders firmly. Conor couldn't stop crying; Ned couldn't still his own apprehension. "Dad, this is more than a family matter."

"Nonsense. There is nothing wrong with keeping some things private. It's just a cat." If their mother had been alive, it would have been the same. She had always deferred to Gus. And Gus would not budge. There was no need to discuss the cat; it was over and done with.

Ned had carried his guilt and worry privately, but Jim saw through that. Ned's work had suffered. He overcharged a customer and then forgot to order some parts they needed.

Jim's ultimatum was blunt. "Solve your personal problems or find another job." Ned had trusted Jim. After work one night, he'd stayed late and they had talked. Ned had somehow, with great embarrassment, told Jim Polinski about the cat, about his father's stubbornness.

"I'll do what I can to help you," Jim promised. There was no more talk of Ned finding another job, and things had seemed so much better for a while.

Of course, it hadn't lasted.

Ned shifted in the chair and stopped talking. He glanced at Lissa sitting primly on the worn sofa, bundled up in warm sweaters and jeans and socks, her shoes all knotted up and bound tight, just like her. Did she ever breathe freely, he wondered. He stared at her shoes - they were some kind of soft leather - and tried to recall what they'd been talking about before his dissertation on the dysfunctional Marchess clan.

Keep it casual, he told himself. Light conversation with this slight, pretty girl should be a welcome change from his usual fare. "What's graduate school like?" he asked Lissa now. "Do you like it?" He settled back, an intentionally casual pose, to hear her answer.

Chapter 15

LISSA MOVED SLIGHTLY; the quiet that had come over him made her even more uncomfortable than the bizarre story he had shared. A cat was *found dead*? What did that mean? But she realized she preferred his conversation to his silence, so she would answer his questions and keep up her end. Somehow, she would get through this horrible situation.

"School is a little frustrating for me," she said honestly. "I work very hard, but the classes are difficult. The business degree was actually easier for me."

"You must be good in math."

"I am," she said seriously. "But I want to know everything about composing so I can be good at that, too. I spend a lot of time on my school work." And, she thought about saying, alone at night I write music that I hide in brand new, shiny blue folders, songs that no one has ever seen but me. That no one has ever heard.

"It seems odd that you're studying music," Ned said thoughtfully.

Lissa was surprised. "Why?"

"I don't know. Music can be, maybe soulful. Emotional. You seem more. . . ." Rigid? He searched for a more flattering word. "Structured."

"I seem *structured*? What does that mean?"

Ned shifted in the rocker. "Organized."

Lissa stared at him, then laughed. "Music is very mathematical," she said. "It's like most of the arts. You have to know lots of rules before you can begin to get creative and break them."

"That makes sense, I guess. What kinds of songs do you

write?"

She blinked, then stared at him.

"I mean, how would people describe them? Popular? Ballads? Rock?" He shrugged. He didn't really know song types.

Lissa looked away, pointedly ignoring his question.

Ned frowned. Was her music some big secret? He let the topic go.

Lissa was suddenly aware of his eyes intent on her and wondered if her face showed how uncomfortable that made her feel.

She bowed her head. "No one thing. I try different types. I'm not particularly talented, and I got a late start. I've only gotten this far by hard work. I know my father thinks I should quit school and get a job in some business, that I'm wasting my degree. He sees no point in the music part of it. My mother. . . well, she died two years ago. She would have understood me better if I had a passion to teach music or something like that, but I can't bear the thought of spending my days trapped in a room with dozens of Katies demanding attention, sucking the life and soul from me."

"Wow," Ned said. "If you see her that way, it's just as well that you've lost touch."

Lissa could feel her face flush. For Katie's sake, he meant. She knew she must be coming across as self-absorbed. She hadn't meant to tell him such personal feelings, and now she wished she hadn't. "You don't understand," she said. "There was no privacy in my house; I had to get away to become someone."

"So who did you become?"

She stared at him, irritated.

"Is that why you came here this weekend?" he asked. "For quiet and privacy so you could get your work done?"

Lissa frowned. She had plenty of privacy in school, more than she wanted, in fact. She sighed audibly. She just hadn't connected with the other students; they seemed older. Most had full time jobs, too, or had families, or were happily settled in relationships or with roommates who usurped all their time. Even William, the one person she had managed to know, had changed toward her.

She banished William from her mind. "I came here to meet up with some friends," she said tiredly. "I do have friends, you know." She immediately regretted the words and the tone.

"And you brought your homework?"

"Well, yes. I thought I'd do it last night." He grinned at her and she sat up straighter. "It's not funny."

He laughed. "No funnier than carrying a toothbrush in your pocketbook. Not to you."

So he'd noticed that, too. He stretched lazily and she wondered how he could be so relaxed. He probably didn't know enough to take anything seriously. She folded her hands primly.

"I suppose the blizzard spoiled your plans."

"That was one of the things," she said.

He had the decency to laugh, and she smiled slightly. His eyes caught the flame from the fire, reflecting it back to her. He looked past her out the window and gestured with his hand. "Look, it's slowing down a little, maybe."

She felt a burden beginning to lift; the snow was still falling, but it was brightening up outside. The flakes were slower, lazier. "I wonder if I could get to my car," she said, half to herself.

"How long did it take you to walk here yesterday?"

"Hours."

"It would take more of them now. It's deeper and just as cold. You wouldn't be able to move the car anyway. You might not even find it - that little car, all this snow. There's no point in going."

"There's food there, though. And aspirin and clean city water, too. The food you saw in the kitchen is all there is, you know."

He shrugged. "We'll make do."

"Well, stop feeding it to mice then. We can have bread and cheese for supper, I guess. We could have lettuce with it, but I think some of it froze."

"I'm not a big eater. It'll be fine."

"In my car. . . ."

"Melissa, I thank you for sharing your food with me, but don't try to go to your car. You wouldn't make it back during daylight. Or at all. What we have will be fine."

"My friend Pat loves to cook," Lissa mused. "She made up a grocery list, split it three ways, and sent us each a third. We were trusting her to make some great meals from it when she got here. It was supposed to be fun."

"I doubt we'll starve."

Lissa wasn't so sure. The onion was gone, and the cheese and bread would be gone this evening. The water jug was nearly empty. They should start boiling snow to put aside. She got up from the couch. "I'm going to make some tea. Will you get snow for it?" At least he could earn his keep. She regretted her critical thought when he immediately agreed and tracked into the kitchen to put on his boots.

They repeated the process of the morning, bringing handfuls of snow to a boil and bubbling the water for five minutes to kill any bacteria. Four big pots of snow gave them enough water for two mugs of tea. As it steeped, Ned returned outdoors and refilled as many containers as they could find. They set them around the kitchen, letting the snow melt.

Lissa gulped the tea greedily at the table. "This tastes so good, but it takes too long for so little. I wish I could get to my car."

"Maybe it will stop tonight," he offered. A roar of wind rushed around the cabin.

"Even a mouse shouldn't be out in this kind of weather," she muttered. She peered at Ned over the top of her mug. "Are you always so solicitous of creepy little animals?"

He laughed. "I helped out in an animal shelter when I was a kid. The plan was that I was going to choose a dog for my own and wait for my father to come around. They let me clean the cages and wipe up the messes."

She grimaced. "Nice of them."

"I didn't mind. I always picked out which animals I was going to adopt as soon as I got permission at home. It never happened. I learned a lot, though."

"Like how to win over rodents."

"Yes, that. A little gentleness is usually all it takes. You don't think a little mouse like that could hurt us, do you?"

"I'm all right with it, I guess."

"He's more scared of you than you are of him."

"Everybody says that about animals," she said. "I doubt it's true."

"What about you? Did you ever have a part time job in school?"

Lissa thought briefly. "In the cafeteria in college. Same deal, wiping up messes others left behind. I've been doing that all my life."

He laughed appreciatively. "Volunteer work? You look like the volunteer type to me."

"I'm not sure what that means."

"Fresh and wholesome, giving to all mankind. You know."

She wasn't sure if it was a taunt or a compliment. Was he mocking her? She decided to give him the benefit of the doubt. "Through a club in high school. I helped deliver Christmas gifts to children, to families one year; you know the kind of thing. I didn't organize it or do much to help, but I felt all warm and fuzzy after it was over."

"You took things to their homes?"

"Well, occasionally. We took them wherever our advisor told us to take them. We dropped off some at a church, some at a prison." She could feel her face blanch as she saw the clear vision of Ned's fitful rest in her spare bedroom. *Jail.* "For the inmates' children," she said hurriedly. "It was through a civic club."

Ned was staring at her, saying nothing. Eventually, he swirled the tea in his mug, then met her eyes again. "It's hard to picture you near a prison."

"Well, I just went along. It seemed like a good idea. I can't take credit." She was stumbling over her explanation. His frank stare was making her very uncomfortable.

"It's always nice to help the unfortunate," he said. She couldn't tell if he meant the words sarcastically. "Didn't you ever worry, though, that some convict would remember you? I'd be concerned about young girls coming around a prison with their charity and their good works. You could actually put yourself in danger doing that."

Her blood froze. "It was years ago. Of course I didn't worry," she added primly. "They were locked up."

"And maybe they still are." He sipped distractedly once or twice more, and then pulled Lissa's pill case from his shirt pocket. He fingered out two ibuprofen, shut the case, and poured from the water jug into a glass. She watched him swallow the pills, distressed at the level of the water, and wondered what he was thinking about.

"My arm is starting to throb," he said, rising from the table. "I'm going to lie down for a bit. Is that all right?" He pocketed the pillbox and left the room.

"Sure, of course." Her words trailed after him.

His strange comment about prisons had frightened her. She shouldn't be surprised that he sounded so knowledgable; he knew about some girl's dead cat, too, and was being intentionally cryptic about it. Lissa shivered. Maybe she didn't want to know any more after all. She rested her head on one hand and realized she had the beginnings of a headache. And if it was like others she'd had, it would be fierce and lasting. She wished she had brought the rest of her pills from the car.

She also wished she hadn't given Ned all of her aspirin, and she wished fervently that the snow would stop.

Most of all, she wished she had stayed in Albany in her clean, sparse apartment, alone and enjoying her own company. Being grateful for William's coldness and her friendless existence and the muddle that was her family, the things that made her life so tiresome, but so carefree in comparison to this.

Chapter 16

LISSA WAS SURPRISED to see that it was nearly four o'clock as she listened to the melting snow hissing on the stove. Ned's arm seemed better than last night, but maybe it had been a mistake to send him out to lift and carry packed buckets. She was glad he'd gone to his room. She would enjoy her camp without tripping over Ned Marchess and his evasions and mysterious comments every time she turned around.

She placed her empty mug into the sink and glanced at his on the table. He hadn't finished his tea, a waste of the water they had collected and boiled. She scooped up the mug, knocked on his door and heard his tired voice telling her to come in.

He was lying fully dressed on his back on top of the blankets, his arm looking awkward and uncomfortable as he tried to find a restful way to hold it.

"I didn't want to throw this out," she said. "Do you want to drink it while it's still warm? You probably need the fluids."

He propped up on his good arm, took the tea and finished it off in two gulps. "Thanks."

Lissa looked around for the pill case. If she saw it, she would take it with her, but the case was not in sight. Ned moved on the bed, trying to get comfortable, grimacing every time his arm contacted the mattress.

"It hurts, doesn't it," Lissa said.

"It could be worse."

She closed the door, took the mug back to the kitchen, and stood at the sink, peering out at the afternoon sky. The snow was gentle now, softly falling flakes that should have been Christmas card cheery. Puffy, lovely snowflakes piling up, fencing her in. With Ned Marchess.

His appearance and injury had convinced her that he was the driver of the Grand Marquis, but there was nothing frightening about him now, she thought wearily. He was helpful, agreeable, even grateful, and she couldn't help responding to that. Or was it an act? She admitted she was beginning to trust the man in the next room.

A sudden gust of wind shook the cabin. Lissa could hear it whistling through the makeshift window cover in the living room. She turned off the stove burners, covered the pans, and stood watching the snow fall, shivering in her sweater and turtleneck. It had suddenly become darker.

The camps on Arrowhead Lake had one thing in common; each had been built on at least a double lot, and between the cabins, thick woods created privacy and a feeling of desolation that Lissa had never noticed during the summers she had spent here.

She noticed it now. The snow had started driving sideways, blustering angrily, and the sky had turned to pearl gray.

A sudden flickering movement near the woodshed surprised her. An animal returning to the dog pen? A bear? Maybe a fox or a coy dog. She thought of the disturbed straw; something had made that depression.

She had always heard stories of bears and foxes, of course; these were the mountains after all. She recalled a bright week of summer in her tenth or eleventh year when the whole string of Arrowhead Lake camps had been abuzz with news of bears roaming the lake road, upsetting trash cans and leaving a trail of fruit peels and tattered garbage bags in their wake. Very few children had played far from their own front doors that summer.

When she caught the movement again, Lissa's breath snagged in her throat.

It was a man! Perhaps he was a hunter or part of a group of hardy winter hikers. He could help her!

He had disappeared behind the shed again and lest she lose him altogether, Lissa flung open the kitchen door. Oblivious to the sheet of snow that drifted into the kitchen, she called out. "You there! Hey!"

There was no response. Her long hair whipped around her face and she pulled it back with one hand, shivering. She motioned wildly with her other hand to attract his attention, and called again. "Mister! Hey!"

She was rewarded when he stepped out from behind the shed and stared at her. She could see curls of dark hair peeping out from under a knit hat, snow pummeling his dark jacket. She caught her breath. His lips were not twisted in the angry snarl she remembered, but she was sure, as sure as she had ever been of anything, that this was the driver who had hit her. His look was prolonged, his mouth a flat line, his eyes boring into hers. He stood in snow nearly as high as his knees. He started toward her.

Lissa moaned as she tried to force the door shut. Snow clogged the threshold and she kicked at it, clearing enough that she could slam the door & lock it. She leaned back against the wall, willing her heart to stop pounding. When she crept to the window again, he was gone.

The sweeping snowflakes settled on the ground and shed roof, stuck to tree branches, and pelted the property that sloped to the frozen lake. There was no one, nothing, a bit of disturbed snow the only sign that anyone had ventured close to the cabin. But she knew she had seen him. And that meant that Ned was not the driver of the Grand Marquis, the driver she had assumed was speeding away from a robbery in Gorham.

Lissa laughed suddenly, but the sound that escaped was a whimper of confusion and dismay. Closing her eyes, she sagged against the wall.

"Are you all right?"

Lissa's head snapped up and her eyes shot open. A steady pulsing pain began at the back of her head. Ned was standing in the doorway between the kitchen and the living room, his face looking gaunt and strained. He held his right arm with his left, a posture she hadn't seen since the night before. His glance took in the drift of snow just inside the door, her tracks from door to window melting in slushy puddles across the floor.

"What are you doing?" he said. He noticed her ragged breath and came closer, his eyes narrow. "Maybe you ought to sit down, Lissa."

Still gasping for air, she sank into the chair he had pulled out and stared into his eyes. Who was this man? More importantly, who wasn't he?

He crouched before her, looking at her with great concern.

"What happened?"

"Nothing."

"I heard you call, Lissa. Was someone out there?" He rose and looked out the window, checked the door lock, and came back to her. "If there was someone out there, Lissa, you should tell me."

"There was." She spoke numbly, as if the words were torn from her against her will. "I thought I saw someone. I might have imagined it."

Ned was staring into her eyes. "Maybe."

Suddenly she buried her face in her hands. She could feel wet tears squeezing from her eyes and seeping through her fingers. Her head pounded. "It was the man I thought was you." She looked at Ned. "I thought you were the one in that car. But he's out there."

Ned sucked in a sudden breath and glanced again at the window. "I don't see anyone. Are you sure you did?"

She nodded.

"What did he look like, then? Did you get a good look?"

"Good enough to know. It's the same guy. I know it."

"Okay," he said soothingly. He put his left arm around her shoulders awkwardly and she leaned into him, avoiding the makeshift sling, allowing the heat of him to comfort her.

"I thought you robbed the gas station and that you might. . . you might. . . ."

"I didn't rob the gas station, Lissa. I told you that."

"I know, but your arm is hurt, and. . . what are you doing here? And you let me believe the Grand Marquis was your car."

He kneaded her shoulder, then turned her head to face him. Their eyes were inches apart. He placed his hand under her chin and tilted it up. "I'm just a guy, Lissa," he said softly. "A completely average, ordinary guy. There's no mystery to me."

Her words were hushed. "But you broke in and then you wouldn't tell me. . . ."

"You imagined a lot of things about me that aren't true," he said gently. His eyes gazed into hers, dark brown eyes that searched deep within her and took her breath away.

For brief seconds, Lissa actually wondered if he were going to kiss her. The thought shocked her, but not as much as the one that followed. She would have let him.

His thumb caressed her cheek until he pulled his hand away and began to stand up. "I need to check the fire. It seems cold in here."

Her emotions roiling, Lissa grabbed at his sleeve, pulling him back. "No, you need to check outside." She hadn't meant her words to sound so demanding, so full of fear.

"I looked out," he responded. "There's no one there now."

"But you should *go* out. He might be hiding. We might not be safe."

"All right. I'll check. Let me tend to the fire first." He started for the living room. Lissa glanced around the kitchen, its yawning emptiness suddenly sinister in the waning light. She scurried after him.

He was right; the fire had begun to die down and the camp was chilly. She had turned the stove low to conserve propane. From the couch, she watched Ned throw another log into the fireplace. Embers glowed and burst, orange and red. "I told you to trust me," he said at length.

"I made a mistake," she said. "*Please.* Are you going out to look around?"

He sighed heavily, said, "Stay here," and headed back to the kitchen. She heard the door close and jumped up to secure the kitchen door lock. In a few moments he was back, shaking his head. "Nothing."

"Did you check in the shed?"

"Yes, and the outhouse. He's gone."

"I'm sorry, Ned," she said. "It was the color of your hair and jacket that I noticed first. And when I found you hurt in the kitchen, I mean, you broke in, after all. . . ." He led her back to the fire and sat next to her, frowning. He glanced at her in surprise when she clutched his arm. "I didn't know what to think," she said.

"Well, tell me what you did think. Start at the beginning."

Her fingers fisted, still gripping him. It was a relief to finally confide in him. "When I was driving up here," she said, "my car was hit by the car you saw on Rice Road." She glanced at him, begging for his sympathy, but he was staring into the fire. "The driver stared at me," she went on. "He was angry and looked as if he blamed me for blocking the road, but it wasn't my fault; it was because of the snow.

"When you broke in, I jumped to conclusions. I thought you must have robbed the gas station and were injured there. I was afraid you would hurt me. I didn't know if you might have hurt someone else, or maybe killed them. . . ." She stopped with a shudder.

His eyes remained steady, staring into the flames. "You don't believe that now, do you?"

She shook her head. "I haven't believed it for a while. If you wanted to hurt me, you could have by now. Lots of times."

"That's not going to happen."

"But you wouldn't answer my questions, and that made me more and more suspicious." She leaned forward and covered her face with her hands. "Ned, I've been scared, really scared."

He pried her hands gently from her face. "I know. Tell me about that guy you saw outside."

"He was by the shed. I saw him once, just a flash, and he disappeared. I called to him, thinking he could help me get away."

"Away from me, you mean."

"I hollered to him, but I didn't realize until I saw his face. It was him. That horrible man. I'm afraid of him, and now he's right outside the cabin. What if he recognized me? You scared me before, talking about prisons. What if he was a prisoner and remembers me? I know it's stupid."

"I was speaking hypothetically, Lissa. And I'm here, you know. You're not alone." Ned got up and walked from window to window, holding the curtains aside, looking out at the wooded side lawn, the naked birches and maples and the wintry evergreens that dotted the property in front. "He's not here anymore." He turned back to Lissa, whose eyes were on his every move. She held her hands in her lap, the fingers twisting in and out. "Even if he comes back, he's not going to get in here," he told her.

"You did."

He chuckled softly, and went into the kitchen. When he returned, he carried two juice glasses, one awkwardly in his right hand. He handed her one.

She took it and sipped, then exhaled a big breath. "Pinot Grigio. It's a very versatile wine."

"And one of its many uses is to make you stop fidgeting and

relax a little. We're fine here. Don't worry so much."

"How can I relax when that man could be out there prowling around? Do you think he'll try to break in later when we're sleeping?"

Ned shook his head. "No, I don't think so."

"But you don't know that," Lissa said.

Ned sat beside her again. "We're fine, Lissa. If he did try to break in, I'd stop him. Drink that. You need it. We'll talk about something else."

"We can talk about my headache," she said. "I know I gave you my aspirin, but are there any left? If I don't treat this, it will just get worse. I get these a lot." She felt a spasm of guilt just asking for the medicine.

He pulled the tiny box from his pocket and opened it. One insignificant aspirin sat alone in the metal-lined box.

"The last one," she said guiltily. "I'll leave it. Arm gash trumps headache."

He smiled, picked up her hand and dropped the tablet into it. "I was taught to share," he said. Lissa placed the pill in her mouth and washed it down with wine. She tossed the empty pillbox on the table, took another swallow of wine and leaned back, taking a big, steady breath. "This is my favorite kind of wine. I don't drink anything else."

"I thought beer was the college kids' drink of choice."

She made a face. "Not for me. I gave Katie a beer once when I was in high school," she continued with effort. "I was punished for that." This was good. To change the subject altogether, to will the irate driver far away.

"How old was she?"

"She's seventeen now. I guess then she was about eleven. I was old enough to know better, and I wasn't even a drinker. I poured her a can of my dad's beer from the refrigerator because I had to study and she wouldn't stop talking. I always had to have her with me. I grew to hate that."

"Tough for you."

She looked at him quickly. "I mean, I didn't mind at first. When we were younger, we were good friends. She'd play paper dolls when all my friends had outgrown them. She loved my jokes. She'd do whatever I wanted to do. I got sick of it, though."

"So you gave her a beer?"

Lissa nodded. "She threw up."

Ned laughed. "That's one way to get some study time."

"I ended up grounded for a month."

"So it wasn't worth it."

"I wouldn't have known the difference."

He took the glass from her hand and held it up to the light. "Well, you finished that off pretty quickly. Feel better?"

"Yes, thank you. Are you really convinced we're safe?"

He smiled a lop-sided smile at her and stood up. "Absolutely safe. You stay here and enjoy the fire; I'm going to start some kind of supper for us."

She reached a hand out to him. "No, don't leave me alone."

He stood looking down at her, silent.

She blushed furiously and looked down at her hands. "I can't make up my mind whether to depend on you or flee from you."

"That's all right." His voice was husky. "Come and help me then."

Chapter 17

SHE WENT TO THE KITCHEN with him and watched him rummage through a drawer for a serrated bread knife. Something had changed subtly in their relationship, and it was all on her end. He wasn't doing anything different now than he had done since she'd first found him bleeding and gasping in pain. Her perceptions had altered.

He found the knife, removed the Italian bread from its wrapper, and placed it on a plate. With his right hand, he held the bread steady; with his left he began slicing. The loaf tore unevenly. Lissa almost laughed. A few hours ago she had raged hysterically when she'd seen him holding a knife that way.

"Ned, wait," she said. "You can't do anything with that sling so loose." He put the knife down and sat, and she adjusted and reknotted the sling.

"I'll cut this," she said. She picked up the knife and cut four or five slices of bread, uncomfortably aware that he was watching her.

"It's been hard with me and my sister," she said thoughtfully. "I started resenting her when I got to high school. I feel kind of ashamed about that, but I wanted a life of my own. I wanted to *be* alone. I've regretted it since then, but it's too late in some ways."

"Why?"

She knew how it would sound, but decided to confide in him. "I had a terrible fight with my mother. I said some hateful things to her. I never apologized, and when I went home for her funeral they were all very cool to me. I've broken the ties, and I don't think any of us wants to mend them. I wanted to be alone, and now I am. I wanted independence, to rely completely on myself and be responsible only for myself."

"That's funny," he said quietly. "I find that lately I want the opposite. I've been on my own since I was eighteen, so I guess I'm tired of it."

"Well, there's probably a middle road somewhere," she admitted. "Your brother doesn't live with you?"

"No. He demands a lot of attention from me, though."

"Well, Katie will take over me if I let her," Lissa said. "It's stifling, but that's the way she is. Do you ever see your brother that way?"

Ned shrugged. "I wouldn't abandon him, if that's what you mean."

"Well, I didn't exactly abandon her." She pulled the romaine out of its wrapper and pulled off all the spoiled leaves that had frozen and thawed. It didn't leave much. She felt uncomfortable and wasn't sure why. Did Ned Marchess see her as a selfish person? Did she care how he saw her? When she spoke, she was thoughtful. "I wanted my own friends, boyfriends, college. People have a right to that, don't you think?"

"Sure."

"I wanted to sit in the bleachers at basketball games and not see my sister down in the doorway in her wheelchair. She used to stop all the people coming through and tell them our family business."

"People were sympathetic, though, weren't they? They understood it was just her way."

"Sure, they'd smile and nod and try to get away. It was embarrassing."

"All younger brothers and sisters can be embarrassing when you're still growing up yourself."

She looked at him. "You're saying I should grow up and get over it?"

"I'm not saying anything. I'm sure you always do whatever you think is best."

"You think I'm selfish, don't you."

There was a surprised look in his eyes. "I didn't say that."

"You didn't need to. You obviously think so."

Lissa concentrated on the food preparation and missed the hint of a smile on his face. "Well, one of us does," he said quietly.

When tree branches squealed overhead, rubbing together in

the wind, they both looked up suddenly. "Oh, it's the trees," Lissa said tightly. "I hope a branch doesn't fall on the camp."

Ned chuckled. "I'm sure that tree's lasted through worse storms than this one."

"Probably," she agreed. She forced herself to exhale a breath. "Anyway," she added, "I'm planning to take Katie with me when I finish grad school. It won't be easy, but it's a decision I've made."

Ned shrugged. "It sounds like a decision that makes you resentful."

"I'm not resentful!" Lissa retorted. "I'm happy with the choice, but it will mean sacrifices on my part."

"Great, I admire you." He didn't sound particularly admiring. He sounded sarcastic, and it infuriated Lissa.

"Well, what about your brother?" she said. "You mentioned that he needs a lot of attention. Don't you ever have any deep, resentful thoughts about him?"

He grimaced. "Every day of my life."

"Did they shower him with attention and lavish all the family energy on him like my parents did with Katie? Did they expect you to take care of him?"

"No, nobody expected much of anything. I kind of took that on, though. Sometimes I'm the only one who can manage him."

"Then you know what I'm saying," she said righteously.

He nodded. "I guess I know what you're saying. You got tired of being on call all the time. You'd had enough. How was it for her when you left for college?"

Lissa could feel her lips pursing tightly in defiance. She recalled that day as if it were yesterday. Her parents ushering her into the overloaded minivan, Margie and Steven trying to get their father to solve an argument about somebody's CD found in somebody else's room, Katie sitting sullenly in her heavy steel chair, her fat arms crossed over her chest, demanding that Lissa stay another hour, another two hours. Demanding that Lissa call her that night.

Her mother had chastised her. "It wouldn't hurt you, Lis, just to tell her you'll call. She'll look forward to it for the rest of the day."

"And be disappointed," eighteen year old Lissa had said. "What if there isn't a phone convenient to my room? What if it's tied up all evening? You're the ones who wouldn't spring for a cell phone." The truth was that she wanted a clean break. She had outgrown Katie just as she had outgrown the paper dolls they had played with together in the middle of the living room floor. She wanted no more Katie tied to her apron strings, giggling and talking non-stop. No more constant companion. No more washing Katie's dirty face or tying colorful ribbons in Katie's hair. No more.

"Can we get going?" she had asked her father. She knew she sounded belligerent, but she didn't care.

Her father ran a distracted hand through his hair and yelled at Margie and Steven to go inside and settle their differences. They were both too old for childish bickering, he said.

"Could we just *go*?" Lissa demanded. She slumped in her seat and breathed a sigh of relief when her father finally started the engine. Katie cried and caterwauled from the back door, watching as the van backed out the driveway. Her brother Daniel was trying to soothe her and was already looking exasperated when Lissa gave Katie a quick, perfunctory wave, the car backed out to the street, and Lissa lost sight of them.

Her mother had kept up a monologue all the way to Pennsylvania about Lissa's priggish attitude lately, giving unwanted advice and reminding Lissa of all her blessings, all the things she had going for her that Katie would never have.

It had all fallen on deaf ears.

Oh, she had spent time with Katie since then - brief conversations when Lissa was home for vacations, a few phone calls in which Katie did all the talking - but it was all superficial. Lissa had managed to force the split, replaced Katie with Pat and Shelly, welcome replacements, and made it through college without having to explain her sister to anyone.

And now, today, she was trying to justify it all to this virtual stranger sitting across the table from her, eating precious crackers he pulled out of the box with a hand that wouldn't perform as he wanted it to.

"Lissa?"

"I'm sorry. I was thinking about the day I left for college. It was hard for Katie. Really hard."

"So you're taking her with you out of guilt?"

Lissa stared at him. "Yes, I guess I feel guilty about losing sight of her. I know it hurt her. And my dad really can't do it anymore."

"And once again you'll have to give up your freedom."

"I can't think of any other way. I plan to send for Katie when school ends in May."

"Send for her? You mean not even visit them?"

"They won't miss me, and my brother Steven won't even be there. He joined the Navy, so he'll be off on some ship, cruising around Spain or somewhere."

"Enjoying a bachelor's wild and carefree existence."

"Right, lucky him." She could feel her own belligerence. "I can't go home," she repeated. "I'll take Katie, but I can't see the others." She hesitated, realizing how mean-spirited and immature she must sound. But she dreaded facing them after separating herself for so long. After the cruel, selfish words she had said to her mother. She glanced at Ned and found a receptive audience. Why not tell him? She'd probably never see him again.

"I was home on a college holiday," she began.

Chapter 18

THE HOUSE WAS FESTIVE with the smells and sounds of the family gathering for a meal. Her mother busily placed dishes on the table, steaming bowls of vegetables, spicy baked apples, a platter of biscuits fresh from the oven.

Katie had been whiny all weekend, and now she sat sulking in a corner of the kitchen, irritated and moody. The ribbon holding her long hair in place had come loose and was hanging, a frayed, bedraggled rope, in her face.

"Lis, tie that for her, will you?" her harried mother asked.

Obediently, Lissa pulled the ribbon loose, intending to retie it. To her surprise, Katie shrieked in annoyance, snapping her head away.

The anger rose in Lissa quickly, and, without thinking, she slapped Katie, striking her hard on her cheek.

A serving spoon clattered to the table. "Lissa!" Her mother's shocked face reflected Lissa's own surprise at what she had done. Then fury rose in Lissa, hot and righteous, and she took a menacing step toward her mother.

"What," she sneered, "Are you shocked? Sure, poor Katie. Tie her ribbons, Lis, and if she reacts like some caged animal, just let that go."

Her mother slammed the plates she was carrying onto the hard surface of the kitchen table. "What's the matter with you!" she reprimanded. "Is this what college does to you? This isn't like you at all, Lissa."

"No, it isn't, is it. I'm the one who always does what she's told. I'm the one who makes a perfect doormat for the rest of the family."

Her brothers had crept into the kitchen to see what the

shouting was about. Katie cowered in her chair, clenching the end of the ribbon. She was crying in hiccuping sobs.

"A doormat?" her mother said, incredulous. "You see yourself as a doormat?"

"I see myself as the person who raised her," Lissa gestured impatiently to Katie, "almost single-handedly. The person who wiped up her messes and had to beg to go to college, and couldn't have any friends, *no friends*, because why would anyone want to be friends with the permanent baby-sitter." Her glance fell on Katie, and she lowered her voice. "You dumped her off on me for years, and now I don't even know how to have friends. Your goal was accomplished."

Her mother stood mute, her eyes wide with shock and bewildered hurt. "But you loved Katie. You love her."

"Forget it," Lissa said, stumbling from the room. She snatched her jacket from a peg by the back door and left. There would be other family dinners, and a few of them she would even attend, but never again would any of them ask her to see to Katie's needs or to sacrifice herself in any way.

. . .

She glanced at Ned, stuffing crackers into his mouth, looking at her curiously. Why wasn't he reacting?

"It's why I needed to make my own way," she said. "I can't be like her; she was sloppy and careless."

"Well, those aren't really flaws. . . ."

"I didn't find out until much later," she said, "that I had hit it exactly. They really did get me to raise her. It was intentional."

Ned frowned. "Why would they do that?"

"Because of the cancer," Lissa said simply. "When Katie was born, my mom found out she had it. It was stage one, very early. They hid it from us kids and decided to teach me how to care for Katie, just in case." She shrugged. "My mother would go for treatments, and spent a lot of time sleeping. We never knew why. I always thought she was tired from raising a big family. My brothers weren't always that easy."

"Wow." Ned whistled softly under his breath. "They groomed you."

"Yes. But she went into remission. I never even knew what was going on. Like most kids, I figured life was all about me. I knew she gave up smoking, but she'd sneak a cigarette now and then. It caught up with her a couple of years ago."

"When did you find this all out?"

"Not until after she died. My father took me aside one day and told me what they had done and why. I don't blame them. They loved all us kids and knew Katie would need to have someone she could count on. They saw something in me, apparently. And now that I'm finishing school and my father needs me to help, I'll help."

"They should have leveled with you, though."

Lissa shrugged. "Maybe. I can't change the past."

Ned agreed. You can only go forward. It puts things in perspective, though."

"They've been talking about putting her in an institution, which is unnecessary. She's not that much work, really. I'm pretty sure I can give her what she needs." She looked up at him. "But I can't go home," she said tightly. "After the things I said, they'll make me feel guilty all over again. And if they're even speaking to me, they'll eventually get around to the usual: telling me to forget a music career and get a job near home."

To place music on a shelf, to forget her impractical love, would fit in with their plans, not hers. And then who would she be? Lissa Tea, the loser who couldn't break away to save her life.

Ned was shaking his head, his lips pursed in disbelief. "They're not going to do that," he said. "After all you did for Katie as a kid?"

"Oh, yes they will. You have no idea."

"I'm sure they're proud of you. Taking Katie is such a good thing. I can see why you're resentful, but-"

"I'm not resentful of Katie! It's the rest of them. I stepped over the line. I dared to try to be different."

"Are they that terrible? That unforgiving of a few heated remarks...."

She made a frustrated sound. "You don't get it. They haven't even forgiven me for studying music, and you think they'll forgive talking that way to our dying mother? You have no idea what it's like to come from a family like mine," she said.

A hint of a smile flickered in the corner of Ned's mouth. "Try me."

"Fine." She stiffened in her chair across from him and stared him down. "There are six of us. Of all six, I'm the only one so far with enough spirit to go away to college, and I had to beg for that. I won a full scholarship, Ned, so it didn't cost them a dime. I took piano lessons at school when no one encouraged me. They were free or I wouldn't have had them. I found out about them, signed up, practiced at school, and made myself learn. Nobody encouraged me, nobody cared. . . ."

"Well, that's admirable, but. . . ."

"I'm not finished." She squeezed the slice of bread she had been cutting. "If you put together all the hours I spent babysitting, it would probably add up to years of my life. My sister Margie is nineteen and married already to a guy who'll never amount to anything." She was working herself up and could feel the thready beating of her heart. She leaned toward him and saw his eyes widen under the verbal attack. "My father is still stuck in the same job he's had all my life, a menial, stupid job. The work he does doesn't matter and he doesn't even know it." Her voice rose on the last words, and suddenly Lissa stopped and leaned back.

"Have you ever heard kids at school mock your parents? My mother was uneducated, had terrible grammar. I cringed whenever other people heard her. And Katie learned from her, would repeat the same inane, incorrect . . . . My mother. . ." Her voice grew husky. "She smoked all through her pregnancies. It was just dumb luck that Katie was the only one. . . the only one of us. . . ."

Lissa looked down at the piece of bread she had been manhandling and tried to smooth it. The crust was indented with her fingerprints and crumbled into small, hard crumbs. She dropped it to the tabletop. Nice work, she told herself. So what was one less slice of bread? They were going to starve to death anyway. Stiffly, she picked up the slice and placed it aside. "That one's mine," she said quietly.

Ned sat silently for a moment. The whistling wind rattled the window panes behind them, and he turned quickly to reassure himself that it was really just the wind.

When he turned back to her, Lissa's face was diffused with pink. She licked her lips distractedly. "I'm sorry," she said. "That was childish. I've been feeling very frustrated by a few things. I didn't mean to rant."

"That's all right. But, Lissa, everybody makes their own choices. Just because theirs are different doesn't make them wrong."

"Smoking while you're carrying a baby?" She rose quickly from her chair; her hands had balled into tight, angry fists. "Their horrid, useless jobs? My mother worked in an office, filing papers all day long. My father supervised in a factory. Big deal. Daniel washes dishes in a pizza place. And Margie, marrying in her teens. It disgusts me that I'm the only one who seems to want to climb out."

"Were your parents happy?"

The question surprised her. She had never really thought about it. "I don't know. Maybe."

"Maybe they never cared about the things you're going after. Did you ever ask them?"

"Well, I. . . ." Lissa started.

"Of course you didn't. You were too busy being Miss College Student."

"What?"

"Sure, they pushed your sister off on you all those years. It was hard on you, but so what? People live through worse things. So you had to convince them to send you to college." Ned laughed shortly. "And you convinced them, and you went. I don't see what the fuss is all about."

"The *fuss* is that my family thinks it's hilarious that I want another music degree, such an impractical thing. They laughed when I chose a double major. It was twice as much work, and I did it, and they laughed. They don't understand me at all. They never have."

"I guess I don't understand you either." He tried to close up the cracker box, found it nearly impossible one-handed, and pushed it away from him. "I'll stop eating these. I'm sure you have something planned with them for breakfast."

She was staring at him. It was true, and it disturbed her: She had now met yet another person who couldn't possibly understand her. "Breakfast will consist of a healthy order of snow," she said.

"Fine by me." He stood up lazily, stretched, and scratched his head. "Sorry," he said. "It itches, probably because I haven't been able to take a shower." His hand clawed around under Uncle Jeff's shirt; he scratched his belly in slow circles.

"Do you have fleas or something?" she seethed.

"Me?" He looked around at the cluttered room and grinned. "Maybe by now."

. . .

He wandered off to the living room, stretched out in the rocker smiling tightly to himself, reached for the book of poetry and pretended to engross himself in it. He could hear Lissa in the kitchen shoving the chairs in, clattering plates.

What was he doing, he thought, baiting her like that? It wasn't his way. He knew how to act and was usually far more reserved, especially around women. But her outburst had set him off; suddenly, everything about her annoyed him. Those leather shoes of hers - soft and supple with good, tight laces done up to her neck. Who was she trying to kid? That prim, buttoned-up exterior hid all kinds of passion she didn't even know was there. Anger. All kinds of things.

She was self-absorbed all right, an egomaniac. And he hadn't appreciated the slight, superior flaring of her nostrils when she spoke of her father's factory job. Good God. Half the people in the country would be thrilled to have any job at all, and here she was, looking down her nose. She'd *send* for her sister to avoid saying a couple words to her own father. Who was she, the Duchess of Tea-World?

Ned turned in the chair to get more comfortable and forced himself to concentrate on the poetry. He liked Frost, always had. He wondered if Lissa Tea was impressed.

But hers was quite a story, he admitted to himself. Her parents had taken away her childhood, making her responsible for her sister like that. No wonder she seemed older than her age. No wonder she kept such a tight control.

"Ned?"

He looked up. She was standing over him with a plate of sandwiches. "I'm sorry. I didn't mean to go on like that."

He shrugged. "You see things from your point of view. But it isn't the only one."

"I know that. And I love my brothers and sisters. I love my father, too."

"Then maybe you should just accept them for who they are." She nodded. He was shocked to see tears forming in her eyes. "Hey, come on. Don't cry. I was tormenting you on purpose."

"I loved my mother, too. And Katie. I'm not taking her out of guilt, no matter what you think. I love her."

He straightened up in the chair. "Lissa, you don't have to confide in me. And I'm sure not anyone you have to apologize to."

"I know." The first tear crept from her eye and rolled slowly down her cheek. With her sleeve, she swiped at it.

"Lissa," he said, "please. I'm not anyone you want to cry in front of either. Really."

Ned felt like the sixth grade playground bully. He abandoned Robert Frost, took the plate of sandwiches from her and placed it on the floor. Then he reached for her hands, both of them, and held them in his good one. They were cold and small.

"I'm not crying," she said, her voice wobbly. "It's being here like this. I'm afraid and worried. And I don't know what I think about anything."

"Then don't think at all," he said. "Just let it go."

Chapter 19

NED HEARD THE SOUND FIRST, and the sandwich he was eating turned to dry ash in his mouth. A soft whishing sound repeated again in the kitchen, not a camp sound he'd heard before. As his eyes met Lissa's, it was clear she'd heard it, too.

"It's him." Her voice was a frightened whisper.

Ned put his plate aside, swallowed the food in his mouth and stood up slowly, motioning Lissa to stay still, grimacing when she ignored him. She jumped up from the couch, her plate clattering to the floor.

Someday, he thought, that independent streak of hers might cause her some real trouble. He hoped this wasn't the day.

They heard a quick slam. In a few steps, Ned was in the kitchen.

"Oh, no," Lissa's cry behind him was of anguish, fear, a whispered response to the telltale puddles by the door. One window curtain was yanked sideways. Ned was sure they hadn't left it that way. Someone had been there.

Ned rushed to the window and peered out.

"He came in the door?" she said. "How could he? It was locked."

Was it? Ned wasn't sure. At her insistence, he'd gone out to check for an intruder. When he came back in, what had he done with the key? He turned to her. "I. . . I may have forgotten to lock it."

"Forgotten?" Her eyes were the size of saucers. "My God, are you kidding?"

Ned examined the door. "It's unlocked, and I don't remember locking it when I came in." The key should have been hanging on its peg. He felt in his coat pocket- no key there either.

"Where's the key?" he asked her.

Lissa thought. "I locked the door when you went out and opened it for you when you returned."

"Then...."

Her face flamed as she reached into her jeans pocket and produced the key. "It was unlocked all that time," she murmured. "And it was my fault."

"Both our faults," he said. "I never thought about it either. He didn't break in," he reassured her. "At least there's that. Is anything missing?"

"How would we even know?" Lissa glanced around at the Tea family clutter. Odd, chipped dishes were heaped on the countertop; cloudy glass jars held clothespins and twist ties. A rusty tackle box, an abandoned boat motor, a few tattered life jackets piled in the corner. On a chair sat old windbreakers and fishing hats; mismated flip-flops protruded from a torn cardboard carton behind an old wooden highchair. "Even if he took something, it can't be much. We don't leave any valuables at camp."

"The food," Ned said suddenly. "That's what we have of value."

Lissa opened the refrigerator, but nothing seemed disturbed.

"Do you want me to go out and see if he's still here?" Ned asked. "If I were him, I wouldn't be hanging around. You startled him when you dropped that plate."

She had no answer, just stood staring at the new puddles by the door, the curtain pulled sideways.

Ned yanked on his boots and jacket and exited the camp. She locked the door - again - and watched from the window as he checked the shed, the woods, the outhouse. He even fought the deep snowdrifts on the hill behind the camp and peered behind the boulders under their white caps of snow. "He's gone," he told her when he returned. He was breathing heavily and clutching his right arm in pain. "But someone was here. The snow is messed up."

Lissa locked the door and hung the key on its peg. "Let's finish eating," she said dully. She flicked lights on as she retraced their steps to the living room.

"Are you okay?" he asked her. He retrieved her sandwich; it had fallen into messy bits on the living room floor. She put it back together the best she could. When she looked up at him, he could see the tears forming. "Hey, it's okay, Lissa," he said. "He was probably after food, and he didn't get any. The door is locked now. I don't think we need to worry."

She nodded, but her mouth quivered slightly. "Talk about something else," she said. "There's nothing we can do about him."

"Well, there's one thing we can do." Ned quickly retrieved the key from its kitchen peg and held it out to her. "Why don't you hang onto this? There's no point in leaving it so accessible."

She took the key and pocketed it.

Chapter 20

"I THINK YOU WERE LUCKY to have so many people around," Ned said conversationally. "I would have liked having a few more." He was hungrily eating the sandwiches stacked on his plate. Between bites, he massaged his injured arm.

Lissa sat stiffly in an overstuffed chair, trying to relax, watching him devour the food and wondering what they would eat tomorrow if the roads remained unplowed. He didn't seem ready to make the hike back to her car or the nearest town. She had caught him wincing when he moved his arm, and she felt guilty having taken the last aspirin. He hadn't once mentioned needing to see a doctor, but she would feel far more at ease if he could have his wound checked by one. She would insist on it once their ordeal in the cabin ended. Once they escaped from the frightening stranger and the deceitfully sparkling, entrapping snow.

"What happened to your mother?" she asked now.

"She died when I was twenty. It was hardest on my brother. I don't think he ever got over it completely."

"Was she sick?"

"Never. She was playing with my brother and had a stroke. It was pretty quick."

Lissa shuddered. "That must have been awful for him."

"Yeah, he was only seven. He's always felt responsible, I think. He never understood what happened."

"What's wrong with him, Ned?"

Ned shrugged. "He does weird things now and then. He can't really be trusted on his own because he sometimes skips the medication he's supposed to take."

She sat forward, interested. The wine had begun to relax her and she admitted to herself that she was dependent on the company of the stranger who had broken into her camp and into her life. In fact, she was grateful he was here. "What kinds of weird things?"

"Oh, just... School was hard for him. He couldn't seem to sit still long enough to learn much. His behavior was what they call 'inappropriate,' which means obnoxious and out of control."

"That sounds like Katie."

"He drove everybody nuts until Jim stepped in, the guy I bought my business from. I think my brother had more suspensions than anyone else in school." He took a big bite of bread and cheese, chewed, and swallowed. "For things like acting out in class, fights, pranks that were funny only to him. In schools, they call it attention deficit. The thing was," said Ned, warming to his topic, "my brother really didn't understand how bad he was. He just didn't get it. It was like asking a two year old to be mature."

"He was seven when your mother died?"

Ned nodded. "It kind of fell to me to take care of Conor. He eventually joined me in my business."

A whisk of wind shook the rafters of the camp, and they both inhaled a breath. Ignore that, Lissa thought.

Ned set his plate down and toured the windows quickly, peering outside into the darkening dusk.

"Conor. Nice name," she said distractedly.

"Yeah, he got the movie star name; I was named for our grandfather, Edward. Anyway, Conor was lost to the family a long time ago." He caught her dismayed look, returned to his chair by the fire. "I don't mean like you. You chose to separate yourself. Conor can't help himself. He alienates people; he and my father are out of touch. It's just too much for my dad; he has problems of his own without Conor. I make it a point to know what my brother's up to, where he is, and I can usually tell when he's about to show up on my doorstep in the middle of the night. He works with me, so I can usually see things coming. Then I take him in and try to straighten him out."

"You're good," she said simply.

He looked at her in surprise. "I'm good? What's that mean?"

She smiled. "It just means that you're good, a good person. You care about your brother even though he makes your life harder. I wish I were that generous." She picked up her sandwich and took a dainty bite.

He didn't speak for a moment. "Well," he said finally, "thank you. That's nice of you to say. But you have to realize that I'm older than you. You have dreams and goals, and you don't want to lose them. See, we're different, Lissa. I haven't had any dreams for a long time."

"You could have if you didn't have to worry about Conor. He's not really your responsibility, you know. He's an adult, and if he's supposed to take some kind of medication and just doesn't bother, then why is it your problem?"

"I can't answer that. I just know that it is. And he's only nineteen, that's not really an adult."

"Of course it is," she said righteously. "At nineteen, I was on my own." She had earned an impressive college scholarship, made the decision to get two degrees, and was holding down a job for her spending money. If she could do it, then any nineteen year old should be able to. "He's only your responsibility because you let him be."

Ned was looking at her strangely, and she realized that she might sound a little self-satisfied. "I mean, all people have their own problems," she said demurely, "but we all have to face what we are and work around those things. Don't you think so?"

"I guess," Ned said.

Chapter 21

WHY WAS HE EVEN TELLING HER about Conor? She was successful and accomplished. Full power and straight ahead. It was obvious she had escaped a situation that drove her crazy and was making something of herself. She would never understand or sympathize with someone like Conor. Or even someone like Ned himself.

And yet, hadn't she spent her childhood looking after a sister a lot like Conor? And intended to take her sister on again.

Ned vividly remembered the day of his mother's death. Hearing his father's hoarse shouts, running into the house to find his mother slumped on the floor, the glittering silver medal around her neck, and Conor sitting near her, rocking back and forth, his eyes blank.

Conor's eyes were often blank now, and it had started at around that time. Of course, there were still good times, too, and Ned loved Conor's periods of normalcy. In fact, Ned lived for those times. When Conor would come bursting into the shop after lunch and wheedle Ned into going fishing for the afternoon, when he'd beg Ned to take some time off so they could drive into Marcy Falls for a movie. They'd close up the shop, and Ned would take his losses, counting it a small price to pay to have the old Conor for half a day.

Ned appreciated the lucid looks and sadly accepted the empty ones, but more often now, he had begun to notice a new look in Conor's eye, a frightening slyness. Deception had never been part of Conor's make-up. He would pull pranks and skip classes, but he was cheerfully honest about it when caught. The slyness was something new, and it disturbed Ned more than he cared to admit.

He blamed Cassie and could pinpoint the day when that look

had emerged in his innocent younger brother's eyes, could still see Cassie grinning insolently, clutching Conor hard until he turned and followed her out of the shop, against Ned's instructions.

He had spent all those years making sure Conor got up and off to school, fielding phone calls from his teachers, drilling him for final exams, walking him through everything he needed to do in order to make it to graduation. And Conor had made it. He should have been much more, but at least he was a high school graduate, and it hadn't come easily. It frustrated and sickened Ned that a piece of trash like Cassie Sillington now controlled Conor.

He erased these thoughts from his mind. There was nothing he could do about it here, locked into this snowbound cabin.

The feel of Lissa's gentle fingertips on his arm surprised Ned and brought him back to their conversation. The fire was burning low now, and their chairs faced it, nearly touching. The camp felt warm and safe. How he wished he could always feel this safe.

"Ned?" she said quietly, "I'm sorry. I shouldn't be judging your brother. I'm sure he has problems that I don't know anything about. I sounded arrogant. I don't mean to be."

He stared at her hand lying softly on his sleeve. Was she afraid of him or wasn't she? She sure didn't seem it now.

"It's all right," he said, and then he had to repeat it because the words came out a rough whisper. "You have a lot to be proud of. You *should* be proud." He cleared his throat and said, "When he doesn't take his meds, that's when he gets into trouble. It doesn't happen often. Jim got my father to take him for a physical and counseling, and things were a lot better for a while. It's too bad because Conor's not dumb," he continued, trying to convince her. "He's a little screwed up, but he's not stupid."

Ned stopped talking. Why was he doing this? Telling Lissa Tea all about his weird brother. She had escaped from family troubles of her own. She sure couldn't be very interested in hearing about his.

He still had bread and cheese on his plate, and a leaf of wilted lettuce, but he hated to pick it up and disturb her hand lying there so trustingly. He ignored the food, glanced at her, and felt startled again at the peculiar color of her eyes, gray, like the soft feathers of a mourning dove.

She met his gaze and looked down, pulling her hand away.

"He's not happy the way he is, Lissa, and it kills me. No one should have to suffer the way my brother does."

"He's lucky that you care so much about him," Lissa said. "Who would take care of him if you didn't?"

"I don't know. Who takes care of Katie?"

Her brow furrowed. "That's not the same at all," she said firmly. "Katie was forced on me. I had to make a clean break."

"Was it worth it, though?" he said.

"Absolutely, I needed to be on my own," she said stubbornly. "That's why I'm afraid to go back. If I do, it's like admitting they were right."

He shrugged. "Lucky you. You decide when to leave, you decide when and whether to return. With me there wasn't much choice. My father lost interest, and my mother's dead. If she were alive, she'd be right there for Conor. She always said she'd take care of him. To him, it looked as if she just up and left."

"Well, my sister had plenty of people to cater to her," Lissa said shortly. "And anyway, I'm fixing it, aren't I? I'll fit her in; I'll make it work. But I intend to become someone, too."

. . .

Lissa stopped, annoyed with the pleading sound her voice was taking on. What difference did it make if Ned Marchess sympathized?

"How can you make it work?" he asked. "How can you pursue all these dreams and still give her the kind of attention she needs?"

"Oh, I don't know." Lissa was exasperated. He was voicing the same obstacles she had butted up against every time she thought of taking Katie away with her. "There must be some kind of people you can hire for that."

Ned was quiet for a moment, considering. "Well, I'm sure you'll get everything you want," he said finally.

"Well, that's not wrong!" Lissa said vehemently.

He smiled gently. "No, it's not. It's a choice. Some of us don't have that choice."

"Everyone has choices," Lissa insisted.

"Well, maybe. But sometimes a choice that feels good isn't necessarily right."

"What's that supposed to mean?" she demanded. "That I was selfish? People do what they have to do."

Ned stood and wandered to the window. The snow still fell quietly. "You're so cold," he said, turning to her. "Always cool, in control, so sure you have it all figured out. Maybe you should loosen up and admit that not everyone is just like you."

Lissa stared at him. "Cold?" she gasped. She'd hardly heard his other words, had become stuck on the one that made her throat clench. "I'm not cold. I'm not."

"Of course you are," Ned replied. "Sitting there passing judgment on your brothers and sisters and parents and everybody else. Margie's too young to be married. Everybody should make sure to go to college. Your mother shouldn't have smoked. Judging them all. And me, too, I'm sure." He turned abruptly, poked at the fire, then sat on the couch and stretched his feet to warm them.

They sat in awkward silence for a few moments, listening to occasional gusts buffeting the cabin. Lissa felt uncomfortable, as if she had just been reprimanded, yet she knew she was right about her future. It was too bad Ned Marchess was one of those people without any dreams of his own. If he had any, he would understand how important hers were.

"My turn to apologize," Ned said suddenly. "Speaking of judging people, I guess I really let you have it, didn't I. I shouldn't have said those things."

The fire was flickering shallowly, and Lissa glanced at the diminishing woodpile near the hearth. It would be so easy to just stop talking to him, to ignore his ridiculous misjudgment of her and wait in silence until the road crews arrived. But she'd take the high road. "Is there enough wood there to last a few more hours?" she asked.

"Should be. I'll get more if you want me to."

"It doesn't matter; we can burn this and then let the fire die down." She stole a furtive look at the man beside her. He seemed utterly convinced that her decisions were selfish. Yet he had broken her window and made himself comfortable in her camp. He was evasive and secretive, and she couldn't help recalling the things she had heard him muttering in sleep earlier.

Who cared what he thought? She would think of getting back to civilization, to William Brashue. William was forthright and intelligent, had educated opinions about important topics, which he vocalized in class. A far cry from this backwoods clod. William was sensitive and talented and intellectual.

And found the idea of Katie so distasteful that he hadn't had time for Lissa in weeks.

Lissa swallowed and got up from her chair. She wandered to the window and gazed out at the thick cluster of trees on the slope that led to the lake.

"It's too bad you don't have a wife," she said idly, her back to Ned.

"What?"

She faced him. "You don't, do you?"

"No."

"I could tell. If you had a wife, if you had someone looking out for *you*, she would have convinced you that you don't have to give up everything for Conor."

"I wouldn't want that kind of wife."

Lissa laughed, a short, sharp sound. She turned back to the window and followed a flurry of snowflakes as they danced to earth. "There's a guy at school that I've been seeing," she said. "We haven't committed to marriage yet, but that will come, I think. William, that's his name."

"Why are you telling me that?"

She turned to him again and smiled. "I don't know. Just thinking of how people match up. My parents - they were actually a perfect match. I can't imagine either of them with anyone else."

"So, a good marriage."

"Right. No hopes, no dreams, no plans, same old thing every day."

"Whereas you and *William*. . . ." He dragged out the name, accentuating the formality of it.

"He's an artist. He takes his art very seriously. He's brilliant."

"Ah, so you're a perfect match, too." He laughed when he saw the flush stain her cheeks.

"I didn't mean that," she said.

"But there's someone in the world for everyone, is that it?"

"I think, maybe."

"Gosh, even for me, do you think? A boor like me?" He stuffed food into his mouth and looked at her quizzically. "A nothing?" Crumbs dropped from his mouth. "All set in my ways, no education, no future. Even for me, Melissa?"

She turned aside, refusing to acknowledge him.

"Well, he sounds horrible," Ned continued. "*William* sounds boring and stuffy, but perfect for you, just as you said." He crammed another big bite into his mouth and chewed glumly.

"You don't know him," Lissa said simply. "He's not boring. We have a good time together; everything is very harmonious."

"Harmonious?" he scoffed.

"You know, controlled. Predictable." Except for the recent confusion over Katie. She squelched that thought.

"Predictable is another word for boring," he said.

"You're misunderstanding me on purpose."

"No, I'm not. Your love affair is controlled and boring, just like the rest of your life." Ned grabbed a paper napkin and swiped at his face.

"William is. . . courtly, kind of." Lissa was staring into the dying fire with a vague mistiness in her eyes.

"Oh, I see," Ned rolled his eyes. "*Courtly.*"

"It's a trait some men have." She glanced at him and pursed her lips. "And some don't."

"And what does *William* think about you taking on your sister? Assuming you've shared that little secret with him."

Lissa blushed. "It will take some time, obviously." She glanced over to find Ned smirking. "We've talked about it. How we'd do it. Ways we could make it work."

"So you really plan to marry this guy."

"Well, he practically asked me."

"Practically? How does a guy practically ask you to get married? Did he propose or not?"

"Not in so many words. He's more subtle than that."

Ned scoffed. "Wow. That's seeing the glass half full."

Lissa turned away. "You're insufferable." She shouldn't have mentioned William and regretted earlier moments when she had followed Ned from room to room as if he were some kind of saving hero. She sighed audibly, wishing the snow would stop, the plow would come, that she could come to terms with being stuck here with Ned Marchess. She didn't know why he was here, but in spite of his sarcasm, she believed him when he said he had nothing to do with the Gorham robbery. She would feel so much more comfortable if he would only fill in the gaps. Why did his conversation skillfully maneuver around certain issues?

"Ned," she said, turning back to him, "I want to ask you some things, and I'd really like you to be frank."

His eyes narrowed and he put the sandwich down. "What things?"

"Earlier today, you were talking in your sleep, and you said a couple of things."

He relaxed and picked up his plate again. "No kidding. Like what?"

"You were talking about jail. I almost had the impression it was familiar to you." She stopped. She could feel a flush rising up her neck.

"It's familiar to me. What else?"

"You've been in prison?"

"I said it's familiar, not that I've been inside. I know about jails the same way you do."

She couldn't keep the sarcastic tone out of her voice. "You brought gifts to the inmates' children?"

"Not exactly." He finished off his last sandwich and glanced at her plate.

"Have it," she said. "I don't want it." It was dry and tasteless, unappetizing.

"Okay." He helped himself to the remaining half on her plate and ate it in three big bites. "What else did you hear me say?"

She decided to drop the prison question for now. "You were talking about a medal and you sounded sad. You said 'It's mine, my medal.' What were you dreaming?"

"I said that, huh?"

"Does it mean something? Our dreams sometimes indicate things we're worried about; they can help us. . . ."

Ned snorted a laugh, licked the remaining sandwich crumbs from his finger, put the empty plate on the floor, and grinned at her.

She was quiet, looking back at him, waiting.

"Okay, Dr. Tea. I'll tell you about that, and then I don't want to talk about it anymore. Agreed?"

"All right."

Chapter 22

"THERE'S A REAL MEDAL and a story behind it. I've dreamed about it before." He stared at the fire, gathering his thoughts. "The medal was a First Communion gift from my mother. It's a medal of Saint Luke I got when I was seven. When Conor made his First Communion, he got one, too, just like mine. I was twenty and working for Jim Polinski at the time, but I still lived at home. Shortly after that, my mother had the stroke and died." He paused. "Well, Conor's mixed-up mind got the medal all confused with her death. He had this idea that if he got rid of his medal, she'd come back, so he threw it into the Hudson River where it runs through Gorham."

Lissa flinched slightly. "So you *are* from Gorham? And you were coming from there yesterday, weren't you."

"Lissa, lots of people live in Gorham, and a lot of them drive that road all the time. It's the main road leading out of town toward Albany and Saratoga. There's nothing to get excited about."

"But when I asked you before if you were from there, you didn't answer."

He ran a frustrated hand through his hair. "Well, you were so suspicious, and you were obviously afraid of me. I didn't need to give you any more facts to hyperventilate over."

She drew herself up straighter. "Hyperventilate! I was merely asking you-"

". . . if I was the guy who robbed the gas station in Gorham, I know. And I told you no."

"So you do live there?" she repeated doggedly.

He looked at her for a long moment, deciding how to answer, how much of the truth to tell. "Sure, I live there."

"What were you doing on that road yesterday? Was it really coincidence that you were driving south just at the same time...."

"Oh, for God's sake. I had an AC unit in my car and-"

"What's that? An AC unit."

"That infamous air conditioner you don't believe in. I have to transport it to Glens Falls and I've been driving it around for a week. When my car hit a snowbank, there was a jolt. The unit slid into me, or else I slid into it. I'm not sure which, but this was the result." He indicated his injured arm with its ragged sling.

"So your car is there on the road, too?"

"My car is there, too. It's farther down than your little compact, but yes, it's another casualty of the blizzard."

She was looking at him peculiarly. "Who would want an air conditioner delivered in the dead of winter?"

"I don't know," he said irritably. "Customers get things repaired on the off season. I don't quiz them about their reasons for wanting things at certain times. I just do the work." He dragged in a frustrated breath. "Do you want me to continue this story about my brother and the medal?"

"Yes," she sniffed, "but I still think you should have told me all this before. It would have helped me feel a lot more confident."

"Fine, I should have told you before. So, Conor threw his medal into the river, thinking it would somehow bring our mother back, and it caused problems for him, as usual." He paused, searching for words.

"Go on."

"My father was fuming. Conor figured he was in hot water for getting rid of the medal, so if he got ahold of another medal, he'd make up for what he did and Dad would back off."

"So he took yours?"

"Yes, and it was pretty much the only thing my mother ever gave me. We never had a lot of money, and there's no such thing as a family heirloom in my family."

"But why does that give you nightmares? You were twenty. You could have made him give it back, right? Or your father could have. Or even let him keep it, or buy him another one. It's only a medal, after all."

"It was the way he took it. You have to understand, Conor

doesn't know. . . . He stole into my bed one night and instead of lifting the thing off my neck and whisking it away, like any normal kid might have, he tried to cut it off my neck with scissors."

"He brought scissors into your bed?"

"Yes, and tried to cut the chain off."

"Were you hurt?"

"Yes, of course. I woke up, I jumped; he pierced me and drew blood. I started screaming bloody murder, my father burst in, and there was a big scene. That's the way we do it in my family."

"He drew blood?" she whispered. "That's terrible!"

He gave her a blunt stare. "The whole thing was terrible."

"Where is it?" she asked. "You're not wearing it."

"Conor has it."

She thought a moment, staring at him. "That's not exactly fair, is it."

Ned smiled at her tolerantly. "It's not fair. It's safe. I wouldn't dare wear it now. Conor loves that medal and he's a lot bigger and stronger now. He's proud of it and if he likes people, he'll sometimes offer to let them wear it. He lets me wear it sometimes. He puts it on me, and a few minutes later, I give it back. I should have handled it differently that night, but it was a shock to wake up with my brother clipping away at my neck."

"How could you have handled it differently? He might have killed you."

"No, that would never happen. I could have just talked him down; he always responds to me if I stay calm and quiet. If I get excited, he gets excited. That's why he and my father can't be in the same room. It always ends up in fireworks. My father yells at Conor to calm down, to think before he acts." Ned shook his head regretfully. "That's a laugh. My father ought to remove the plank from his own eye before he tries removing the speck from Conor's, so to speak."

Lissa nodded at the familiar passage. "So does he try to do that?" she asked.

"He goes right on berating Conor, who doesn't understand half of it, and I spend my evenings separating them. It's a tradition. That's why they don't see much of each other."

"Is your brother dangerous?" she asked.

"No, no, not at all," he insisted. "He just lacks sense. He was letting my mother wear his medal just before her stroke."

"And he - what? Tried to get it back?"

Ned raked a hand through his hair again. It flopped into his face in damp waves where he had tried to wet it down; a few spikes stuck up on top. "I don't know. No, I don't think so."

Lissa was aghast. "What are you saying, that he killed your mother?" she whispered.

"No, no, that's exactly what I'm *not* saying. He may think he did, but he couldn't have. There were no signs of it; she was still wearing the medal when we got there. No marks on her neck, nothing like that. But he had just put the chain on her when the stroke happened. You can see how he would have seen cause and effect where there was just coincidence. He was only seven."

"Did a psychologist ever talk to him? A counselor?"

Ned looked away guiltily. "Yeh. Not for long. My father doesn't believe in that stuff."

And that was another sign of the kind of uneducated fools they were. All Ned had to do was look into Lissa's eyes and he could read her thoughts. He didn't like the direction the conversation was taking. "The things Conor does are stupid, and he gets confused, but he's never done anything violent or caused any real harm. At least not intentionally."

"Well, what has he done by acci-"

Chapter 23

NED'S EYES NARROWED SUDDENLY. He put a quick hand up to quiet her and was off the couch in a flash. "Did you hear that?" he whispered.

"No." Her blood felt icy and her voice came in a short, quiet gasp. "Did you hear something? What was it?"

"I heard a grating sound," he murmured. "Be quiet a minute." He went from window to window, holding the curtains aside and peering out, checking the living room, kitchen, bathroom, and both bedrooms.

Lissa strained her ears but heard only the occasional brief gust of wind from the storm. It was already dark, and the snow outside the windows had deteriorated to a few hopeful puffs blown about by a fitful wind.

"Hear it?"

She wasn't sure. Did she hear a soft, far-off sound? Her heart began to gallop. Maybe it was the wind. She stared at Ned.

He glanced around the room warily. "I don't hear it anymore. I might have imagined it."

Lissa bit her lip and nodded. "It's mean out there," she said. "I guess we should be glad we're in here."

"Yeah, it makes you count your blessings, doesn't it."

Lissa nodded distractedly. He had been about to tell her.... She'd been asking him about Conor, his violence. Had he fabricated a sound outside to stop her questions, or had the sound been real? Did she have the nerve to ask him again? She glanced at him and found him staring at her. Talking of violence seemed suddenly like planting a seed.

"Did you have enough to eat?" she asked instead. She knew he hadn't. The rations were meager and he was a big man. "There are still some crackers in the carton if you want them."

"And spoil breakfast?" he said. "Nah, I'm fine, Lissa. In fact, I think I'll turn in pretty soon."

She glanced at her watch. Darkness had fallen outside the little cabin, but it was early by civilization's standards. "It's only seven-thirty," she said. The fire was dying down; a few bright embers sparked and glowed. "We should melt some snow tonight, so we'll have water in the morning."

. . .

"This ought to get us through breakfast at least," Lissa mused. They had four saucepans of snow melting on the stove. She stirred and added snow by handfuls while Ned sat at the table leafing through her Aesthetics textbook. "What I don't understand," he was saying, "is why people actually study art. Isn't it just something you either enjoy or don't?"

Lissa shrugged. "There are different schools of thought on that."

"What I've always wished," Ned said thoughtfully, "was that I could visit a place like New York City and see some of the great paintings. I'd love to see some of those Impressionists I've read about-"

He was interrupted by a sudden muffled pop. The cabin was plunged into darkness.

Lissa gasped as the wooden spoon she held clanged against the side of a pan.

Ned said quietly, "What the hell?"

"We've lost power." She felt a sputtering spark of panic and forced herself to speak calmly. "It could be a wire down; that's probably what it is." Her voice sounded disembodied in the blackness.

She heard Ned push his chair back and stand up. He made his way to the stove and stood beside her, a ghostly presence she could hear but not see. "Please don't be thinking someone cut the power lines," he said. "You know how easy it is to lose power during a storm up here, right? It'll probably be on again in a few hours."

"I hope so," she answered. "I need to get these burners off in case it comes back on while we're asleep. She felt for the stove burner knobs and one by one moved them carefully to the upright position. "I think they're off now," she said. "I need the flashlight to tell for sure."

"I think it's over here." Ned maneuvered around the kitchen table and felt around for the flashlight on the edge of the countertop. "Here." He felt his way back to her and shone the beam onto the burner knobs. She peered at the knobs; all were off.

The familiar background noise of the refrigerator motor had ceased; the melting snow hissed quietly to a stop. Only the screaming wind pierced the stillness inside the little cabin.

"Now I'm sorry we didn't keep the fire going," Lissa said.

"Do you have candles or another flashlight?" His voice loomed over her in the dark.

"My mother and Aunt Louise never let anyone bring candles here; there were too many little kids. There might be another flashlight somewhere, maybe in a dresser? Or in the shed."

"I'll check if you give me that one so I can see."

Lissa handed the flashlight to Ned. Their fingers fumbled together until he had a grip on it. He left the room, bouncing the shallow beam before him. Lissa was in pitch black. She stretched out a hand to find a kitchen chair and sat down, waiting for him.

He called back to her. "I'm not finding anything in here. Let me check the other room."

A few minutes later he returned. He had a flashlight, but neither of them could make it work. "The batteries are probably corroded," he offered. He tried taking them out and putting them in again. The light remained dead, the room inky black. "Are there more batteries?"

"I doubt it," she said. They put the extra flashlight aside.

"But, look," Ned said, "I did find this." He shone the working light onto a candle stub. "Someone sneaked one in anyway. I bet it was that old romantic, Margie."

Lissa smiled, found matches in a tin box above the stove and lit the candle. The tiny flame flickered eerily, creating a small circle of dusty light. She could see Ned's face, his features leaping and changing with the candle flame's movement.

"I hope we get the electricity back soon," Lissa said. "I don't like this."

"Let's go into the living room," Ned suggested. "I can get the fire going again; that will give us some light." He started away from her, holding the flashlight. She followed with the candle, walking gingerly, unsure of her footing. He turned around. "Okay?"

"I'm okay."

"Here, give me your other hand," he said. He maneuvered the flashlight, felt for her hand and held it close to his chest; the sling made it impossible to do otherwise. She could feel his hard muscles under the soft chamois of Uncle Jeff's shirt. Her breathing felt shallow and she had a moment's gratitude for the darkness hiding the embarrassed flush she could feel creeping up her cheeks.

With slow steps, they crept to the living room. Lissa sank onto the couch while Ned got the fire going again and added the last two logs from the hearth. "That should burn for a little while."

"You know," said Lissa, "we could put pots on the gas heater in here and keep melting snow. Should we get them?"

"It will probably melt down on its own if the camp stays warm enough. The food in the refrigerator might be a problem, though."

Lissa shrugged. "There's a vast refrigeration unit right outside the door. All we need is some kind of secure box to put the food in and the snow will keep it cold." She thought briefly. "In the shed I bet there's something."

"Are you volunteering me to go out there right now?"

"We should put the food out in the snow, but if we don't put it in something, animals will get it." Or people, she thought. One very bold and angry man. "We'll have to hide it, too."

"All right," Ned agreed. "I'll go look. After that, I'm going to get some sleep. I feel achy and tired."

He took the flashlight with him to the kitchen and started putting on his jacket and boots, winding his ripped flannel shirt around his neck as a scarf. She followed him with the candle. "Do you want to come to the outhouse?" he asked her. "There's safety in numbers."

To go with Ned now or alone later, that was her choice. She felt for her boots and jacket, her warm mittens and scarf and hat. He grabbed the flashlight, and together they went out the door and up the hill. More snow had gathered before the door, and together they swept it aside by the light of the flashlight. "Ladies first," he said. "I'll be right out here." He handed her the light.

This was no time to feel shy. Lissa used the outhouse first and dragged in a relieved breath of cold air when she found Ned still outside, waiting for her. She washed her hands in the cold, biting snow, then put her mittens back on.

"I'll walk you back down," he said.

"That's not necessary. I'll wait here for you."

He took her arm with his good one, propelled her down the bank and out of the woods, and deposited her at the kitchen door. She had locked it against intruders; she fitted the key and entered the dark, eerie kitchen. "Lock it," Ned said. He closed the door behind her and was gone.

She crept to the window and strained her eyes. Ned retreated through the deep snow. She could see the flashlight's beam and the white in the plaid of his makeshift scarf, comforting beacons in the night. Lissa felt beads of sweat form inside her sweater and trickle down her sides until she saw him returning to her, bobbing down the hill and across the wooded yard.

He veered left and went in the direction of the woodshed. She peered through the window, but darkness shrouded her sight. What would he find in there? The hair on the back of her neck felt prickly.

When she saw his figure lumbering back across the property, she sighed in relief. She unlocked the door and flung it open. A quick gust of frigid air entered along with Ned. Lissa shivered.

He was breathing heavily, but smiled a half smile as she closed the door behind him. His arms were awkwardly full. "I found this," he said triumphantly. He handed her the bulky item he carried. It was a metal box with a hasp, perfect for keeping their food safe from animals. "And I got a little more wood," he added. "We'll want it in the morning." She heard the loud rumble as he dropped four fat logs to the kitchen floor.

"Good," she said. "I'm glad you're back. So there's no one out there?"

She could hear him unzipping his jacket and pulling his gloves off, draping things over chairs. She tried to hold the flashlight to help him see. The candle on the table wavered thinly. "There's nothing to worry about and no one out there," he said. He stepped closer to her. His breath came roughly. "I need to get some rest, Lissa. I hardly got any sleep last night, and without any more pain pills, this is really throbbing."

"I know."

"Lissa," he said, "whatever you may think, and whatever happens here, I want you to know that I'll take care of you. I won't hurt you."

And that would be a first, Lissa thought. Someone who would take care of her for a change. She was glad Ned couldn't see the raw gratitude on her face. "Thank you," she said. "I believe you."

"And I won't let anyone else hurt you either. There's something I want you to promise me."

"What is it?"

"When you go to your room tonight, I don't want you to push the dresser against the door like you did last night."

"How did you know I. . . . Don't do it?" She was confused. She hadn't planned to do that tonight; she trusted Ned. She sucked in a tiny breath. A twinge of fear took root in her stomach. "Why not?"

"If he should show up, and I'm not saying I expect him to, but if he does, and if he should come in through your bedroom window, I want you to be able to get out of there."

She had never thought of that possibility, and alarm twisted through her. "Do you think. . . ."

"Hey, hold on, now." He reached for her hand in the dark, found it and drew it toward him, holding it firmly. "I don't expect it to happen, but I'd feel a lot better if I knew you could get to me if you need to."

"All right," she said in a small voice. She pulled her hand away, opened the refrigerator door, held the candle aloft, and started placing their meager food collection into the metal box.

He started for the bedroom, taking the flashlight along.

The kitchen plunged into blackness, the only light the wavery glow of the candle flame. "It's really dark without that light," Lissa said quietly.

He turned back. "Sorry. I'll stay. I'll wait until I know you're not going to die of panic during the night." He sat in his usual chair. "Here, let me hold the candle for you and think of a way to ease your mind."

"I'm okay," she reassured him. "But I'm scared. I'm worried about that man out there. The darkness is creepy, and the weather outside-"

"*. . . is frightful, but the fire is so-o-o delightful!*"

Lissa's eyes opened wide in the darkness and she dropped the bag of bagels she was holding. A laugh burbled up her throat. "Are you *singing*?"

"Just practicing my math," he said. "I should watch myself. I forgot for a minute that you're a music major."

She laughed again, surprised that he had such a rich tenor. "You have a good voice," she said.

"*And since we've no place to go-o-o. . . .*" he sang. The cheerful tune lingered in the air. "Come on! You know this!" His voice was merry.

Lissa giggled again and then joined in, feeling lighter than she had in days. "*Let it snow! Let it snow! Let it snow!*" Their voices blended, piercing the darkness. The last note rang out and died; silence crowded in. Lissa stooped to feel for the bagels on the floor.

"Wow," said Ned, "You should be singing songs, never mind writing them."

She felt herself blush with pleasure.

"Want to try another one?" He began humming another Christmas tune. Frosty the Snowman.

Lissa chuckled and continued storing food in the box.

"Okay now?" he said. "Will you be able to sleep?"

She smiled. "As soon as I put this food outside so it stays cold." Once again she donned her outer clothing. Ned stood in the doorway and shone the light for her. She half buried the box in snow behind some bushes near the door, made sure the latch was secure, and came back in, stomping off her boots.

"Good night, Lissa," he said. "Melissa." He flashed the beam ahead of them, smiled over at her in the dim, wavery light and said softly, "It will be fine tonight. We'll get through this. The snow has nearly stopped. The plows should be coming through, maybe even tonight. I'll see you in the morning."

"Leave your door open tonight," she told him. "There won't be any heat in the bedrooms because of the electric baseboards."

By flashlight, they groped their way to their rooms. By mutual agreement, they would leave the flashlight on a table near both bedroom doors. She heard him return to the living room and check the fire, then go to his room. The old bedframe creaked as he lay down on it.

Suddenly a thought occurred to her. She stumbled from her bed, grabbed the flashlight, and fumbled her way back to the kitchen. Yes, she had left the candle burning there, and Ned hadn't thought to blow it out either. She extinguished the flame with a single breath.

"Oh, you have it," he said behind her, making her jump.

"I thought you were in your room."

"I was, but I wasn't sure if we had blown that out."

"We're not very successful pioneers," she admitted.

"But we could go on the stage," he said thoughtfully.

Lissa laughed and guided them back to their respective bedroom doors.

Last night she had lain awake, fearing for her life with Ned in the cabin. Tonight she lay awake again for more than an hour. *Let it snow*, she thought. It had been a nice interlude, but it didn't change the fact that the power was out, the food was nearly gone, and the driver who'd hit her car was prowling the premises. It had been a relief to tell him about her mother, about Katie, but she still didn't know any more about Ned than she had this morning. And anyway, he was exactly like her mother in some ways. She groaned and rolled over in the sleeping bag. No plans, no future, taking life as it came with no motivation to change for the better. Was that her mother she was describing? Or was it Ned? She should be more careful, she thought. Too much trust too quickly could only invite trouble.

But she felt safer knowing he was in the next room.

Chapter 24

WHEN NED AWOKE in the morning, the lamp by his bed was doing battle with the wash of sunlight filtering through the window. He breathed a sigh of relief; the power was on. He heaved himself from the bed, gingerly touching his arm to reassure himself; yes, the pain was still there. The room felt cold and he rubbed his hands together and put on a double layer of socks.

He wondered what was for breakfast, but didn't hold out much hope. He'd been feeling hunger pains for days.

He passed by Lissa studying her class notes at the kitchen table, shrugged into his outdoor clothing and left the camp. The snow was deep, the air frigid. It couldn't get much colder, he thought.

She had seemed a lot less afraid of him last night, and that was a good thing, but he didn't know how much longer the two of them could stay holed up here. He thought about the singing and smiled. That had been a good moment. A lot better than having her go to bed scared and worrying. If she could just stay calm and not be in such a rush to get out of here, that would be the best he could hope for.

He brushed his teeth with the used toothbrush she had given him, trudged to the outhouse and shed, grabbed some firewood with his good arm, and returned to the camp.

"So, the power's back," he said.

"Such a relief," Lissa said. "I guess it really was a downed wire somewhere."

"Probably out on the highway. They got to it pretty quickly." He spotted the carton of crackers on the table and sat, grabbing a handful and gulping them down. He looked around the little kitchen and spotted a rustic sign on the wall. It spelled out

T-E-A. The letters were made with birch twigs and fastened with rawhide and glue to a white birch backing. "Did someone in your family make it?" Ned asked.

"My cousin Neal probably." Lissa dumped the remainder of the crackers on a plate and pushed it toward Ned.

"I was perfectly happy eating these out of the box," he said. "Why wash a plate?"

She stared at the plate, nonplussed. "I don't know. I always put things on plates."

"Oh, well, I guess I'm lazy because I live alone."

"I live alone," she shrugged. "Anyway, Neal also took the photograph I nailed over the window."

She'd brought the metal box inside and emptied it. She was cooking mushrooms. The smell was tantalizing; he could feel his mouth watering.

"Is there any more of that hamburger?" he asked.

"About one spoonful, and it's all yours."

She pushed the mushrooms aside and added the lump of meat to the pan. It sizzled invitingly.

"What else is there?" he asked.

"It's all right there on the table." She unwrapped the small packages and they both stared at the bits of leftover food. He divided things as evenly as he could between two plates.

She plopped the meat onto his plate with the crackers. He gestured to her, inviting her to share.

"No, I've been eating them while you were asleep. These are yours. And, except for six slightly stale, frozen bagels, that officially ends the food supply." She set the empty cracker box aside to burn in the fireplace. "From here on in, we gnaw tree bark."

He had told her he was a light eater to keep her from going to her car, but the truth was that he was starving; nothing pleased a meat-and-potatoes guy like him more than a big meal, but she didn't need to know that. He could manage.

When his plate was empty, he leaned back, telling himself he was full, and stretched against the painted chair. She wore the same sweater she'd had on the day before, but he noticed the turtleneck was missing. So, she was feeling more comfortable around him, beginning to trust him. Or maybe she thought it was warm in the camp. Maybe she was just cold-blooded.

Outside, the crisp air still seemed to be hovering around zero degrees, but the snow had turned to small, twirling wisps. The brunt of the storm was over, and weak morning sunlight painted the windows of the cabin.

Ned stretched again, shivered, and started to rise. "I'll get snow for the dishes."

"I have a better idea, Ned. If I walk to my car, I can bring back more supplies and water. These lake roads are the last to be plowed, which means our cars are stuck for a while. We could be here for a couple more days. If I'm going, I'd rather start now and give myself all day to get back."

His eyebrows rose. "Aren't you afraid?"

"Of course, a little. But we haven't seen any signs of him. He can't still be out there. I think I could make it."

"You talk as if I'm not invited."

"No," she shook her head decisively. "You're not invited. You still have a washed out look sometimes; I can't take a chance on you collapsing somewhere along the lake road. How would I get you back here?"

He dismissed her fears. "I won't collapse. We can get twice as much if I help."

"Right, with one arm that sets you howling in pain when I try to change the bandage."

"You're exaggerating."

"Let me see it, then."

Obediently, he pulled his arm from the sling and rested it on the table. Lissa pulled the bandage up as gently as she could. He yelped. Without an ointment, the gauze had stuck to the healing skin. She moistened it with warm water, but it pulled, tearing the scab and making him bleed.

"I'm sorry," she said. She swabbed at the wound with water and tried to staunch the flow of blood. She poured on hydrogen peroxide; it fizzed and bubbled over his arm. She glanced at him for a reaction. "Does it hurt?"

"No. Keep going."

She poured a little more. "An antibiotic ointment would help." She applied fresh bandages and tightened the sling. "The first thing you do when we get out of here is see a doctor. I still don't know if I treated that correctly."

"You treated it perfectly. I have no complaints."

Chapter 25

"I'LL GO WITH YOU," he insisted again. "You don't know if that guy's still out there, and why not get twice as much food? And, Lissa, you shouldn't hike alone in weather like this anyway. What if *you* collapse?"

She ignored him. "When I come back, I have to work on that paper for my class, too. I feel guilty that I haven't even started it yet."

"You said you have the whole week off."

"I do, but I always get my work done early." She knew she sounded ridiculous. "There's really no excuse for ignoring it," she said, trying to convince both of them. Ned grinned, and Lissa scowled at him. "Well, as long as I brought it, I should do it. I've been stuck here for days with nothing else to do."

"You had to boil water," Ned argued, "plan meals, keep the home fires burning." He grinned at her. "And you had me to take care of."

Her heart gave an unexpected lurch as she lifted their breakfast plates from the table and turned her back on him, hiding her furious blush. She added the dishes to those from the night before already in the dishpan.

"We do need snow," she decided. "These pots melted a little overnight, but you should have more for today, while I'm gone. I'll try to bring two gallons of water back, but we'll use that just for drinking and cooking and to take care of your arm. For dishes and washing we should still melt snow, don't you think?"

"Yes, ma'am, I do," he said lazily. He was sitting back, lounging against the stiff chair. Behind him, through the window, she could see the fresh mounds of clean snow, piled up against tree trunks, sloping gently to the lake. The pines stood straight and tall, sugar-coated.

She said a quick prayer of thanks for the clear sun and daylight; they desperately needed supplies and she craved time away from him to think.

"It's Sunday morning," she said thoughtfully, "and I would normally be in church."

Ned looked surprised. "You usually go?"

"Yes, why are you so shocked?"

"It's not typical, I guess. Most of the people I know don't think about religion much."

"Well, we always went as a family, so it seems right to me. Do you still go to Mass?" She was leaning back against the sink now, her arms crossed over her chest. "Or did you give that up long ago?"

"I go. But I'm giving us a dispensation for today."

She laughed. "Yes, obviously." It warmed her to know that he still practiced his faith. He was right; some of the best people she knew didn't bother anymore. And for some it was a conscious choice. She smiled at him, pleased. "It's nice to meet someone who sees church as a serious responsibility."

He chuckled and looked away, and she regretted the prim words. Why couldn't she ever just be cool and offhand instead of so ultra-proper and rigid; she was growing to hate that about herself.

"A serious responsibility," he murmured. "Is that the way you see it?"

She straightened her shoulders, ready to do battle over her point of view. "Well, yes, don't you?"

He shrugged. "Not really. A privilege, I guess."

"A privilege?" Mass had been a requirement growing up in the Tea family. She valued it, but still saw it as a dutiful chore. His attitude sounded novel to her. "With all that fasting and abstaining and confessing? All those shalt nots?"

He laughed. "There were times when my father didn't let me go because he needed me around to help him."

"What does he do?"

There was a long pause as Ned considered how to answer. Then he grinned, slightly embarrassed. "He collects junk. He rides around the countryside in his truck and buys up people's cast-offs, then sells them. I never liked helping him."

She smiled weakly, wishing she hadn't asked.

"But the Marchess men are definitely coming up in the world," he said cheerfully. "From junk collector to business owner. That's not too bad. Anyway, I guess going to church started to look like a break from junking. That's what he calls it, junking. And if he said I had to go, I had to go. I spent a lot of Sunday mornings rooting through people's trash wishing I could be sitting in those nice, polished pews hearing the choir sing."

"Maybe I don't appreciate it enough," she mused.

"Maybe none of us appreciate things like that until we lose them somehow."

"Maybe so," she said thoughtfully. "Well, I guess if we have to miss Mass, we could at least pray for our safety, not to mention an end to this storm." She was only half kidding.

"Hey, it worked for the apostles. Go for it. I prefer to pray privately but I applaud any public demonstration you wish to make."

She laughed. "No, I'm not an evangelist, just a mixed up kid trying to stay on the right path."

"You seem to be doing pretty well to me. Lissa, why don't you put off going to your car until tomorrow. I don't like the way the wind is gusting out there. It's still bitter cold. We can manage for one more day."

"Six stale bagels," she said. "And it's clearing up. I can get more food and some aspirin for you."

"I don't need it. I'd feel a lot better if you didn't go. You're safe here. With me."

Lissa cursed the pink tinge that she could feel climbing up her neck. Why did she take his most innocent comments so personally? Well, maybe because her fear had turned. He had grasped her hand last night, and she had let him. He was nice, at least he *seemed* nice, and it was more comfortable to treat him as a friend than a threatening intruder. Yes, her new friend, her pal, the junk collector's son.

"So," Ned said, "Tell me more about this music degree of yours. How does a composer make a name for herself? Do you perform your songs in coffee shops or send them around to people in the music industry?"

She met his eyes briefly. What was he doing? Introducing another topic of conversation to keep her from her car? She banished the critical thought. "I guess so. Maybe I'll do that when I'm ready," she hedged.

"When you're ready? I thought you were about to graduate."

"I am."

"Shouldn't you be doing something to reach this successful career you're so bent on?"

"Well," she hesitated, "yes, but I guess I haven't started yet."

His eyes were on her, waiting.

"I just keep them," she explained. It sounded lame, she knew. "I mean, someday I'll share them, of course. But actually, no one's really heard my songs yet, except in class, when we have to."

He looked interested, the hint of a frown bisecting his brow. "William?" he asked. For the first time, he said it as just a name, without the mocking sarcasm.

"Umm, no; he's never asked to hear them." She gave an embarrassed laugh. "No one has."

"Then how do you know if they're any good? I suppose you'd know, but isn't the whole point to have an audience?"

She nodded slowly. "Someday, sure."

A quiet loomed between them until Ned broke it. "I'd want to hear them," he said simply.

Lissa swallowed a choking laugh. It took a stranger to encourage her. No one had ever shown much interest before, but here was Ned, who hardly knew her, asking to share this most intimate and sacred part of her life.

"I don't let people hear them," she said with finality.

Ned frowned again, and opened his mouth to argue the point, but Lissa turned her back to him and fiddled with the plates in the dishpan. "I guess I could use some water for these dishes," she said.

"Okay." He lumbered up from the chair. She could sense him standing there wanting to say more. She didn't encourage him. He turned away, and she watched him through the window, stuffing snow into pots, pushing it down, adding more. It was odd now to visualize him holding up a gas station; she couldn't picture it. He had been nothing but gentle toward her, grateful for her help, understanding of her fear, curious about her life. Too curious.

He looked the picture of the backwoods, small town citizen, a hard worker who would never amount to much more than he was right now.

She knew of Gorham only from that one visit with her family, and the outing had bored her. Now she wondered what it must be like to live there. The town was small, no movie theater, no stores to speak of, no cultural outlets of any kind. It had winter sports and the river in summer, and that was about it. So what did people in Gorham do?

They repaired air conditioners and then rode around with them in their cars. They wore big, cumbersome rubber boots and let their hair get too long and broke into people's camps. They went junking.

She turned from the window. She wasn't being fair. He was so willing to do whatever he could to make his presence bearable. And it was definitely bearable.

Why on earth were her thoughts running this way? As she lifted her hands to her hot face, the door opened and Ned shoved the pots inside, stomped off his boots, and shut the door behind him. "Man, it's freezing out there. It's one of those deceptively pretty days. You don't realize just how brutal until you get out in it."

She began moving fistfuls of snow. It began its slow melt. She turned to watch Ned remove his coat and hat. His face was ruddy with cold.

"Why Saint Luke?" she said suddenly.

"What?"

"Saint Luke. Your mother gave you medals with Luke on them. Why him? Is there some significance?"

"Well, yes, as a matter of fact." He sat down and toed his boots off. When he had worked his feet free, he stood the boots up near the door, grabbed one of the dirty dish towels, and wiped up the excess snow and water.

"He was a physician and also a painter. He's the patron saint of artists. His name means 'Bringer of Light.'"

"Are you an artist, then?" This had never occurred to Lissa. Perhaps she had underestimated him. Was it possible that this man had the same talent as William Brashue? It would give them something in common, she thought idly. In other ways they were so different. She recalled Ned's words the night before, *I'll take care of you,* and pictured him feeding crumbs to a mouse.

William, by comparison. . . . She brought herself back to their conversation.

Ned was chuckling cheerfully. "An artist? Not at all. Neither is my brother. But my mother's father was, or thought he was. She had very lofty ideals for us. She figured one of us would end up a doctor or an artist. Or something. Even if we were just average guys with no particular talents."

"I'm sure that's not true," Lissa said politely. "I'm sure you're good at repairing things."

He gazed at her and said nothing for a moment. "Right. So, tell me about graduate school, Melissa. How does it work? Do you have a job, as well, to support yourself while you earn yet another degree or does daddy send the money or does the school give you a free ride because you're such an intellectual? Or what?"

She felt the derision in his voice and turned to the stove, picked up a wooden spoon and stirred the snow in the pots to hasten the melting. A few clumps of snow floated on the surface, melting rapidly.

Ned was up and standing behind her; she could feel his breath on her neck. "I'm sorry," he said. "That was crummy. I know how hard you work. You deserve whatever you can get out of it."

"No, it's fine," Lissa answered, stirring the snow. "Don't be silly. I shouldn't have said that about repairing things. It sounded. . . pompous. Anyway, you do have a talent. I've heard you sing."

"Turn around," he said.

She didn't dare.

She felt his hand on her shoulder. "Lissa?"

"They hire you," she said. "Instead of paying them for the classes, you're assigned a job on campus and you work for them and get the tuition for free. I'm a tutorial assistant. I get schedules of all the undergrad students who need tutors and all the seniors and grad students who can tutor them, and I match them up. I co-ordinate all that, I proctor exams, make schedules, that kind of thing. Sometimes they have me fill in for people, taking tickets and setting up for campus events." The words came all in a rush.

The snow she was stirring had melted and she removed the

spoon. His hand was on her arm now, his touch gentle. He turned her to face him and took the spoon away from her.

"I admire what you do," he said. "I'm a little envious because my circumstances never allowed me to become much of anything. If I sound jealous, it's because I am."

Lissa laughed nervously. "You should never be jealous of me," she said. "My office is a little cubicle stuck in the back corner of a building no one uses, and my job has nothing to do with what I'm studying. It's boring, and I stay quiet so people will assume I'm competent. I'm not even sure I am. What I do really shouldn't excite much envy from you. I'm sure no one else in the world would see it that way."

"You make it sound so insignificant," he said. "But I suspect there's more to it."

She shrugged. There wasn't more to it; she had summed up exactly what her grad assistant position was like for her.

"I'm lucky I stumbled across you," he said. "I like the way you share your food with me, and take care of things, and I like talking to you. I even like arguing with you. You're smart and motivated, too. You represent all the things I would have liked to be."

"Well, thank you," she said.

"Don't you wonder if we'll ever see each other after we get out of here? If our paths might cross again?" He wandered to the table and sprawled in his usual chair.

She thought a moment. "Well, I guess that's unlikely." She was surprised that the thought troubled her. "We don't have all that much in common."

"I'll be in Gorham fixing people's washing machines. I wonder what you'll be doing."

"Good question," she said quietly. "There are so many things I want from life."

"Like what? A house in the country? A New York loft? A Mercedes?"

"Sure," she admitted. "Why not?"

"No reason, if you think they'll make you happy."

"William is planning to work at a gallery in Los Angeles, so I'll probably be there," she said. "If you want to envy someone, envy him."

Ned slouched back in the chair, massaging his injured arm.

"And what will you do out there?"

"Compose, maybe support us if I can get something in marketing."

"And take care of Katie."

"I don't know how that will work out," she admitted. "He's not - he's not sure. He thinks it will be a burden to us."

"Really. So he's telling you to make a choice between your sister or the life you want with him?"

"We still need to talk-" she began.

"That's nonsense, and you know it. You can have both. Just because I didn't bother finding someone crazy enough to share my life doesn't mean you shouldn't. But you need someone who will support that. And he isn't it. I'll probably never see you again after this week, but I can tell you this: That guy is not right for you. If he loved you, he would never ask you to make such a choice."

"It's not-"

He didn't let her finish. "And by the way, I saw you this morning, washing the blood stains out of my shirt. And you know what I thought? I thought, that is a really nice girl. She's kind, and she wants to do right in everything. Yeah, she's opinionated, but look at her in there, washing out my shirt, no rubber gloves, getting my blood on her hands. Would William do that for you?"

Lissa had no response. Of course William wouldn't do that for her. She suspected, though, that Ned would. Her breath was caught in her throat. Ned was creating havoc with everything she thought she believed in, and she had known him only three days. In fact, she *didn't* know him. He puzzled her. And worried her. What on earth was happening? She could feel herself trembling.

"Sorry," Ned said. "Not my business." He stood up and went into the living room, and she felt the cold intrude. She gripped the edge of the kitchen counter and collected her panicky thoughts.

She couldn't be having these thoughts about Ned Marchess. That would never do. She had her future all mapped out. She wanted a man of dignity and substance, someone successful, an educated professional. She intended to move to L.A. or wherever William went and write music that people all over the world would recognize. She intended to have money and status. Someone like Ned did not fit into her plans.

She would keep him at a distance. She had to. There would be no thinking about the alluring stranger who had broken into her well-planned, organized life.

She rubbed a hand over her arm and felt the searing heat where he had touched her.

Chapter 26

NED HAD DISCOVERED a pile of last summer's news magazines and amused himself leafing through articles on current events that were anything but.

Lissa dragged her Aesthetics books to the big chair in the living room and sat before the crackling fire, making notations in a notebook, chewing on the end of a pencil, and screwing her mouth up in dismay when points in the readings eluded her.

He peered over the top of the magazine he was reading and wondered what it must be like to be that educated. He was a little in awe of Lissa Tea and would have liked to see the way her mind worked as she studied the books and picked out details that would eventually form the basis for her paper. She would definitely be a success. It was clear that nothing was going to stand between Lissa and what Lissa wanted.

He wondered how she would react if she had a Conor in her life, popping up every week or two with a new dilemma for her to solve. You had to be flexible to handle a brother like Conor. Flexible and a little bit insane yourself. Lissa could never do it. Rules were gods to her, and they were not made to be broken. She would go nuts if she had the pressures on her that he had. It made him feel slightly superior to realize it.

Of course she'd had Katie. Interesting, a sister a lot like his brother - troublesome, demanding, maybe a little spoiled by a family that overlooked a lot. But Lissa had escaped the responsibility.

He would never escape Conor, would probably never have much of a life of his own. He could never subject a wife to his roller coaster of a life, and Conor wasn't exactly good husband material either. Ned shifted his position on the sofa. The

Marchess line would end with the progeny of old Gus and his junk shop. And that was no great loss to the world. Wasn't it ironic that Good Saint Luke was also the patron saint of unmarried men. Maybe his mother had had some foresight after all.

Lissa's voice broke the stillness. "Why are you staring at me?"

Ned started. He hadn't meant to stare, had forgotten that he was. Lissa's gray eyes stared boldly back, and he gave an involuntary sputter. "Sorry. I didn't mean to. I was just thinking."

"About what?"

"About my brother. As usual."

"What does he do besides work for you? Does he have a girlfriend? Friends that he goes around with?"

"Sort of a girlfriend. She's not great for him, though."

Lissa held a finger between the pages of her book and looked at Ned with interest. "In what way?"

He looked away uncomfortably. He hadn't intended to mention Cassie, but here he was, jumping in with both feet. "She manipulates Conor. She's a pain."

"That's too bad," Lissa said, and he could have sworn that she was sincere.

"He met her two years ago when her cat died." Lissa stiffened almost imperceptibly, and Ned plunged on. "He was very. . . sorry about it, and since then he's always trying to please her to make her feel better."

"It seems like someone might be over the death of a cat in two years."

Ned laughed. That was the Lissa he was coming to know, matter of fact, pragmatic. "How long would you allow for that kind of grief, Lissa?"

She smiled, accepting his teasing tone. "One month, tops. We had a beagle once. I cried when it died. I was over it within a week."

"You're a sane, sensible girl. Cassie isn't."

"Seriously?"

Ned shrugged. "I don't know. Around my brother, everyone takes on bizarre characteristics. Maybe Cassie's fine and I'm all screwed up."

Lissa smiled again.

"It's true," he continued. "You begin to doubt yourself when you spend too much time with my brother."

"How did the cat die?"

He hadn't expected the question, and he hedged at first. "Well, we found it, you know. I guess it died from natural causes."

"Natural causes?" Her eyes narrowed. "Then why do you look like that?"

"Like what?"

"Like it didn't."

"Because it didn't, I guess." He drew in a ragged breath. "My dad and I found it lying in the field across from the house. The cat had a cut so deep that it bled to death."

Lissa frowned, gazing at him, through him. "Maybe another animal got it," she said generously. "Cat fights are vicious."

He let out a breath. "That's nice of you, Lissa, but it was my brother. He used to carry a Swiss Army knife. That was my father's doing. I always worried about him having it, but you can't tell my father anything. Conor tried to play with the cat, it started scratching him, and he had to get it away. He struck out with the knife."

Why was he telling this proper girl such an awful tale. He should keep his brother buried and secret; that had been his plan.

Ned had pleaded with Conor to come clean about the cat. "Conor, tell the truth," he'd begged. "You know about this, and you have to tell me."

"I didn't do it," Conor had insisted at first.

"I can't help you, buddy, unless you tell the truth."

Eventually Conor had cried and told him. Seventeen years old and Conor had cried. The tears had startled Ned; this was something new in Conor. Always before, Conor would smirk and admit the truth, and go happily on his way, vowing to be a better boy.

But, of course, this was different. The death of an animal. . . . An accidental death, of course - Ned had known that from the beginning - but Conor truly felt sorry. Ned had hugged Conor and told him he would take care of everything.

He did. He buried the cat in the field, explained things to the cat's owner, Cassie Sillington, and considered the chapter closed.

Cassie had seen it differently. She lived in a rat-trap bungalow down the road from the Marchess men and started to come around suddenly, showing up on their front stoop, asking for Conor, flirting shamelessly with both brothers. Eventually she had gotten her talons into Conor to the point where he'd skip work and even lie to Ned about it.

"She takes advantage of Conor," he told Lissa now. "If she can get him to buy her something or do a favor for her, she does it. She has him twisted in knots, and Conor doesn't know what he's doing half the time. First it was promising to get her another cat. Well, he did that, and things were all right for a while. Then she wanted him to supply the cat food and cat toys, all that junk that people buy. So he did."

Lissa had placed her books and notes on the coffee table and was leaning forward, resting her chin in her hands, listening raptly. "Then what?"

"Then she started needing rides here and there. My brother doesn't drive, so it fell to me. I didn't mind a few times, but it started to be an imposition. Finally, I told her she was asking too much of Conor. I tried to explain to her that he's different, he doesn't always use good judgment. She told me to mind my own business and let Conor make up his own mind what he wanted."

"So what did you do?"

"Talked to him a couple times. He couldn't listen, though. He'd be jumping around all agitated, just waiting to get back to Cassie. She's in her twenties and Conor's nineteen. She gets things from him, cheap jewelry, clothes." He grimaced, remembering. "Fortunately she has terrible taste and likes cheap junk; I guess I should be happy with that. Conor moved in with her. He spends all the money I give him on her."

Lissa tilted her head. "Well, you don't really give him the money, do you? He earns it, right?"

Ned stood up, agitated. "I'm on the verge of losing my business since I took him on. He's lost me so much money I don't even like to think about it." And the way the customers looked at Conor. And lately at Ned himself.

Ned had tried to teach Conor how to deal with people, how to help keep the books, a little something about the goods they dealt in. It was impossible; Conor would never learn, and Ned was watching his own good reputation draining swiftly, methodically away.

"That's too bad, Ned." Lissa sat hunched forward, eyeing him sympathetically. "What can you do about Cassie?"

"That's the big question. If she had his best interests in mind it'd be one thing, but she doesn't. She thinks of Cassie first, last, and only."

"I'm sorry," said Lissa. "That must be hard for you when you've invested so much in him. Does he realize that she's taking advantage of him?"

"Of course not. He's not capable of that."

Chapter 27

LISSA WASN'T SURE what to say. She felt sorry for Ned and his troubles. To be saddled with an unpredictable brother, stuck in Gorham with no way to escape. She was sure he stayed only because Conor was there. She felt guilty relief that she had extricated herself from Katie and the ties that surely would have strangled her just as Ned was being slowly strangled by his love for Conor.

And that made Ned a better person than her. She felt humbled looking at him. "Isn't there something in the Bible?" she asked. "There is no greater love than to lay down one's life for one's friends?"

He looked at her, surprised. "John's Gospel."

"So you're doing the right thing sticking with him."

"Well, I'm not exactly laying down my life, Lissa. That sounds pretty dramatic."

"What's it like to live in Gorham?" she asked.

He exhaled a big breath, clearly happy with the change of topic. "It's okay."

"I was there once for a vacation."

"Yes, the resort center of the upper Adirondacks."

She laughed. "There was nothing to do. But the motel was cheap, and my parents kept trying to convince us that we were having a great time. I was about fourteen, I think."

"It's quiet there, but it isn't that bad. It's just a regular small town."

"The river is probably nice," she mused.

"Yep." He was distracted; he stalked to the window and gazed out at the still dancing snow. "You wonder if this is ever going to actually stop. Are these new snowflakes or the same old ones getting blown around over and over again?" He turned back to her. "I'd probably leave there if it weren't for my brother. And my business." He thought a minute. "I guess I'll never leave there."

Lissa was watching him with interest. He obviously didn't relish the thought of living out his life in Gorham, New York. Who would? "I used to feel that way, too, when I was living in Binghamton," she said. "Sometimes you have to just make up your mind to get out."

"You were pretty young to be left in charge of your sister all those years."

"I was young, but she was easy. Katie couldn't do much. I'd prop her on the floor and play around her. When she got her wheelchair later, she'd sit and watch me. I was a weird kid. I didn't require much interaction from her. She was more like an audience."

"The opposite of my brother," Ned said. "He was always into everything. Nobody could keep up with him. My mother never worked; it would have been impossible with Conor. You should have seen us going into town, like when Conor needed shoes or had to buy supplies for school. I'd make him sit still and my mother would jam shoes on his feet. He'd keep shaking his feet until the shoes fell off, then he'd laugh and she'd stick them back on. He'd shake them off again. It's a wonder he ever had shoes that fit."

Lissa couldn't help laughing. "It sounds sort of funny, though."

"In a way, I guess. I remember we stopped for lunch one time when my mother wasn't too exasperated, and she let Conor order cocoa. He started blowing the whipped cream off the top, and spots landed on the shirt of some guy sitting in the next booth. We didn't even finish our lunch; we had to get out of there before that man noticed. And Conor was just a little kid. I always worried that he'd end up in jail one day. My whole life has been like that."

"Did he? I mean, is that why you dream about it?"

"No," he said slowly. "Conor's never been in jail. He's pretty harmless." His eyes met her questioning glance, and she could tell there was more. "My dad, however, is a different story."

She was startled. "Your father was in prison?"

Ned retreated to the window again, turning his back on Lissa and watching the snow swirl and dance over the tree-studded property. "You know, he shouldn't have been. He took some things from a woman's lawn. These gnomes." He caught her eye and grinned sheepishly. "He really believed it was junk out for the garbage collection, but she went nuts and had him arrested. By the time I knew about it, he had already spent the night in the county lock-up. It was pretty humiliating. Not for him, for me."

He sat down heavily on the couch and gazed at Lissa. "I seem to be the only one in my family who has any conscience. I just spend my time going around bailing my relatives out." He stopped speaking and exhaled a heavy sigh. "And now that I've painted this appalling picture of the Marchess family, I think I'm going to lie down. My arm hurts." He struggled back up and glanced around at the comfortable furniture, the blazing fire, the shelves of old books and mounted fish on the walls, all so far removed from his usual surroundings. So foreign. "I know you can't figure out why I don't climb out of my miserable existence and make something of myself, but you don't have a clue what it's like to be me." He stalked from the living room. The bedroom door closed tightly behind him.

Lissa sat gazing into the fire. He was right; she had no idea what it must be like. Her family wasn't rich, but they were wholesome and normal. Mostly.

Ned's father and brother certainly sounded eccentric, sick even. She wondered if maybe Ned was troubled, too, in his own way. Maybe everybody was.

. . .

Outside, the sun was sinking rapidly and the sky was quickly turning dark. She hadn't made the trip to her car, and although she felt mildly guilty about that, she felt relieved, too. Maybe by tomorrow the plow would come by. Maybe the man who'd violated her kitchen would be even farther away.

She donned her coat and mittens, let herself out the kitchen door, and trudged toward the outhouse. Her gaze swept the woods on either side, but all she could see were mounds of clean, unbroken snow, swirling snowflakes sweeping past in their lazy descent. Near the woodshed, she paused and listened, hearing only the tree branches creaking together. Had Ned really heard something out here? She peered around, aware that her heart was skipping a faster beat.

Did she dare go in? The man was gone; she was sure of it. And Ned was right inside the camp and would hear her if she needed him.

With a shaking hand, she opened the shed door, stood still and listened, allowing her eyes to become accustomed to the relative dark. Nothing. She bent to the under-counter door, quietly turned the latch, and gazed into the space beneath. The air hung cold and stale. The dog opening at the other end let in some light, and she could make out the same pile of old blankets stuffed along the side, the rusted tools and broken bits of metal and crockery she had seen before. The straw was disturbed, just as it had been, but the indentation might have been made weeks or months ago. Even years ago.

She let out a heavy breath. The space was, at least, empty of life. If an animal - or a man - had been nesting here, it or he was gone now. She bent to close the latch and her breath caught in her throat. Something was different.

The olive drab army blanket wadded up in the far corner had not been here yesterday.

Lissa closed her eyes briefly and sucked in cold, stale air, willing her heart to stop hammering. She had seen that blanket recently - in the camp kitchen, folded with a couple of lightweight jackets and fishing hats, all piled on a chair in the corner.

A quiet scrabbling sound startled her - a mouse. At the unwelcome noise, she ran from the shed, slamming the door shut behind her.

...

In the guest room, Ned lay on the bed, wishing he were far from the Arrowhead Lake cottage and the determined, successful girl in the next room. She was so pretty, so controlled and soft-spoken, even when she was lit by passion. Her boyfriend sounded like a complete jerk. Ned groaned. Why did he care that an immature girl like Lissa Tea was enthralled with some smart artist from school. They probably *were* a perfect match.

He shouldn't have opened up to her like that either. What must she think of him? Ah, what difference did it make? Chances were he would never see Lissa Tea again. That would be one thing gone right.

The door to his room burst open and Lissa stood there in her boots and jacket, dripping snow on the floor and gasping for breath.

"It was a blanket," she said. "He took a blanket from the kitchen. It's in the dogpen."

Ned propped himself on one elbow and stared at her. "You went out to check?"

"Maybe he took other things, too, but definitely that."

"Okay. But he's gone, right?"

"There's no other sign of him."

"You went out there?" Ned repeated. He was still processing her foolishness. What made her like this? "That was probably not a great idea, Lissa."

She waved away his opinion. "He's been sleeping there, I think."

"Maybe."

"I think you're right," she said. "He's probably not a threat. He hasn't tried to hurt us in any way." She thought briefly. "If we had food to spare, I'd leave some out for him."

"Oh, for God's sake-" Ned began.

"Well, we don't know, Ned. If he's starving he might break in again. And what if it turns out he's some. . . homeless person. . . ."

"Here?" He gestured around the wild forests surrounding them. "Driving a Grand Marquis?" Crazier and crazier, Ned thought. A part of him wanted to laugh. She could go from terrified to sympathetic in a heartbeat.

"I guess you're right," she said. "Can you imagine how cold it must have been in the shed? What do you think we should do?"

"Nothing," he replied.

Lissa began to close the door, then popped her head back in. "Well, I just wanted to tell you. The more we know, the safer we are. All he wanted was a blanket."

Ned corrected her. "All he got was a blanket. If you hadn't dropped that plate, he'd have been after the food, too, don't you suppose?"

"So I did a good thing then." She grinned very briefly, then her face became serious again. "I wish we knew who that guy is and why he was here." She came in and sat on the edge of the bed.

Ned maneuvered around to accommodate his throbbing arm and peered up at her. "He's gone, Lissa," he said. "Did you bring the blanket in?"

"No, I left it." She chewed her lip distractedly, then stood up. "I'm getting everything wet; I'll go take off these things. Do you need anything?"

"No."

The door closed after her.

It was a lie. He needed many things. Ned turned on his side, propping his arm, trying to get comfortable. Suddenly he laughed aloud; he had to admire her spirit. What could have possessed her to go exploring out in the shed?

Man, though, it was getting so obvious he didn't belong here, had nothing in common with a smart, capable girl like Lissa. And he had business to attend to. The sooner he got out of here the better. For the first time since he'd stumbled through the broken window and staggered into Lissa's life, Ned realized he was feeling anxious to leave.

Chapter 28

LISSA'S EYES FLEW OPEN and she sat up, struggling for breath. The room was dark and she was drenched in sweat. The dream had been so vivid.

Katie sat slumped in her wheelchair, soaked and shivering. The wheels were caked with mud, and slimy aquatic vines wove in and out of the spokes. Steven held the chair, but the wheels began to slip away from him, down the bank, toward the river. He grabbed more forcefully, threw his weight against the front of the chair, and reached out to scrabble his fingers over the smooth surfaces of two good-sized rocks and secure them under the wheels. He stood up, breathing heavily with the exertion.

Lissa stood across the river and watched the drama, feeling great relief as her brother arrested Katie's chair and leaned over her, soothing her agitation. Katie plucked at the rank vegetation that bound her and wrinkled her nose against the putrid smell of the weeds.

Lissa knew she had to reach Katie and called to her, her voice echoing off the mountains and bouncing back, rhythmic and clear.

I have her, Steven shouted, but Lissa knew Steven wouldn't have the slightest idea how to fix ribbons to Katie's satisfaction. Besides, to her surprise, Lissa had the ribbons clenched in her own hand. Steven might think he had everything under control, but Lissa knew.

I'm coming, Lissa called. *Be patient, Katie. I'm trying to get to you.*

Ned was there, holding one hand out, gesturing to Lissa. He was standing on a water-drenched log that stretched across the river, creating a fragile bridge. Bugs crawled in and out of holes in the log, and murky water squeezed up through the rotten wood.

This way, Ned said. *It's the only way you can reach her.*

The log sat submerged in the water, moving up and down slightly with each breath Ned took. Water drained from holes in the log's sides, miniature waterfalls sheeting back into the river. This flimsy bridge was holding Ned now, but what would happen if Lissa stepped on it?

You don't have a choice, he urged her.

Across the river, Steven was now removing the rocks holding Katie's wheelchair. He had piled so many in front of her wheels that it was taking him a long time. Katie sat patiently, watching him, unaware that her chair had begun inching, so slightly, toward the river.

Wait, screamed Lissa. *Steven!*

Ned held both arms out to Lissa, encouraging her to step onto the log.

She looked up in great relief when she heard the drone of a small plane and flagged it with great sweeping movements that she felt sure would lead to her rescue. The plane, glinting silver in the sun, would take her to the other side. The plane played in the air currents, its wings fluttering like a bird's, and dipped down; one wing touched the surface and sent a spray of cool water splashing over Lissa and Ned. With a surge of joy, Lissa stepped forward into the river. Murky cold drenched her sneakers and socks and seeped up her ankles. The plane was so close she could almost touch it, but it couldn't get close enough for her to board. It circled above and tried again and again, always dipping close to her, never quite close enough. Finally it circled lazily, then soared off and out of her sight.

This way, Ned kept saying. Insects still rushed in and out of the log's wormy holes as it bowed with Ned's weight. The bugs frightened her, and she didn't dare step over them. The log bridge was mostly submerged now; Ned's boots were soaked. The surface looked slippery; the passage seemed far more dangerous than it had just moments ago.

Hurry, he told her. *It's the only way.*

Katie opened her mouth in a petulant grimace. *I need you*, she whined.

Lissa's chest ached as she wondered if she would ever reach

Katie, ever tie her fistful of ribbons in Katie's long hair, ever brush the tangles out.

The plane had come so close, but the sky remained empty and still.

Ned held out both arms. *I'll get you there*, he said.

No, Lissa wailed. As insects burrowed in and out, the holes grew larger, caving in and rotting away.

It's the only way.

She placed one foot on the log and felt it bob under her. The wood sagged and bits crumbled off into the water. She pulled her foot back.

Try.

She tried again and felt the log sink slightly.

He nodded. *Take another step.*

As she walked to him, he backed up imperceptibly, always slightly ahead of her, the log bobbing, his dark eyes fastened on hers.

They had reached the middle of the river. The sky was pale blue and all along the shore, reeds and wildflowers sprouted. Katie was closer now, watching her progress. Steven had stopped his work and was watching, too. For now, Katie's chair was secure.

Another step, Ned insisted.

He held both hands outstretched and she was surprised to see that he was wearing his own clothes. It was thoughtful that he had returned Uncle Jeff's shirt, and it was such a nice surprise that his shirt had been mended and cleaned. There was no blood-encrusted gash in the sleeve.

The log jolted suddenly, and Lissa struggled for footing. A quick look passed over Ned's features, then he calmed. *Come on*, he urged her. *Step right here*. He gestured to a spot on the log; the wood looked soft and wet. Lissa cringed.

I'm waiting, Katie called.

Lissa looked up at the sudden sound of the plane returning. Its wings dipped and soared, and Lissa, blinded by sunlight, stepped ahead. The log twisted and Ned's hand was upon her arm, hard, a quick grab, pressure, and gone. Cold, bitter water grasped her ankle, working its way up her body. She felt herself tumbling, somersaulting in the deep river, while water fizzed around her. She tried to feel for Ned, for the bottom, and realized in a panic that it was hundreds of feet below her. Yards, miles below.

She gasped and took in a mouthful of water. Her eyes shot open.

The dream had seemed so real that for a moment she sat, breathing hard, telling herself she was fine.

She was at camp; Katie was safe at home, Ned sleeping in the next room. She flung her sleeping bag aside and dangled her legs over the side of the bed, her heart racing. She turned on the dresser lamp and looked at her watch. It was five a.m. How would she fill this day if she arose so early? She turned off the light and lay back down, pulled her sleeping bag around her and closed her eyes, then opened them again.

Maybe it was true that dreams could help people deal with their troubles. Well, she didn't have any troubles, she told herself. It was the guy in the next room who had troubles. It was Conor and Katie who had troubles. And anyway, she was taking Katie on again, wasn't she? She didn't need some dream to shake her into doing the right thing.

Images from the dream had already begun to fade, but several of them crystallized, and each time she closed her eyes to sleep, there they were, burned into her mind. The ineffectual plane, those bugs. She tried to dismiss them.

Katie, calling plaintively, needing her.

Ned, with two good arms, urging her forward.

And herself, against her better judgment, responding, trusting, putting one foot before the other, terrified but walking forward. Toward Katie. Toward Ned.

Ned had grabbed her, just as she fell. To rescue her? To save himself? Or had he pushed her?

She burrowed into her sleeping bag and muffled her head with her pillow. She would not start analyzing this dream. She knew her own mind; going toward Ned could be the worst possible choice. That route was not an option.

Chapter 29

BY THE TIME NED EMERGED on Monday morning, Lissa's dream had faded to a blur, and she had put it out of her mind. She had spent a few minutes in front of the bathroom mirror, pulling her long hair into a knot on top of her head. No shower, no hot water. The same clothes she'd been wearing since Saturday.

Camping out was getting old.

She had make-up in the car, as well as shampoo and her hair dryer. She could get a change of clothing, and they needed water and food and aspirin. Regardless of the man from the Grand Marquis, she could not put off walking to the car for another day. She would have to assume he had gone. There was no way he could survive this long in the woods or holed up in her unheated woodshed.

Lissa shivered and set her mind to the task at hand. She was tearing a sheet of paper from her notebook and getting ready to write Ned a note when he appeared in the kitchen doorway, his eyes bleary with sleep and his hair sticking up in greasy spikes.

Three days trapped in the camp had been no kinder to his appearance than to hers. Black, unshaven stubble made his face look gray, and the gold shirt was untucked, dirty, and wrinkled. Lissa glanced at him briefly, then watched him put on his jacket and boots and trudge outside, where he took a mouthful of snow and jabbed the borrowed toothbrush around inside his mouth. She made a mental note to grab the toothpaste in the trunk, too. She should make a list.

Ned had boiled the toothbrush, she knew, and she supposed after using it a few times, it had come to seem familiar to him. Even the worst of circumstances could start to feel normal if it was all you knew.

When Ned returned, he went into the bathroom for a moment and emerged with his hair carefully combed and shirttails tucked neatly into Uncle Jeff's oversized jeans.

Lissa couldn't help laughing.

"Do I look that funny?" he said.

She couldn't stop. "We both do. We're dirty and tired and hungry and cross and sick of being cooped up inside."

Ned smiled, too. "Well, at least I made my bed," he said, "I'm trying to do my part. And the snow has stopped. With luck, the plow will come by."

"That would be great, but I'm not planning on it. I'm walking to my car to get more food and water. I'm leaving you here to keep the fire going and rest."

"I don't need rest," he insisted.

She smiled at him. Even now, as he sat across from her with his hair slicked down and wearing dirty clothes, she found him appealing.

All the more reason to get out of this cabin into the fresh air and take a long, arduous walk through the knee-high snow.

"I ate the bagels you brought me," he said. "I know I wasn't great company last night."

"Actually," Lissa said, "I think we've done quite well, considering the circumstances. We haven't killed each other yet."

He smiled at her. "And we've shared very nicely."

"And pitched in on chores," she added. "Here, this is the last bagel." She pushed the bag across the table to him. "I had one this morning. This is your breakfast and lunch, so savor every morsel."

He fingered the bag. "Thanks. I really owe you for everything."

"No, you don't."

"Yes, I-"

She reached a hand across the table and placed it over his, interrupting him. "No, Ned, you don't owe me." She smiled. "Really. But I do need to get to my car. It's a nice day; look how clear the sky is."

"You know better than that. The temperature is just as bad now as it was two days ago."

"Well, I made it here a few days ago. I can make it again.

Maybe I'll run into someone on a snowmobile or cross country skis who can help us out."

"I'll go with you, Lissa. At least I could carry an extra couple gallons of water back."

"I'll be quicker alone. I don't think you should risk a four mile trek, round trip, through deep snow in freezing weather."

"Exactly. You shouldn't go either."

"Forget that," she said defiantly. "I'm hungry."

He glanced out the window. "I'm coming, too."

. . .

It was eleven o'clock when they set out. They were well bundled against the elements, and Lissa carried the camp key, her car keys and the empty bags. Ned seemed preoccupied, his glance darting into the woods on the side of the road, his conversation stilted. Lissa wished he would stop. She had convinced herself it was perfectly safe. Sort of.

Within fifteen minutes, it was obvious that Ned would not be able to complete the trip. Lissa could hear his labored, gasping breaths as he fought against the pain in his arm. She stopped in the deep snow and looked at him. "You are not going forward one more step," she said.

"I'm okay. You know what it is, though? I can walk it, but with every step my arm rubs against my coat. It's throbbing and I guess I've broken the scab again."

"Which means it's bleeding under the bandage," she said. "You need to go back."

"We should both go back. This is impossible." He turned and took a step toward the camp, then looked back at Lissa. "Aren't you coming?"

"No," she said. "I'm going to my car."

"Lissa, be reasonable. You'll never make it. Besides, I need your help with my arm."

"I'm going to my car, Ned. Here's the camp key."

He took the key and hesitated, glancing into the woods again. "I'd feel a lot better if you'd come back with me."

"I'll be fine. You'll be fine, too."

He hesitated, then said, "Okay. You were right; I'm not up for this."

"Take care of your arm as soon as you get there," she instructed him. "You should remove the gauze and put a fresh bandage on it. The medical tape is on the counter over by-"

He was grinning at her in spite of the pain. "Poor, poor William," he said. Laughing, he turned toward the camp, then on impulse, took a step back toward Lissa. "Hey," he said quietly, "take care of yourself. If you're not back before dark, I'm coming to find you."

"I'll be back." He was standing near enough to touch, but she didn't. "I'm not going to abandon you." She smiled. "I'm going to bring you goodies."

She watched him trudge back along the trail they had just broken.

Alone, she pushed the man from the Grand Marquis from her thoughts and began to enjoy her solitude as she gulped in big mouthfuls of the fresh pine air. The snowdrifts were thick and fluffy; her spirits soared. She walked steadily, her thoughts humming.

As a half hour became an hour and an hour became two, Lissa's pace was noticeably slower, and her hands and feet were numb. She had covered her nose and mouth with her scarf, and her steamy breath had soaked through, making it scratchy, wet, and uncomfortable. Her legs were sore and ached as she lifted and pulled them. She wondered, as she had two days before, if she would actually make it.

She did not expect to see the driver who had hit her, but she couldn't help peering around her as she walked. This was supposed to be a fun weekend with her best friends, pelting each other with snowballs and eating Pat's delicious cooking, toasting their new careers and gossiping about their lives. And what had it turned into? She was hungry and tired, and confused by the tangled emotions overwhelming her. The unanswered questions overlapped and knotted, and at the center of the web was the flickering attraction to Ned that she kept trying to squelch.

Lissa exhaled a long, cold breath. She liked Ned very much, and it still surprised her. She'd known him three days, and she usually made friends slowly. She had always tried so hard not to be one of those foolish, sentimental women who fell for a handsome face. Well, this particular handsome face had puzzled her from the moment she'd set eyes on him. Was it simply their forced togetherness that had forged such a quick friendship from two most unlikely people?

She was glad to be out of the cabin and wanted desperately to get back to school, to resume her normal life, to see if Ned even crossed her mind. She would see William again, hear his intelligent, insightful comments in class, gaze at his artwork in the student gallery. She would gain perspective. Ned Marchess would fade into a vaguely pleasant - or maybe a vaguely disturbing - memory.

And she needed sleep. Friday night, he had kept her up all night as she worried about his motives. Saturday, she had kept herself awake trying to puzzle out the mystery of Ned. And Sunday night, she had dreamed fitfully. Dreamed. . . what? She couldn't remember, but she knew it had something to do with Katie and with Ned, that it had left her confused. So much for the helpfulness of dreams.

It occurred to her to look for her cell phone and the steak she knew she had dropped, but she had no idea where along the road they might be. Some animal had probably found the steak already, and the phone would lie there until spring, rusting and useless.

Lissa pulled in a cold breath and looked down the unbroken road, a pristine, white expanse stretching far ahead of her. She could see the cloudy puffs in front of her face each time she breathed out, could feel the harsh, painful cold when she breathed in.

Behind her was one lone trail through the snow - hers. Where were the snowmobiles? The cross country skiers and snowshoers? Well, she knew the answer. They were home, plowing out. And when they finished, they would hibernate back inside their homes with their hot chocolate and cookies. They would flick on the television and doze in front of the game; they would eat a big chicken dinner and read to the kids. No one would venture out on such a day.

The thought of the cookies and chicken made her stomach ache. She looked forward to having more food and vowed to carry as much as she could, in spite of the heaving pain in her legs.

Chapter 30

WHEN SHE REACHED HER CAR at a little after two, Lissa was exhausted. The little vehicle was buried under a mound of white and she used her arm to brush two days worth of snow off the door so she could force her key into the lock. The door appeared frozen shut at first, but finally it opened, sending a sheaf of snow onto the front seat and floor. She grabbed her snowbrush, plowed her way to the back end of her car and cleared the tailpipe of snow, then sank gratefully into the driver's seat. Her journey was half over.

Lissa turned the key in the ignition and was relieved that her car started. She turned the heat on and sat for a while, allowing her frozen extremities to warm up before she set about getting her things from the trunk. She turned on the radio and waited patiently throughout the news broadcast. There were no stories about the robbery in Gorham. It was old news.

The time had come. Lissa forced herself to exit her car and close the door, brushed off her trunk, forced it open, and stared in at the bags of clothing and groceries and supplies, massive items that looked suddenly too heavy to carry all the way back to camp. Well, this was what she had come for. She began to lift items into her canvas bag. Two gallon bottles bulging with ice, not water, nearly filled it, but she tucked her aspirin and make up kit in at the sides. She picked up a small packet of cookies, tore it open and wolfed them all. She rummaged through, searching for something else to eat. Frozen cheese, frozen potatoes. She found a chocolate bar and bit into it, letting the frozen chocolate melt on her tongue. She ignored the spices Pat had requested, but chose a bag of frozen blueberries and three potatoes to carry back. She would cook the potatoes immediately; maybe they would be okay. She filled a plastic bag with rolls and some canned goods, remembered the toothpaste, shampoo, and hair dryer, and then picked up the old family photo album she had brought to show Pat and Shelly.

She smiled, wondering if Ned would be interested in seeing her family. Pictures of a young, irrepressible Katie, herself as a little kid. She felt a little foolish packing an unnecessary album, but forced it in anyway. Well, so much for careful, in control Lissa Tea. Ned seemed to have awakened another side of her, and she wasn't entirely sorry.

She went on packing the bags until she worried that they might be too heavy, then looked thoughtfully down the road leading eventually toward the highway miles away.

The road, of course, was unplowed, so it would be impossible to move her car. Ned had said his car was stranded just down the road from hers, and she wondered if it might be visible if she walked around the bend just a few hundred yards away. She decided to see. The few steps it took to get there would be worth it if she could report that his car was still where he had left it, safe and snug, awaiting his return. He hadn't told her the make or model, but how many cars could there be snowed in along Arrowhead Lake Road? She could warm up again and rest a little in her car before starting back.

She left her bags in the back seat and slogged through the deep snow farther down the road. She made the right hand turn onto Rice Road, surprised that she had not come across a third car, Ned's car. The only car she could see was the Grand Marquis, still buried on the side of the road. She made her way to it, her legs screaming with the pain of the walk, and leaned against it to rest. Catching her breath and turning around, she brushed snow from the side windows of the car and peered in.

Leather upholstery, but used looking. A fancy dashboard, lots of knobs and buttons, but the car looked as if it had been driven hard. In the back seat, a big square box caught her attention. The front of the box faced the rear of the seat, and the surface she could see was metal. Metal fins protruded; an electrical cord snaked over the upholstery. It was an old unit and the metal was bent on one corner with a razor sharp edge sticking up.

Shocked, Lissa stepped back. Red crystal stains blurred the

edges of the bent corner and streaks of frozen rust marred the upholstered seat. The air conditioner had seen better days, especially now that it was smeared with icy blood.

Her mind whirled as she tried to digest this new information. Did this mean that the Grand Marquis was Ned's car after all? An air conditioner in the back seat. So had he been injured in the back seat of his own car? Or had someone moved the air conditioner from the front seat to the back? Her mind fogged over. Who had been driving this car on Friday? Was it Ned after all? Or the other man? Perhaps they had been in on it together.

The worn edge of something caught Lissa's eye, a small black triangle protruding from underneath the back of the driver's seat. She scraped snow from the back door of the Grand Marquis and tried the latch, surprised when it opened.

The item was a wallet. With frozen, mittened fingers she opened it. Ned's driver's license, a picture of him, those clear brown eyes, that dark hair. *Edward T. Marchess, 14 Middletown Road, Gorham, New York.*

Fumbling, she opened the wallet and sucked in a sudden breath. It contained money. A lot of money. Her cold fingers were clumsy as she tried to count it, and tears blurred her vision. Fifty dollar bills, tens, twenties, several one hundreds. She guessed there were close to fifteen hundred dollars; in fact, she was positive it amounted to that much.

And he had left it in his unlocked car. Because he was tracking her down and couldn't take a chance on her seeing the money from the gas station robbery in Gorham.

So, he had lied to her about this, too. About the money, the car, all of it. Except for the air conditioner. Somehow the injury from the air conditioner was the one kernel of truth in all the lies he had spun.

Why that? Why bother with the truth about that one ludicrous, hideous fact?

Numb with shock, Lissa pressed the bulging wallet deep into her jacket pocket and closed the car door. Tears pricked her eyes as she sank into the snow and sat there uncomprehendingly. None of it made sense. She had grown to trust Ned, to genuinely like him. They had sung together in the dark, waiting out the storm. Had he been deceiving her all along? He'd done everything possible to dissuade her from making this trip. Of course. He knew what she might find. The deep hurt of it made her gasp aloud.

She stumbled to her feet and gazed down the length of Rice Road, at the frozen woods and untouched snow. Her breath formed gray clouds before her face.

How dare he.

She must go to the police now and report everything he had said to her, turn over his wallet and give them explicit directions to his car and her camp. Her heart pounding with anger, she stepped forward, then stopped. It was late in the day; the roads were filled with difficult snow. It would be dark long before she reached the highway. She would never make it.

Lissa returned to her car slowly and in great pain, her legs aching, her mind numb. Tears frosted on her face, hurting her.

She hauled the photograph album out of the plastic bag and threw it onto the back seat of the car. She would be damned if she would share any more of her life with him. She dragged the two filled bags toward her, gripped them, and kicked her car door shut.

She took one step, then a second. Back toward her cabin on the easier, trodden path she had broken earlier. She would confront him; how dare he make such a fool of her. No, that would make things worse. She couldn't let on that she knew the truth. She would pretend ignorance, act as if things were fine between them, sit and talk, joke with him, trade stories of their lives while they waited for the plow to come.

She couldn't do it. It would destroy her to pretend affection. She felt a sudden sob travel up her throat. It wouldn't be pretense.

Suddenly she let the bags go and covered her face with her snowy mittens. She sank into the snow and cried, as ice particles stung her face and her nose ran in drops that froze like tiny, glistening icicles. She wiped them away and groaned in despair.

Sniffling, she picked up her bags and started the long, painful journey back to her camp. Burning anger, hurt, and crippling sadness consumed her.

The sun sank lower in the western sky.

Chapter 31

IT WASN'T DIFFICULT to wash the wound by himself, but he admitted that he liked it better when Lissa took care of it. As he had guessed, the bandage had torn away from his skin, leaving a bleeding, raw patch that had to be cleaned up and rebandaged. The cut looked deep, and he hoped the delay in seeing a doctor wouldn't cause extra problems with healing. It didn't look infected, but how could you know? He maneuvered his arm around, back inside the sling, and wished there was food in the camp. There was a small amount of water in the big pot by the stove, so he placed it on a burner to heat for tea.

He was sick of tea.

He wasn't too happy with Lissa hiking to the car by herself, but the tension in his gut certainly wasn't a new feeling. He lived with it, day after freaking day.

He worried over how much about himself he had told her. That innocent expression in her eyes did something to him, and he found himself going into detail about family matters that were nobody's business but his. Conor's problems, Cassie's involvement, his father's pitiful excuse for a legitimate business. He had ridiculed her for judging her family. He sat equally in judgment of his own.

If she had liked him at all, he had certainly given her every reason to reconsider.

At least the details of Conor's First Communion party hadn't come spilling off his tongue like ash from Mount Vesuvius.

Their mother had been very much alive then, her deadly stroke just a few months away. She flitted around the rubble-strewn landing that passed for a yard at the Marchess house, setting things down on two picnic tables borrowed from neighbors. She had done her best to make it a nice reception for Conor. Potato salad and rolled up ham, deviled eggs, soda, dishes of nuts. Some neighbors had stopped over, as had his grandmother, who'd been alive then, too. A few people from church brought Conor the obligatory children's Bible or envelopes with a few crumpled bills inside.

At seven, Conor didn't really understand much about the sacrament, and Ned had followed him around all day like a prison warden, keeping a firm hand on his shoulder in the church, sticking by his side while the guests sat in webbed lawn chairs, eating and chatting with each other.

What a good big brother that Ned Marchess was, what an ideal role model. He wondered how many of them realized that his smiling looks at Conor had been tinged with an anxious fear.

The First Communion medal swung on Conor's neck, and Ned had seen him removing and replacing it, trying it on various friends and relatives. Aunt Libby, Mrs. Johns, they all reacted the same way, a smile and dip of the head as Conor placed the chain around their heads, then his quick, feverish grab when he decided they'd worn it long enough. Aunt Libby had been startled and swatted at Conor with her broad hand, although she'd missed. Mrs. Johns had curled her lip and said something to her husband, then patted her hair back into place.

He knew. Little Conor was out of control. Someone should really do something.

No one wanted to wear the thing anyway; it was Conor's imagination that everyone was out to steal it. Ned had tried to talk to him. "Hey, buddy, let's put the medal in the house for a while. Keep it safe."

Conor stared at Ned rather than answer him.

"Shall we, Conor?"

Conor laughed and ran off, a sturdy boy, the chain swinging wildly.

Later, when he crawled into Ned's lap clutching his gift envelopes in his fist, Ned had held him securely. The splintered slab of the picnic table bench cut into Ned's rump, sending spiking pain through his legs, but still he sat there. If Conor needed to be held, then Ned would hold him.

Conor was shaking.

"What's the matter?" he had asked.

"I don't like that man," Conor said.

Jim Polinski. Ned looked over at Jim, innocently shoveling potato salad into his mouth. Jim was the closest thing to a role model Ned had ever had, and Conor's words surprised him.

"Why not?"

"I don't like the way he looks at me," said Conor.

Jim happened to glance up at that moment and caught both Marchess brothers looking at him. He smiled a tentative smile and went on cutting into a deviled egg before he popped the halves, one at a time, into his mouth.

Later in the afternoon, Ned found a few minutes to approach Jim. His employer was a forthright, honest man, and if Ned trusted anybody on this earth, it was Jim Polinski. "My brother said something weird today," he said to his boss.

Jim leaned one muscle-bound arm on the wooden fence dividing the weedy Marchess property from the weedy vacant lot next door. "Yeah?"

Ned gathered up his courage. Jim had given him the first real job of his life, let him help out in the shop, meet with customers, tinker with the appliances, learn the trade. Jim trusted him to make deliveries on time, was even letting him handle the money. It wasn't easy to repeat Conor's words.

"He said you look at him funny."

Jim stared at Ned, then nodded. "I do look at him funny. A lot of people look at him funny. That fever seems to have hit him hard this winter. I notice something, maybe a little oddness that wasn't there before."

"An oddness?"

"He acts peculiar. Everything seem okay to you?"

Ned shrugged. He was worried sick about his brother. Conor hadn't been the same for months; the carefree, happy kid had become a stranger, timid at one moment, garrulous the next. He'd become clingy, always hanging on to their mother, and if she were busy, to Ned.

But family matters are private. Gus Marchess's dictate was the law Ned had grown up with; this was a family matter. It wasn't Jim Polinski's business no matter how compassionate or wise Ned believed Jim to be.

"Yeah," Ned said heartily. "I think he's okay. I guess he noticed you watching him."

"Course I been watching him. So have you," Jim said. "Some kids aren't lucky enough to have a big brother. You want to keep watching."

His mother was exclaiming over Conor's First Communion gifts, circulating from table to table, replenishing plates, dressed in some clingy-looking apricot-colored dress flounced with ruffles. Ned wondered if it felt as out of place to her as it looked to him. He squelched a flicker of embarrassment. His family was always doing things, dressing in certain ways or acting out, attracting attention. His father's voice was the loudest, his mother's dress the most flamboyant. He looked down at his own tan pants and navy blue shirt. Conservative and subdued. He tried to balance their need for attention with what he hoped was a quiet grace. Usually, he simply got overlooked.

Conor was running around the yard with two neighbor kids, spinning wildly, making himself dizzy. "Conor!" he yelled to him. Conor ignored him. "Conor!"

Suddenly one of the children was crying, and a mother was running into the mix, scooping up the little girl and patting her back, rubbing her neck where Conor's chain had dug into her delicate child's skin.

The little girl was pointing at Conor. Her cheeks were smudged with dirt, the sash on her soiled pink dress floating loose in rumply ribbons down her backside, the wrinkled points hanging below her hem. "He scared me," she told her mother.

Ned avoided the angry glance of the concerned mother, darted after Conor, and scooped him up. Conor struggled away from him. Ned picked him up again and flung him over his shoulder. A fun ride into the house, but Conor wasn't buying it. His screeches intensified as Ned neared the back door and yanked it open, marched into the living room, and tossed Conor onto the threadbare sofa. "You can't, Conor," he said. "You can't tease other kids."

Conor's eyes were wide. His fingers fumbled with the shiny new Saint Luke's medal around his neck. "I'm not teasing anyone. I let her wear my medal and it was time to give it back." He meant it. He didn't even know.

And in the intervening years, it hadn't gotten any better. In fact, it had gotten worse. Conor talking back to teachers at school, sitting through detentions. Bringing Cassie around to their father's house, to Ned's house, encouraging her. Ned couldn't help remembering the time Cassie showed up on his doorstep right after he'd closed on his house. She'd parked herself on Ned's front stoop, wearing Conor's medal, *Ned's* medal. It made him sick the way she kept twisting the chain around her fingers, flaunting it, grinning sideways. She had no idea what a religious medal was. To her it was an ornament, just a shiny bauble. And Conor was no better.

Ned had opened the door to leave for work, and there she was, sprawled on the stoop, looking disheveled as if she'd just awakened from a lazy sleep. He nearly tripped over her.

"Hey, Ned," she said sleepily.

"I'm on my way to work," he answered bluntly.

She stood up slowly, uncurling herself like a lithe snake, stretching her limbs, thrusting out her barely concealed breasts in their gauzy cropped shirt. Her intent was obvious, and she gave him a sultry look from her smudgy eyes.

"I have to get to work," he said again, and he pushed past her, down the steps and into his car.

It would be a lie to say he hadn't thought about her at work that day, and on other days, too, but thoughts were as far as it went. She was big trouble, and he wasn't stupid enough to show even the slightest flicker of interest. He didn't *have* any interest in her.

He wished he could have convinced Conor to share his disdain.

. . .

Gray dusk was tainting the trees on the mountain across from the Tea cabin, and Ned stared restlessly out the window. Lissa had been gone for hours. He should have forced himself to go with her. It wasn't right that she was out there, making that arduous journey to bring food and medicine back for him, an unwelcome intruder in her life. He wondered if she had gone as far as the Grand Marquis and hoped not. She mistrusted him enough as it was.

And why wouldn't she?

On Saturday, though, something had changed. Maybe it was the power outage, maybe something else. But he could feel it in the air between them, a charge. She'd recognized the driver who'd hit her car and suddenly saw Ned as the lesser of two evils. He'd been relieved to get inside after the bitter cold, and there she'd been, waiting for him. Then later, making their way through the camp in the dark. He'd sensed a spark, a willing tension in her, but a hesitance, too, as if she wouldn't allow herself.

Ned jabbed a hand through his hair. Her indecision. Her quick, shallow breathing. What was it? Was she still afraid of him? Did she feel something between them, the way he did? Or was she actually just scared to death?

He wouldn't blame her. But she was exactly the kind of girl he had always wished he'd find - smart, pretty, sensible. Classy.

And how classy did he appear to Melissa Tea?

He wished he were anywhere but here. Even Gorham was starting to look like paradise, a place where he could just live life as it came and never mind trying to measure up to the arty, superior ways of the level-headed girl who had basically saved his life.

Ned walked through the camp, noticing the displays on the paneled walls, kids' paintings, photographs of the lake, of people sitting on the dock, smiling, gathered around picnic tables. There was a lot of furniture so that lots of people could crowd in here. A big, comfortable family, lots of noise, congestion, confusion. He could picture it. Lissa clearly didn't know how good she had it. Imagine giving up a family like hers just because of one slightly demanding sister confined to a wheelchair.

Try having a bizarre father and a weird, demanding brother, and a neighbor like Cassie who infiltrated the family, horning her way in until people didn't know if they were coming or going. Katie couldn't be half the trouble Conor was. He'd trade his brother for a Katie any day.

As soon as he had the thought he knew it wasn't true. He wouldn't trade Conor. He loved his brother and would stand by him, no matter what he did. No matter what he had done. Their father was right to hush up a lot of Conor's pranks. Family pride was everything; the idea was ingrained so deeply in Ned that he couldn't think any other way.

But he was worried to death about Conor.

Ned gazed out the window at the pewter sky turning to slate, gripped the window sill and stared out into the coming dusk.

He wished Lissa would return soon.

Chapter 32

IT WAS DARK, and Lissa had just thrust out a shaking, mittened hand to insert her key into the kitchen door lock. She was numb with cold, her heart hardened with pain and humiliation. She'd had hours to consider all that she now knew, and the truth deadened her: Ned and the driver of the Grand Marquis were involved in the Gorham robbery together.

It explained so much, Ned's nervous apprehension when she told him she'd seen the driver near her shed. His constant checking of the windows, his reticence to talk about the robbery or even admit he lived in Gorham. He had escorted her to the outhouse, insisted on accompanying her to her car. And hadn't he seemed agitated even then?

How could she face him after making such a fool of herself? How could they remain in the cabin together now that she knew the truth? What would she say to him?

The kitchen door opened.

Staring back at her was the driver of the Grand Marquis.

Lissa fought dizziness, shrinking back in terror, preferring the numbing cold to the sight of the man she had been fearing for the last seventy hours.

There were shadows under his eyes, and his clothes were rumpled and damp. He wore a sweat-stained blue denim workshirt open at the collar. His face was not enraged now; he smiled politely at Lissa and welcomed her in.

"Miss Tea?" he said.

She stared dumbly.

"Come in."

She considered turning and running back down the lake road. How would she hold out against both of them? A low whimper crept up her throat and she entered the cabin. To stay outside for one more minute would kill her. Her feet were frozen, and her hands and arms shook with the pain of holding the bags she carried.

He took the bags gently and hung her jacket to dry on a hook. Stiffly, she allowed him to lower her onto a chair. "I'm here to help you," he said. "You're frozen. Let me get you something hot to drink." He looked around and spotted the saucepan Ned had left on the stove, still holding a quantity of melted snow. He turned the burner on.

"Who are you?" she breathed, terrified. "Where's Ned?"

"He's all right. Are you?"

"I'm fine," she said numbly. She pulled off her boots and rose, her eyes on the stranger.

"Sit down," he said gently. "Ned is in the bedroom; he can't hurt you now."

"What?" she felt confused.

"Let Marchess rest," he said. "He fainted and fell, hitting his head. He's restrained, but comfortable. He's done some injury to himself, but we'll get him to a doctor as soon as we can get him out of here. I'm more concerned about you."

Lissa sank to the chair and faced the stranger. She was tired to the bone, angry, humiliated, and confused. She had no patience for the driver of the silver Grand Marquis, nor for the liar lying on the bed beyond.

"There's nothing wrong with me," she said through clenched teeth. "What's going on? Who are you?"

The man smiled gently at her. "I'm Lieutenant Miller."

Lissa stared at him, shocked. A police lieutenant? His clothes were wrinkled and dirty; his face showed the same three days' growth of beard that Ned's had. But here in the woods. . . .

"Can we talk in the other room?" Lieutenant Miller asked her. "That tea is almost ready. I think you need it. How far did you walk?"

"To my car," she said, biting back anger. "You remember my car. You hit it on Friday." Miller was guiding her into the living room. "It's stuck in the snow a couple miles down the road. I went there to get the food and things you saw in the kitchen." Against her will, she sat on the couch before the fire.

"Let me get that tea."

Lissa didn't answer. She rubbed her ankles, trying to activate the circulation. She could hardly move. It had taken her seven hours to make the round trip, and she wasn't convinced she didn't have frostbite, at least the earliest stages of it. She shouldn't have sat in the snow all that time. She wasn't even sure how long she had sat there, crying her eyes out over a con man, a thief. Her head was pounding, too.

Lieutenant Miller returned with a cup of steaming tea. In spite of herself, Lissa sipped gratefully. She cupped her hands around the mug and felt the warm steam invading her nose and mouth. She began to breathe more normally.

The lieutenant eyed her carefully and allowed her a moment to drink from the warm, fragrant cup. "Miss Tea, do you realize who that man is who's lying in the other room?"

She looked up painfully.

"His name is Ned Marchess. He's wanted for a robbery that took place last Friday in Gorham, and two other ones as well."

"He told me he didn't commit that robbery," she said dully.

"My main objective is to make sure you haven't been injured in any way."

She met his eyes finally, deep set, dark eyes that looked deep into her own. Numbly, she lifted the mug and sipped at the hot, soothing tea. It scalded her throat, and she greedily drank again.

"We've been after Ned Marchess for some time, and we had him on Friday. That was when you saw me from your car. I had apprehended him and had him in the back seat. When we hit that snowbank, he was injured and became unconscious. There was an air conditioner back there and the metal siding sliced his arm. It looked nasty, and he was in no position to walk, so I went for help. When I returned, Marchess had left the car. We've been searching for him since then. Has he been here the whole time?"

Her tea was almost gone, and Lissa looked longingly into her mug. She wanted her cup refilled. She stood up and walked fuzzily toward the kitchen. There was a little water left on the stove, and she poured it into the mug, then added the damp tea bag, swirling it to hasten the steeping.

Lieutenant Miller followed her.

"How did you get here?" she asked. "I didn't see a snowmobile."

"It's behind your shed," he answered easily. "You saw me

there and called to me, do you remember?"

Lissa nodded distractedly. She had done that, and then Ned had told her the stranger was gone, that there was nothing to worry about. Had he been there right along? She hadn't heard a snowmobile, but there had been sounds. . . .

"I didn't want to frighten you. If you were suspicious and let him see that, I was very afraid of what might happen. Today, when you left to walk to your car, it was the opportunity we needed. We've been watching your cabin, you see."

"You've been watching my cabin?" It would explain his damp, wrinkled clothes and the tiredness around his eyes. She'd read enough novels to know about stake-outs. Could the blustering storm have covered the sound of a snowmobile sent to help her?

A forlorn feeling took root in Lissa. Maybe he really was a police lieutenant. Maybe help had been there all along and she hadn't known it. After a while, hadn't even wanted it. She sank into a chair and put the cup down suddenly. Her tears began fast, and once she started, she couldn't stop. She grabbed a dish towel flung onto the table top and held it to her face, willing the tears to cease.

They didn't.

She lifted her face to the lieutenant. Her damp cheeks ached from crying. "I saw you driving the car," she muttered nasally. "You were angry. Why were you so furious at me? It wasn't my fault that you got your car stuck. You hit my car, not the other way around."

"If it frightened you, I'm sorry," he said. "I was angry, absolutely. The roads were making it impossible to get anywhere; you were blocking the road; I needed to take Marchess in. I was trying to avoid exactly what happened - Marchess stalking the woods, breaking into one of these camps. The worst case scenario was that he'd have a hostage, and that's exactly what occurred."

"I. . . I was a hostage?" she gulped. Yes, held by her own fear of two men, one inside the cabin and one outside. She wiped the tears away with her hand, felt more tears slide from her eyes and run down her face. A hostage, believing Ned Marchess and his quiet, solicitous ways. A stupid, willing hostage in her own home.

Her head sank to the kitchen table. The slippery oilcloth lent a cool comfort to her hot cheek. She was too tired for this. She could hardly think.

"We were hoping you might have a CB radio or a phone, that you would find a way to contact someone."

"I didn't have any way," she said.

"You must have heard the radio bulletins, though. You knew about the robbery, didn't you? Marchess had been injured. Did you hear the description?"

"No," she said, her voice thick with tears, "I only heard part of it. I turned it off. I really don't know anything about the robbery. Anyway, he was injured in the car. There's blood. . . ."

"Okay," he said soothingly. He patted her shoulder. She forced herself not to flinch away from him. "You may not have heard that Ned Marchess also killed a man."

Lissa raised her head. Could that be true?

"He's highly dangerous. If you had listened to the whole news report, you would have recognized him immediately as that man. You wouldn't have allowed him access to your camp."

Except that he had simply broken in. And she was too stupid to leave. In fact, she had left and had come stumbling back. She had known right along who Ned Marchess was, but had decided to fall for him anyway. He seemed so kindhearted and gentle. He had spoken softly and had made her feel safe.

"He didn't seem like that kind of person," she murmured finally. "He seemed like a decent guy."

Lieutenant Miller leaned over her, handing her his handkerchief. "Are you all right now?"

She nodded, taking the handkerchief and blowing her nose.

"Take heart. You certainly aren't the first person he's fooled. Now that we have him, maybe you'll be the last."

"Yeah," she rasped, "I sure hope so."

It surprised her that she felt so little fear. She felt drained and aching from a hurt so deep and so painful that it shocked her. She had watched Ned with that mouse when he hadn't known she was there. He had listened to her frustrations over her family and grad school. He had told her stories about his family, about his job. Lies, probably.

He was a darn good actor, and like many a willing audience, Lissa Tea had been completely and happily fooled.

"Miss Tea," Miller was asking her now, "do you know where

the money is? He stole fifteen hundred dollars on Friday; if he has told you anything about it, I'd like to know."

The wallet. It was still in her jacket pocket. She stared at her mug of tea, willing herself not to glance toward her jacket on its hook. This man might be exactly who he claimed to be, but if he were Ned's partner, perhaps they'd had a falling out. She looked at the lieutenant, sniffled, and pulled the mug half full of hot tea toward her. Where was Ned anyway? Was he really resting in the bedroom? Had he fallen? Or had the good lieutenant knocked him out when Ned was unable to produce the spoils from the robbery? Was Ned even in the cabin? Alive?

Lissa's head was throbbing. She sipped her tea again slowly, collecting her thoughts. She needed to be lucid and stop giving in to the exhaustion that consumed her. People said she was smart. There would never be a better time to prove it.

"No," she said, "he never told me about the money."

"Did he tell you anything that might help us? Was he working alone? With someone?"

"He told me he didn't do it. I don't know anything." And wasn't that the understatement of the year. Some judge of character. What an idiot she was.

Chapter 33

"LISSA?" Her head spun quickly at the familiar sound of Ned's voice. He had emerged from the bedroom and shuffled groggily into the kitchen doorway, rubbing his left hand distractedly over his bruised, swollen jaw. His face looked red and chafed through the stubble on his chin. "Lissa, are you all right?" His words were thick and pained. He turned his head toward the other man. "What are you telling her?"

The lieutenant was beside him in a flash. "You shouldn't have gotten up," he said sternly. "You need to be lying down."

"No, I don't. I need to know what's going on in here." He took a step toward Lissa, and she shrank back. "Lissa?"

It was too much to bear. Scruffy, dirty Ned Marchess, the junk collector's son, with his badly fitting borrowed clothes, his discolored jaw and his tattered sling barely holding up his injured arm. She had somehow seen something to admire in this man. She turned her face away.

"Don't go near her," Miller warned.

Ned ignored him. The lieutenant grasped Ned's left arm and pulled it behind him.

"I thought he was restrained," Lissa said carelessly.

Miller ignored her and concentrated on twisting Ned's arm painfully. "If I had cuffs, you'd be in them," he said, "but there are other ways."

Ned winced with the sudden pain. "Take your hands off me."

Lissa was surprised at the unexpected gentleness in Ned's voice as he tried to shake the bigger man loose.

"Why did you lie to me, Ned?" she found herself crying. "I walked to your car. I saw the air conditioner. That was *your car*." Lissa began to cry again, large, soft tears that rolled from her eyes and tasted salty on her mouth. "Everything you said to me was a lie."

Ned licked his dry, swollen lip. "That's not true."

"That's enough," Miller warned, tightening his hold.

"Lissa, I admit it's my car. I was in the back seat, and when the car crashed, the unit sliced my arm. But I-"

"That's enough, Marchess," the lieutenant thundered, as Ned tried to break free. "Leave her alone. Miss Tea, go into the other room, please."

She stared at him and made no move to leave. She didn't have the energy to walk ten steps. It hurt, a pain so searing that she had never felt anything like it before. She simply sat and stared at the two men struggling before her.

Lieutenant Miller still clutched Ned's arm behind him in a tight grip. He was taller and broader than Ned, although he looked younger, and Lissa could see how muscled he was through the denim shirt. Ned spun around suddenly and stared at his captor, then shook free of him and lurched toward Lissa. "Don't-" he began, but whatever words he intended to say were torn from him. The tall lieutenant grabbed him easily, spun Ned to face him and hit him solidly in the face with his strong fist. Ned went down, collapsing like a rag doll. A knife skittered across the kitchen floor.

Lissa backed up in horror. Had Ned been coming at her? Why now? If he had wanted to hurt her, he'd had so many chances.

Miller was massaging his knuckles, and bent slowly to retrieve the knife from the floor. "I'm sorry," he said to her. "I should have seen that coming. I didn't know he had this until a split second before he lunged for you."

Lissa couldn't stop staring at the knife. It was the one she had washed the day before. Ned had tried to cut carrots with that knife, and she had ordered him to put it down. She had been afraid. . . .

"Leave him for now," Miller said. "Come with me." He gave Ned, inert on the floor, a long look. "I'd better bring this," he said. He carried the knife away from him, so as not to cut himself or her, and nudged her out of the kitchen.

Lissa shut her eyes briefly in horror and told herself to move forward. She glimpsed Ned lying crumpled on the floor, her emotions colliding and crashing. Ned might have robbed a gas station, may even have hurt or killed someone, but it frightened her to see him sprawled across the floor that way. She was completely at the mercy of the other man.

"I want you to stay in here," Miller said to her, leading her to her own room. "Come on. I'm going to call for help and get him out of here. Someone will stay with you until you feel calmer."

Someone? Who? The whole camp had been in her view as she walked from the kitchen to the bedroom. There was no-one else in the building but herself, Ned, and this man. Why was he still pretending that Ned had been restrained? What *someone* did he expect to stay with her?

Mutely she went toward her bed, watching the kitchen knife glint in Miller's hand as he guided her. She needed to stay alert, to think, but she was exhausted from the lack of sleep, the seven hour trek through the snow, the shortage of food. The emotional upheaval. She sat on the edge of her mattress. Her arms felt like lead. "Why were you driving his car?" she asked.

"He's lying about that, Miss Tea. That Grand Marquis is an unmarked department car."

She stared up at him, watching the burning tip of the knife. A department car? With an air conditioner in the back seat?

"You don't believe me." He shrugged and pulled a cell phone from a tab on his belt. "Here, call 9-1-1, then. Ask them about me." He held it out to her. "Go ahead, take it. Call anyone you like."

She took the phone and clicked it on, waited and listened, then threw it aside heavily. There was no cell service from within these woods. Miller retrieved the phone and hooked it onto his belt.

Tears leaked from Lissa's eyes. How much had Ned made up? Did he own a business? Have a brother? Was his father really a junkman? She remembered his quiet conversation, his soft voice, the quality she had labeled humility. And the other things - volunteering at the animal shelter, and Cassie. Had he made up the medal his mother had given him? It had evoked Lissa's sympathy, and maybe that was his whole objective. Maybe he had simply fabricated stories that would win her over. And she had been so very easy to fool. Lonely Lissa Tea. So desperate for friendship that she would believe anything a stranger told her.

Look at the facts, she told herself. He smashed a window. He terrified you. He kept you here, with gentleness, yes, but how easy to keep a hostage when you convince her to keep herself.

She slumped forward on the bed. Ned, whoever he was, was out cold on her kitchen floor. Maybe he had tried to attack her with the knife, maybe not. Either way, she needed to keep her wits about her, since another man now held her hostage in her bedroom.

But she was tired, so tired.

She stole a quick glance at the bedroom window. If she could distract him, she could break the glass and run madly through the snow. . . .and collapse with hypothermia before she was a quarter mile away.

"You've been through enough," Miller was saying from someplace far away. She let her eyes close and felt his hands gently grasp her shoulders. "Listen to me."

She forced her eyes open. The knife was gone. With peripheral vision, she could see its shape lying on the chair near her bed, just out of reach. "Ned Marchess won't be bothering you anymore. You just stay here. I'll send someone in to stay with you, and we'll get you out of here as soon as we can."

"Is there someone. . . ?"

"There will be a deputy here in a few minutes. We'll take care of everything."

"Thank you," she said quietly. "I didn't realize. I feel very confused." The knife's point glinted and dazzled, stinging her eyes. The rapid beating of her heart began to slow.

"That's right," Miller soothed her. "Relax. It will be okay now." He sat on the edge of the bed, still gripping her arms. "You've been through a hard time here. You lie down and rest. I'll take care of everything."

She forced the stiffness from her body, made herself relax, kept her eyes on the knife. She needed to stay aware. Ned was unconscious and couldn't help her. Would he help her if he could? She choked back a sudden sob. It all depended on her. She breathed in, a cleansing breath.

The knife was possibly within her grasp, if she could lean just slightly toward the chair. She stretched her fingers. . . .

"All right now?" Miller asked, holding her away from him. His glance traveled to the kitchen knife. "Oh. Oh, no, don't touch that," he said softly. He picked up the blade and held it carefully. "That's sharp. You could hurt yourself." His eyes were black, meeting hers with a brilliant intensity.

She nodded numbly.

She could still feel the frightening warmth of his hands on her upper arms, and she sniffled a little as she pushed away from him slightly. He held the knife loosely.

Don't let him hurt me, she prayed. "I'm all right now," she nodded. "I'll be fine. Thank you." She pushed him gently away, her hand against his chest, her teeth clenched.

She wasn't even surprised when she felt something hard, a disc that he wore beneath his shirt, on a chain around his neck. It had become visible as he moved, a tarnished silver medallion with scallops around the circumference. A raised, embossed palette, a paintbrush, the figure painting an icon. She touched it with her hand as she read the inscription. SAINT LUKE, PRAY FOR US.

"Your medal," she whispered.

His body stiffened. "What did you say?"

She leaned away from him, still gripping the medal. "Your medal," she repeated louder. Her mind was suddenly sharp and lucid; she struggled not to scream. "It's a beautiful ornament," she said huskily, spreading her fingers, releasing it. "Where did you get it?"

He smiled down at her. "From my mother. It's one of the few things I have from her."

Stark terror filled Lissa's heart as she looked into the eyes of the man whose strong hands held her captive on her bed. Conor Marchess stared back. Lissa had a wild thought that she could lunge for the kitchen knife and twist it from his grasp. Had Ned come at her with that knife? She knew better.

"Just lie back," Conor said soothingly. "Don't be afraid. It's no wonder you're trembling; you've been cooped up with a madman all this time."

Her eyes locked on his, and she lay back as he directed, terrified by the deep glitter in his eyes.

"There, you'll be all right now," he said. He released her but continued to sit on the side of the bed, staring at her. He stopped suddenly to tuck the medal away inside his shirt and replaced the knife on the chair. "If she had lived, things would be so much different," he said.

"Yes," Lissa whispered. "She would have taken care of you." Her eyes never left his face.

He smiled at her.

"Yes," Lissa repeated calmly. "I know she would want you to do what's right."

"I never do bad things," he said. "I never mean to. She gave me this." He touched the medal reverently. "I'm very proud of it. Sometimes I let people wear it. Good people."

Lissa nodded mutely.

"Would you. . . ." He smiled at her, an appealing, innocent smile. "Would you like to wear it for a while?"

She didn't answer; she couldn't. He slipped the chain off his own neck and placed it carefully around hers. His warm fingers froze her skin. She felt the metal disc fall hard against her chest, burning through her sweater. She flattened herself onto the sleeping bag. Her feet, still in their damp socks, dug in as her fingers gripped the material she lay on. She stared into his eyes.

He stared back, but his gaze had moved to the medal, was no longer on Lissa's face. He reached for the metallic charm and fondled it in his hand, his other arm still holding her motionless.

"*. . . he tried to cut it off. . .*" Ned had told her. Ned was in the kitchen, unconscious on the floor. God, she prayed, bring him to me now. If Ned Marchess is what I believe he is, bring him to me. She willed herself not to glance at the knife.

"Conor, don't hurt me," she said. Her hands clutched at the bedclothes; her gaze was riveted on Conor Marchess; she memorized every movement he made.

"I want it back now," he said, and she sucked in her breath as his fingers reached for her. When she realized how he intended to take it, the air was knocked from her momentarily, and she felt as if she might never breathe again. He picked up the long-bladed kitchen knife from the chair just out of her reach. She made a sudden movement as if to grab it and he tightened his grip on it.

"No," he said. He held the knife scant inches from Lissa's throat.

"Please," she whispered. "I'll take it off and give it to you."

"That's okay," he responded sadly. "It's mine. I'll do it."

Lissa closed her eyes in fear as he began sawing back and

forth on the chain in a leisurely fashion. He intended to cut the chain off, an impossible task. The blade tipped up, then down, as he sawed at the metal chain. Her eyes, slits, could see only fragments of the knife as it came into her view, then dipped down again, out of sight.

"No," she whimpered. She opened her eyes and found her voice suddenly, and she tried to scream, shocked that she couldn't make a sound. "Conor, don't hurt me," she begged softly. Then, "Ned. . . ." It came out as hardly a whisper.

Conor rocked the knife steadily, rhythmically, the blade held taut against the chain around her neck. He cocked his head to one side, concentrating.

Lissa felt her tongue grow thick and fuzzy, and her terrified eyes observed her own destruction from far away. Ned had told her that Conor was never intentionally violent. She understood now. This would not be intentional. This would be the deranged act of a lunatic.

"Ned," she whimpered again, and then she sucked in her breath and screamed his name.

Conor clamped his hand over her mouth; his brows drew together in disapproval. *"Shhh."*

She felt a biting sting and wrenched her head back and away from him, but could not shake his powerful hand over her mouth. The blade dipped down, and she felt a gentle throbbing. When the blade rose again, it didn't surprise her that its broad, sharp edge was bright with a bubble of her own red blood. "Oh, God, help me," she whimpered behind Conor's tight, suffocating hand.

Chapter 34

IN SOME DISTANT, FOGGY PLACE in his mind, Ned heard the familiar shout. It was his mother again, calling to them. He could see himself and Conor, ages twenty and seven, running through the woods near their home in Gorham. Conor ran swiftly, always agile and athletic, his sturdy legs pumping easily.

"Conor, come here," begged their mother from far off, her voice tinged with fear and dread. Then, "Ned!"

The woods were getting darker, and Conor was beginning to cry. It was the nightmare again. Ned knew it, but couldn't shake himself free.

"It's my medal," Ned said, reaching out. His breath came in fast, panting streaks as he ran. "You have to give it back, Conor."

Conor pulled the medal away, crying freely. His hands were strong.

"Give it back," Ned ordered. "You can't steal things, Conor. Do you want to go to jail?" But he knew he would never catch up to Conor.

They reached the clearing in the woods and stopped to catch their breath. Their mother was slumped in pine needles across the clearing, and Ned could hear her cries, louder now and more plaintive. Conor ran to her, and her cries became whimpers.

He was causing trouble again, and, as usual, it was up to Ned to smooth things over and make everything right. But it frightened him that Mother sounded so desperate and her cries so quiet. Then he saw. Conor was winding the chain of his First Communion medal tightly around her neck.

"Don't do that," Ned shouted to Conor, beginning to run again, knowing he had to reach them before his mother's death replayed, before the tragedy of twelve years before repeated itself in the endless cycle of the dream. "You'll hurt her."

"I don't understand," Conor said, his dark brown eyes an unspoken question. He looked down at his mother's face and pulled at the chain of the medal. "Mama? he asked. "Mama?"

Their mother's mouth opened in a round, soundless shriek, and her eyelids flickered. The life was ebbing out of her. "Ned," she called again wearily.

Ned ran faster, trying to reach her.

"Ned!"

Ned opened his eyes suddenly and felt sweat drenching him, plastering his clothes to the unfamiliar kitchen floor in Lissa Tea's cabin. How long had he been unconscious on the floor?

The nightmare faded as it always did, leaving behind only a tense remnant. Would he never dispel that image of his mother dying? The dream embellished it, but the fact was there. It was a stroke, nothing more, but she had been wearing Conor's medal. Conor had sat near her on the floor, rocking back and forth, while their mother tried on the medal, pleasing Conor. There were no marks on her neck; Conor hadn't tried to wrench the chain off or caused the stroke that took her life.

Ned had been over it and over it. Conor hadn't done anything. There was nothing Ned could have, should have done to stop the inevitable.

But guilt was not a rational thing, and his little brother couldn't separate the images. To him, it was all one, the medal, her death, his guilt, and above everything, he needed, always, to remove the medal to set things right.

Ned's jaw throbbed mercilessly, and his right arm was thrumming with a new pain. He felt a sharp, jabbing fire and wondered if his arm might be broken. Had he fallen on it? Conor had hit him; the memory returned in a searing flash. Conor had done that three times in recent days, twice here in the cabin.

The first time had been the most shocking. It had been so completely unexpected.

. . .

When Conor had shown up at the shop early Friday afternoon, Ned knew immediately that there was a problem.

Conor's eyes were bright, his pupils dilated; excitement and fear coursed through him. "You have to help me, Ned." The usual worried beginning and the anxious confession.

There was no point telling their father; Gus Marchess would come up with a thousand ways to cover for Conor, and all of them would involve Ned.

"No, Conor," Ned had said this time. "You have to face up to this. What you did was serious."

Conor's acquiescence had surprised him, but he was so used to his brother's unexplained mood swings that he simply closed up the shop, emptied the cash register into his wallet to deposit later, locked the door, and began the trip to nearby Marcy Falls to help Conor explain himself to the police.

It had seemed far too easy, and as Ned drove cautiously through the thickly falling snow, he watched his brother suspiciously. Their progress was difficult, and they met few vehicles on the snowy lake road. When Conor suddenly demanded that he pull the car over on a lonely stretch, Ned knew his hunch had been right.

"Just pull over here," Conor insisted.

"No, Conor, we'll keep going." Ned forced the Grand Marquis ahead.

"Pull over," Conor repeated. "Just do it." Ned heard the cunning note creep into his brother's voice and glanced at him sideways. The sly look that had disturbed Ned lately was back.

"What is it, Conor?" he asked.

"I mean it, Ned."

Ned could see the change coming over Conor and could predict the lashing out that was likely to follow. Conor might do anything, grab the wheel, slam down on the gas. For safety's sake, Ned calmed him and did as Conor asked. He pulled the Grand Marquis to the side of the road and turned off the ignition.

"Get in the back," Conor said.

"What? Conor, don't be like this. Let me just start the car up and we'll do what we agreed."

"Get in the back with me. I want to talk with you about the robbery. I want to tell you why I did it."

"I know why you did it," Ned muttered gruffly. It was Cassie again. Her influence and her selfishness had put Conor in more hot water lately than in the last five years combined. "Cassie wanted the money for something, am I right?"

Conor nodded. "Get in back and I'll tell you."

He was like a stuck record. His eyes were pleading, and for a moment, Ned almost did climb into the back seat. Instead, he turned to his brother and made his voice as gentle as possible. "Conor, I'm listening. What is-?"

When the blow hit him, Ned was taken by surprise. He stared at Conor, not understanding, then the car's interior went black and Ned felt himself slumping forward in the seat. He was vaguely aware that his head had hit the side window. A stabbing pain pummeled his head.

It was his pulsing right arm and the taste of dirt in his mouth that brought him around hours later. Groggy, he opened his eyes and looked around the interior of the car. Black. It was night. His right arm felt on fire. He felt over the upholstery with his left hand; it came away smeared and sticky. When he clutched his right arm, streaks of flame shot up his forearm, and he felt the jagged, damp rip in the sleeve of the leather jacket he had waited years to be able to afford.

He was bleeding.

Ned sat up, massaging his arm. He was in the back seat of his own car, muffled in by the dark, cloudless air, the forceful snow hitting all around the vehicle. He was freezing. What time was it?

He noted the creeping pain in his arm and tried to see his watch, but the night was too black. He swallowed twice, wishing for water, then felt the dull ache in his jaw.

Conor had punched him.

Ned was still for a moment, thinking. That had never happened before. He had always been his brother's protector and friend.

Sudden panic swept him. Where was Conor?

Painfully, Ned extricated himself from the back seat. Sheets of snow sifted down as he forced open the car door, and he was immediately pummeled with sideways-blowing gusts. The dome light remained black, and he hoped the bulb had simply become dislodged. He crawled back inside, felt around with one hand, and pried open the cap. The lightbulb was screwed in tightly. It must be that the filament had broken.

Anger overcame him and he smashed his left hand into the metal air conditioner, then sat back, gritting his teeth with the new pain. Smart move, he told himself.

By filtered moonlight, Ned could see that the Grand Marquis was plowed head first into a snowbank, and he suspected this was not the spot where he had pulled to the side hours before; Conor had driven here. Ned grimaced. Conor didn't even have a driver's license. What the hell was he doing?

Ned felt his pockets for car keys, trying to ignore the burning in his right arm. He rubbed his arm and felt his hand come away wet and sticky again. He smelled his fingers and nearly vomited. The movement had started him bleeding again.

The keys were not in his pockets, nor was his wallet. He felt mild alarm and checked, with his good hand, the ignition, the front and back seats, the floor, the dashboard. He couldn't see and could hardly concentrate on the search. Every movement sent pain shooting up his right arm.

The keys were gone, his wallet was gone. He squeezed his hands shut in frustration. All that money from his cash register. Gone. And so was Conor.

His mind catapulting, Ned sat inside the vehicle, thinking. His head hurt, and he felt dizzy, maybe from the loss of blood. He pulled his injured arm from its sleeve and gasped at the cold. Clenching his teeth with the pain, he ripped his tee shirt off and wrapped it around the gash, tying it clumsily, then pushed his arm back into his sleeve, moaning aloud in agony.

He wondered how long he had been lying in the back seat, crunched up against the air conditioning unit. He couldn't stay here.

He staggered out of his car again, slammed the door, and lurched off into the night, his mind blurred, hoping to find someone, anyone, who could help him.

And he had found Lissa Tea.

Chapter 35

AND NOW, HERE HE WAS, knocked out again by his little brother, staring at the faded pattern on Lissa's vinyl tile floor.

Ned shook his head, trying to clear it, dragged himself to the kitchen table, and grabbed it. Ignoring the excruciating pain, he hauled himself to his knees. Conor had done some damage with his last blow. Ned's left leg hurt, and he massaged it.

What the hell was happening to Conor? For years he had acted a little odd, and had needed his older brother to vouch for him and clean up his messes time and time again, but Conor had never been violent before, at least not to Ned. In some strange way, Ned realized it actually hurt his feelings.

He had seen Conor out there after Lissa left the cabin. So it was true; it was Conor Lissa had seen loitering around the property, Conor who had stolen the blanket. Relief that Conor was safe overshadowed Ned's resentment at his brother's attack. He had swung the kitchen door wide open and called. If he could get Conor to come inside, there was no danger of him following Lissa. The two of them could talk plainly in her absence.

"Conor!" he'd screamed into the wind, standing shivering at the open door. "Conor! She's gone! It's safe for you to come in."

His brother loped around the side of the woodshed, plowing through the snow with his powerful, long legs. He approached the cabin, eyes weary and gaze darting into the woods beyond the camp.

"Conor," Ned had said, "what are you doing here?"

"Coming after you, big brother; you know that."

"I thought you went to the police, Conor."

"No, I left you in the car because I decided not to go the police."

"You have to turn yourself in. They'll treat you far better if you just tell the truth."

"They don't know for sure it was me."

"That's not possible, Conor. Hasn't it been on the news right along? Someone probably recognized you. Everbody in Gorham knows us."

They had stood there shivering in the doorway until finally Conor pushed past him and entered the building. Ned felt relief flood him.

"You have to help me, Ned."

"I'm trying, but this is a real serious one. I'll go with you; I'll help you through it. But this is serious. You robbed a place."

Conor cringed back against the kitchen wall. "I can't go to the police. I had an accident with your car."

"That's all right," Ned soothed him. "I don't think you did any damage. I'm sure it's still right where you left it."

"I'll be in trouble, though. I hit another car."

"I know you did." Ned exhaled rapidly. Conor had robbed a gas station and he was worried about an accidental fender bender in a snowstorm. "Listen, buddy, the police will understand about the car."

"You can't tell them, Ned. I don't have a license." Fear froze Conor's eyes.

"Listen, I'm going to help you with this, okay?" Ned met his brother's eyes frankly, and felt swift fear creep up his throat as that sly look came into Conor's face.

"Who's the girl who lives here, Ned? Do we know her?"

"We don't know her very well, Conor. She's a real nice girl who's letting me stay here because my arm is cut. We're not going to do anything to scare her."

"What's her name?"

Ned hesitated, absurdly protective of sharing Lissa's name with his only brother. "Lissa," he said. "Melissa. Her last name is Tea, like that sign."

Conor looked at the birchbark ornament on the wall. "She saw us when we were trying to get away," he said.

We? thought Ned. "It's okay," he said. "She'll help you, just like I will."

"Did you tell her what I did?" His eyes looked wary.

"No, Conor. Of course I didn't. She saw you yesterday,

though."

"Did you tell her that was me?"

"No. She feels like a hostage already. I'm trying not to scare her. We've been cut off here. No phone, no radio. It's been frightening for her. I didn't think it was a good idea to tell her what you did. How did you end up here anyway?"

"I went back to the car to help you," he said guilelessly, "but you were gone." Conor smiled shyly, the old Conor. "But I could tell where you went; there were depressions in the snow from your footprints. Then I saw that girl's car, and I remembered when we hit it."

We again.

"I remembered her face, and I thought if you were looking for a place to stay, you might be with her. And, oh boy, you are." Conor laughed cunningly then, and Ned wiped away an image of Cassie in her tight, shifting blouse and sooty eye make-up. "Don't tell her what I did," Conor pleaded.

"Have you had anything to eat since the accident?" asked Ned. "Where have you been sleeping?" Today was Monday. Conor had run from the car on Friday. "Where have you been, buddy?"

"I found a house nearby," Conor said. "The people weren't home."

"Did you find food there? Did you sleep there?"

Conor nodded. "I had a fireplace and everything."

Ned would have to find out which cabin and contact the owners. Just one more thing to smooth over for Conor.

Conor grinned suddenly. "I camped out in that shed, too, until I got too cold." His glance traveled to the Tea woodshed. "When you came out to get wood Saturday night, I was right there, and you didn't even see me."

"You were in the shed?"

Conor smirked again. "That was very chivalrous of you, Ned, the way you walked her to the john and back, and then brought in wood for your fire."

"God, Conor."

"And you didn't even see me. Were you expecting to?"

"I thought I might." Tiredly, Ned sat down at the table. "Here, sit down."

Conor sat. He didn't look well. There were dark smudges

under his eyes and a jittery quality to all his movements. If Conor was tired, Ned might be able to talk his brother into resting in the spare bedroom while he figured out what he was going to do. Conor should be turned in to the authorities, but Ned hated to do it. Even when he thought he had convinced Conor to go to the police, Ned had not really convinced himself. This was his brother, the little boy he had protected his whole life. It wasn't that easy to just hand him over. They had always worked out Conor's problems without outside help. Family matters were private.

Besides, right now, except for a certain skittishness in his movements, Conor didn't seem that bad.

Briefly, Ned had considered setting out on foot with Conor while Lissa was on her journey to the car. A three or four mile hike could get them as far as Marcy Falls, but Ned had hardly made it over the first hill with Lissa; how would he make it to Marcy Falls? He wasn't even sure what the purpose would be. To turn Conor in? To hide him? To beg the Marcy Falls Diner for two steak dinners with heaps of potatoes puddled in gravy?

He had done none of those things, of course. In retrospect, any of them might have been better than what did occur. His back to Conor, Ned opened the kitchen door to look for Lissa trudging home in the falling dusk. "I might have to go meet her, Conor," he said; at least he could finally come clean about the Grand Marquis, the robbery, all of it. He dreaded telling her, but there was no point in covering up for Conor any longer. Conor was no scared little kid now; he was a big, powerful man who could do real harm, and if Ned were to have any hope of a continuing friendship with Lissa he would have to-

Ned never completed the thought and hardly felt the cast iron frying pan that knocked him to the floor. His eyes glazed over as he heard Conor above him saying, "I didn't mean to do it so hard, but you can't go get her, Ned. I'm sorry. Wake up."

And he had awakened, later, crumpled on the bedroom floor, hearing Lissa and Conor talking in hazy tones about the robbery, about Ned's role in it. And getting it wrong, all wrong.

Chapter 36

THE CIRCULATION seemed to be returning to his leg; he rubbed it carefully, not sure exactly how it was injured. He worked his jaw around, too, feeling with his tongue for broken teeth and relieved to find none. His head pounded angrily. Lord, a frying pan! And he clearly remembered now the knife that had slid over the kitchen floor just after Conor had hit him. Ned groaned in agony. What would Conor do next?

A muffled cry assaulted him. "Ned! Oh, God!"

He stopped massaging abruptly. That was Lissa's voice. He shook the grogginess from his head. Lissa was here, and so was Conor, and he'd been lying in a daze on the floor reliving the angst of his sorry life.

Would Conor punch a woman? He had never, to Ned's knowledge, done anything like that, but then Conor had never hit his big brother before either. Painfully, Ned lifted himself from the floor. Conor's behavior was beyond worrisome; his anxiety was controlling his actions.

It was quiet in Lissa's bedroom. Ned gathered his strength and his wits. He knew his brother. Conor would never hurt Lissa, not intentionally. If Ned could just drag himself to Lissa, he could soothe Conor and calm him, just as he always had. Conor had never meant to hurt Cassie's cat; he'd never meant to hurt Ned. But Ned had been a fool to let him in Lissa's kitchen door.

"Don't." It was Lissa's voice, a quiet whimper uttered without much conviction.

Ned lurched past the kitchen table and through the living room, ignoring the anguished wrenching from all his muscles. His jaw felt raw, and he could taste blood. He inhaled painfully, willing to jump to Lissa's rescue, not at all convinced that he was in any shape to rescue anybody. He dragged himself to the bedroom door and stopped short, gulping back a shout that would only startle his brother.

Conor sat on the edge of the bed holding the kitchen knife inches from Lissa's throat. But instead of screaming, Lissa was talking to him now. Her gentle voice was a hypnotic sing-song, and Conor was listening.

"Yes, you can put it down, Conor," she said quietly. "Your mother would want you to put it down." She nodded almost imperceptibly. Her hands were flat and tensed, her fingers splayed, pressed into the sleeping bag that lay rumpled beneath her. Conor sat absolutely still, hunched over Lissa.

"I'll place my fingers on the chain, and I'll lift it off and give it to you," Lissa said. "I'll give you your medal, and it will be whole for you. You don't want to ruin it with the knife. If you cut it with the knife, you'll spoil it. Let me hand it to you instead. Shall I?"

Conor lowered the knife slightly, and Lissa gave him a gentle smile. "That's right," she said. "Shall I remove the chain now and put it in your hands?" Her own hands stayed flat on the bed.

Ned watched, still and silent, afraid to move. Her years managing Katie had placed Lissa in good stead when it came to managing Conor. She was inches away from having her throat slashed, and she was sweetly talking Conor out of the crazed impulse that had made him pick up the knife in the first place.

Conor dropped the knife and it clattered to the floor as he held his hand open between himself and his captive. Lissa moved one hand slowly to her neck and drew the chain over her head. She dropped it with a shaking hand into Conor's open palm.

Ned pitched forward painfully, found the knife with his foot and skidded it across the living room and into the kitchen, where it clattered across the floor. He turned briefly to see it come to rest below the side yard window. His breath was coming hard and pain was shooting up his leg and arm, and his mouth ached, too. And now Conor's more recent victim, Lissa, lay stiffly on her bed, soundlessly crying as Conor hunched over her.

Guilt spasmed inside Ned. Who was he kidding that he could control Conor and solve all his problems if he just had enough patience? Would Lissa ever forgive him for putting her through this?

He forced himself to be still, to watch Lissa taming the beast that was his brother. When he saw Conor clasp the medal in two hands, Ned limped forward.

"Okay, Conor," he said heavily, "good for you. Things are going to be okay now."

Conor stared up at his brother.

"We're going to help you now. Give me your hands."

Obediently, Conor extended his wrists.

"Get those sheets, Lissa, and rip them into strips."

Lissa glanced at the remains of the bed sheet she had placed on the dresser top after fashioning Ned's sling. She gathered up the sheet and began to tear it. Her hands were shaking and she kept her eyes on Conor's now placid face. She piled the strips before her as she tore them, avoiding Ned's fingers as he grasped the strips and tied his brother's wrists together. Conor watched with interest.

"Lissa, I can't get these tight," Ned said as calmly as he could. "I need your help."

She took her eyes from Conor's only briefly as she knotted and tightened the bindings on her captor. Conor sat very still and looked at her. "I wasn't going to hurt you," he said to Lissa. Then he looked up at his older brother. "If I admit what I did at the gas station, will it go easier for me?"

"Yes," Ned said, his voice husky with pain and guilt. "You're doing the right thing. We're going to help you as much as we can."

"How?" Conor asked.

"I'll explain that you forgot to take your pills," Ned said. "Again, Conor. You forgot again. I'll make sure you take them. I'll tell them you never really hurt anyone, you only took the money. And you'll give the money back. That will help, too."

Lissa stood silently, staring ahead. Tears ran unchecked down her cheeks.

"Lie down," Ned instructed his brother softly. "You're going to do what I tell you from now on. Right?"

Conor nodded slightly and lay back.

Ned glanced at Lissa. He felt his insides dry up at the expression on her face and suffered a quick flash of sorrow at the line of blood drying on her neck. He looked away. "No more bad things, Conor," he said weakly. "I can't do this anymore. You just rest there. Sleep if you can."

Conor closed his eyes, then opened them again. "I can't sleep," he said in a small, frightened voice. "Mother said she would never leave."

"I know. She never wanted to leave. She loved you." Ned sat on the bed beside his brother, stroking his back, a rhythmic motion. Conor still clutched the chain and medal in his hands. Ned took it from him carefully and worked it around Conor's neck. "There. Now you can sleep. Try."

From the corner of his eye, Ned saw Lissa leave the room. He could hear her go to the kitchen, the outside door opening and closing, and then, a few minutes later, her return. She was moving around in the living room, then, and he heard the sounds of a log thrown on the fire, a chair pulled forward. He stayed with his brother another half hour until he was sure that Conor's demons were deep in sleep.

Chapter 37

LISSA SWIPED AT TEARS that refused to stop. She had been glad to see Ned in the bedroom doorway, but by then, she had it under control. Yes, under control. Conor had been mere seconds from slashing her throat, but she, Lissa Tea, always in control, always capable, had saved the day.

And then had promptly exited the camp to throw up beyond the birch tree by the kitchen door. She washed her mouth out with ice cold snow, grateful for the stinging ache on her teeth and gums, then re-entered the camp to sit before the fire, where Ned found her.

"I believed you," she said dully. "I didn't really believe him, but I believed you, every word."

Ned sat beside her wanting to clutch her hand, but knew she would not allow it. "I never lied to you." A deep frown etched his face. "I never thought he would hurt you or I would have told you. Conor's never been this bad, though. I'm so sorry, Lissa. I'd give anything to undo it."

She rose from the couch. Ned looked up at her and a part of him wanted to die. The soft feelings he had begun to notice there had hardened into the old, familiar look of distrust and fear. Her dead, flat eyes stared through him.

"Lissa," he said. He stood up and reached for her, stifling the urge to place a hand on her eyes, to obliterate the accusation there, to close them as one closed the eyes of the dead.

"No," she said, moving away from him. "No. Just leave me alone."

"I never expected him to do that," Ned said, "or to hit me the way he did." The words sounded inadequate, even to him. "I thought if I could just help him, like I usually do. . . ." He stumbled to a stop. Lissa was moving away from him, back toward the kitchen. He followed her, trying to convince her. "He's cunning. He gets you thinking he's all right, and he's going along with everything you say, and then all of a sudden, he's someone else. That's what happened on Friday. He wanted me to hide him, and I convinced him we needed to tell the police. Or I thought I did...."

"I don't care about that. He can't help what he does, but you can." Lissa picked up the knife from the floor and stared at it. Her own blood was flecked on its blade. She placed it on the countertop. Outside the window, the pristine snow curled up against the trunks of pines.

"It's your car, isn't it? The Grand Marquis that hit me?" Lissa said.

"Yes, it's mine."

"You pretended it wasn't. You let me believe you had nothing to do with that robbery."

"I didn't." He fought down the plaintive note. She still gazed out the window, and he touched her delicately, urging her to face him. She shook him off, and he was surprised at the sudden sharp sting. She was blaming him when he had done everything right. He had only wanted to protect his brother. He tried to explain. "I was working through lunch when the robbery happened. Conor came to me after."

"Were you trying to help him escape? Except that I got in your way."

"No, I thought we were going to the police. He said he would. He tricked me. He hit me and knocked me out and took my keys."

"He tricked you?" There was disgust in her voice. "How long have you known him, Ned?"

He stood behind her, helpless. She was right, of course. He had only believed Conor because he wanted to. For years, everyone except Ned and Gus Marchess had known there was something very wrong with Conor.

"Lissa, what do you want me to say? I'm telling you the truth. You're right, I shouldn't believe him. I'm sorry. Please don't let it change whatever might have been starting between us."

"Between us?" She looked horrified. "There is nothing between us, Ned."

He turned away from her, swallowing bitter sadness, then pivoted back toward her, angry. "Listen, you have to understand something. You were scared, and knowing everything about me would have scared you even more. You'd have been terrified trapped in here knowing Conor was out there-"

"You knew he was out there, didn't you. You knew it was Conor from the first moment."

"Yes, I thought it was."

"And you never let on. The man who hit my car was Conor. Where were you?"

"I was in the back seat. Somehow he dragged me back there after he punched me. I was out cold; he took over the car. When he hit the snowbank I didn't even know. I woke up later with my arm bleeding rivers all over the upholstery."

"And it didn't occur to you to tell me that?" She stood firmly, badgering him; he allowed it. "What about your wallet?"

"I don't know where it is."

"Well, I do." She reached angrily into the pocket of her jacket and fished out the leather wallet stuffed with bills. "Here." She thrust it at him. "I imagine this money looks familiar to you?"

He looked down at the bills falling sideways out of the folded wallet. "I. . . It's from my cash register. It was too much money to leave in the shop."

"Funny how it's the same amount that was stolen in the robbery."

"Where did you get it?"

"It was in your car," she muttered. She pushed past him, walked stiffly away, and slumped down onto one of the hard painted chairs at the kitchen table. Ned sat next to her, pleading. "This is something new with him, Lissa. Before it was little things, trouble in school, minor problems with the neighbors-"

She interrupted him, impatient. "Someone's dead cat."

"I told Jim Polinski about that, Lissa. Conor got counseling after that."

"How much counseling? Are you going to tell me he was cured?"

He looked away, shame creeping through him. "We should have gotten help for Conor years before we did. I should have done a lot more. The winter he turned seven, he was sick and feverish. My father doesn't like to call the doctor."

"That's stupid."

"Well, in retrospect, of course it's stupid. At the time, it was his call, not mine. Conor wasn't the same after that. My mother's death later that year put him over the top. He's always felt he was to blame, I guess, even though it wasn't his fault."

"Have you ever made him be accountable?"

His silence was answer enough.

"I didn't think so. Even after the robbery, you knew he would try to get away and that he'd come here looking for you, or for me. You expected it, and you let me be a part of it."

"He wasn't looking for you, Lissa. At least believe that. He seeks me out when he's in trouble. He always has."

"And you let me walk to my car alone."

"*Let you?* I didn't *let* you! I tried to go with you! I told you not to go; I didn't *want* you to go."

"You could have just told me the truth," she said sadly. "That your brother might be out there, and that he's dangerous. Do you think I would have gone if you had-"

"He's not really. . . . At least, I didn't think-"

"He might have killed me, Ned."

He shook his head sadly. "He would never have gone that far. You don't know him like I do. Anyway, I would never let him hurt you."

"Right, from your position of authority, passed out on the floor. Do you know what he told me, Ned? That you committed the robbery, and that you killed someone."

Ned closed his eyes briefly.

"And I almost believed him," she said. "It didn't take much to convince me that you're everything you say you're not."

"He was playing a role, Lissa; he watches too much TV. No one was killed in Gorham. Conor demanded money from the cash register. He didn't even have a weapon; he just pretended he did."

"He held a knife to my throat."

"He held a knife to the chain," he said doggedly. "He wasn't trying to hurt you."

"And that makes it ok?" She thrust her head up; the blotchy beads of dried blood on her neck taunted him. Conor had done this. His beloved brother.

"He doesn't have anyone but me." Ned's voice was quiet, a

whisper in the desolate cabin. "He's always needed me. I can't change that."

"Does he still, Ned?" she asked. "Is covering for him still the best way for you to help him?" Lissa left the kitchen suddenly. Sitting near Ned was becoming painful. She had believed him, cared for him suddenly and without reason. His deception was a searing pain; it hurt too much to be near him.

Chapter 38

SHE STOOD IN THE DOORWAY of her bedroom, watching Conor curled on the bed, the tight bindings cutting into his ankles and wrists.

Ned followed and stood behind her. "Lissa, I'm sorry. Sorry for all of it. I only did what seemed right to me."

"You should have told me the truth."

The brittleness in her voice hurt him; he felt his face flush in anger and turned her suddenly to face him. His hand was rough on her shoulder. "That isn't fair," he said tightly. "You're calling me dishonest, but look at you. Look at the girl who plans to whisk her sister away from her family, but can't be bothered to make contact with the rest of them."

"I have the right to choose who I want in my life," she said indignantly.

"Yeah, your rights. You talk a lot about what's best for you, but I don't hear much about what's good for the rest of the folks. Avoiding your own father because of some warped idea of shame. They can't measure up to your standards-"

"They don't even try," she interrupted. "I demand more of myself."

"Of course you do. You're going to be famous and everyone will admire you. What will you do, use your humble beginnings as some kind of sob story in a song?"

"You're hateful!" she said.

"Right, I'm hateful. Because I see right through you. You want independence, but you think some . . . *William*," he spat the name, "is going to charge up and rescue you from your boring existence. You think you'll take Katie back, but it will be such a *sacrifice*. You're all torn up over your mother's death, but you don't have the plain guts to go back there and make things right with the rest of them. What if your father dies suddenly? Or one of your brothers or sisters? Will you mope around feeling sorry for yourself? Wishing you'd mended your fences after all?" He stopped, almost enjoying the look of shock on her face. "If we're going to talk about being honest, maybe you should start by being honest with yourself."

Lissa sputtered furiously. "You have no idea how I feel about anything."

"No? Maybe I have a good idea, Lissa. Maybe I know exactly how you feel. I have a Katie of my own; my roots aren't so glorious either. But people do what they have to do. You said that yourself. And coming up with some stupid plan to send for Katie is idiotic, and you know it." He stepped back from her suddenly and lifted his hand from her shoulder, looking at it as if it were someone else's hand, a strange appendage that had somehow gripped the shoulder of Lissa Tea, gripped it hard. "Ignoring the only family you've got is worse than stupid," he said. "It's. . . it's a sin."

He ran his fingers back through his hair and said tiredly, "Maybe you ought to think about who's evading what, remove the plank from your own eye."

Lissa took a step backward, and Ned kept pace with her, filling the space. "You can't face them, that's all it is. You're so angry with your parents for what they did to you that you can't forgive any of them. That's why you can't go home."

Lissa's chest was heaving with pain and fury. "How dare you!" she cried.

His voice was mocking. "You can't even see the truth if it steps up and slaps you in the face."

"Okay, fine! I *am* angry. I do resent them. I should have been just a little girl having fun, and instead. . . . I'm angry with my brothers for not doing enough, and with Margie, running off to get married without a care in the world-" Agitated, she broke off. Her breathing was ragged, uneven. "Even Katie," she spat. "I tell myself I want to take her, but I'm not even sure why, or if it's even true." She stopped and breathed in a tortured sigh.

"Yeah, and I'm the one in trouble here for not being truthful." Disgusted, he turned away from her.

She stepped aside angrily and stalked across the room before she spoke. Her voice shook. "How dare you even have an opinion about me. No one invited you here."

He sank into the nearest living room chair and looked up at her. It was true, of course. He was uninvited and unwanted. "Look, I'm sorry," he said. "Feelings are tense and we're both exhausted; neither of us is thinking straight right now."

There was no response. Lissa had turned her back and was cursing the hot tears that were flowing down her face. How could he say such things to her? She had tried so hard to make something of herself. How could it be wrong to want a life with a purpose?

"Lissa?" He had come to stand beside her. "I'm sorry. This is a terrible situation we're in, and it's Conor's fault. It's my fault. You're right; I had no right to say what I did; I guess I don't want to be the only one making bad decisions. But look at it from my point of view. How could I be completely honest? How could I tell you everything? People always see Conor as an extension of me. I didn't want that."

There was no reaction from her.

"I guess the truth is that *I* was ashamed," he said. "You're so far above what I am, and Conor. . . ." He hesitated. Maybe he should just be blunt with her. Gently, he turned her toward him; this time she gave in. "At first I was protecting Conor," he said. "But then, after a while. . . I wanted you to know me. Just me."

When she began to speak, her voice was soft and quiet, her words halting. "I left Katie the first chance I got. I wanted to be a success, and if that's wrong, then I was wrong, but I look at you and all you could be, and I don't think it's fair. You will never be anyone as long as Conor runs your life. He needs more than you can give him. You need to let someone else take it for a while."

"I know," he said.

"I wish things could be different," she murmured. She moved abruptly, out of Ned's reach. "I'm so sorry for you, and for him."

She turned from the room and stopped in the bathroom, where she examined her neck in the mirror. She forced back the hot tears starting again behind her eyes. The cuts were little more than surface scratches. Conor hadn't hurt her, not really. It was nothing to cry about.

Ned had come up behind her. She studied his familiar face in the mirror, his dark, unkempt hair, the place on his jaw that was red and raw looking. The straight nose and intelligent eyes.

"Lissa?"

Her answer was an exhaled breath, a sigh that escaped her.

"I better clean those cuts for you. It's only fair."

She shrugged. "It's hardly worth the water, Ned. And I can do it myself."

But he led her to the kitchen and sat her at the table in the chair he usually took. He poured water into a pan and warmed it, then took a clean dishcloth from the cupboard. Dipping the cloth into the water, he moistened it, then rubbed on a little soap. Gently, he dabbed at the cuts on Lissa's neck, working awkwardly, one-handed. The only sound was the gentle swish of the cloth in warm water, the small trickle as Ned pressed the water out. He cleaned the blood from her skin and sat back. The cuts were shallow and didn't require much.

"When this is over-" he began.

She interrupted him. "We'll be glad we parted on friendly terms."

"Is that what you want? Because, I'll be honest, I thought I noticed. . . I hoped. . . ."

"No." She was adamant. She turned away.

"Because you're so busy seeking that life you've always craved? Or because I am who I am."

"Because I have things to accomplish, whether you approve or not, and I need to pursue them."

And, he knew, there wasn't room for the man from Gorham, with his crazy brother, demented father, and small, suffering business that he didn't even own yet.

He put away the makeshift medical supplies, then glanced at the two heavy bags Lissa had brought to the cabin. He peered in and began to remove items. For a few minutes, he rummaged pointlessly, and then caught her watching him. He stared at her for a moment and put down the dripping bag of blueberries he was holding. "Look, let me just say this, Lissa. I don't like the idea of this ending here and now," he said. "I would like to see more of you, and keep on seeing you. At least I want to have a chance. Don't hold my brother against me."

"It's more than that," she said.

"What? You want me to be more sauve? Sophisticated?"

"Don't. Stop making this worse."

"Forget it, then," Ned said. "We've gone from strangers to friends. Let's leave it there." He held up a can of soup. "I haven't eaten all day." He exhaled a sharp breath. "We might as well do what we've been doing right along and eat something weird."

She stared at him. It was domestic and funny, and so like him that it tugged at her heart. She watched him pull meat and dripping vegetables from the bags.

"I have something even better," she said quietly. She poked through the canvas bag and found the bottle of aspirin. "There's enough here to last for weeks. We can keep on hurting ourselves indefinitely."

"Good, then there's no rush for the plow." Ned smiled softly at her and poured water for both of them. They swallowed their painkillers together. "Lissa. . . ."

She stood looking at him. He thought he saw something there. Regret, maybe.

"You'll miss me, you know," he said quietly. He glanced at her sideways.

She smiled in spite of herself.

"Come on," Ned said, "there are some things in this bag that should have been refrigerated. We better take care of them."

But Lissa suddenly wasn't listening. Ned dug into the bags and pulled out packages, opened the refrigerator door and began thrusting things in. He glanced at Lissa; her head was cocked sideways and her eyes held a suddenly focused look.

"I hear something," she said. A slow grin was spreading over her face. "Oh, Ned, I hear something."

"What?" He strained to hear, and was rewarded with the unmistakable clattering of a huge machine churning toward them on the deep, snow-covered road. Lissa's eyes were bright, and Ned swallowed a sudden lump of dismay. The arrival of the snowplow thrilled her. Well, could he blame her? They'd known each other less than four days, and she'd been terrified through all of it. First by him, then by Conor. And Conor still lay in the bedroom, docile now, but it was anyone's guess when his next meltdown might occur.

Lissa was flying around the room, throwing on her boots and coat and hat, her fleece-lined gloves and plaid tartan scarf. "You stay here with your brother." She grinned suddenly. "Thank God," he heard her say. "Help is arriving. Finally, we're going to get out of here." She met his eyes briefly before she flew out the door.

The great roaring beast came up the road, its massive headlights illuminating the yard. Ned stood before the window watching Lissa making headway across the snow. The milky light from the heavens created strange, eerie shadows, but her escape was unmistakably buoyant. She hadn't shown that much energy the whole time they'd been together. He watched her wade happily through the pine grove, across the lawn, to the road.

The plow crunched up the pure, heavy snow; its enormous steel blades pushed it to the side of the road, clearing a scraped path. High snowbanks and a snowy, pebbly road, gray and gold in the light from the moon and the plow, lay where moments before there'd been only a deep field of snow.

He could see Lissa waving eagerly, flagging down the driver. The plow stopped and a man heaved himself out of the cab to get close enough to hear her.

He could read Lissa's animated gestures and imagine her words: There was a man, an injured man inside, and the thief from Gorham, subdued now, and she, too, yes, Lissa Tea, who had been held captive by them all these days.

Ned turned from the window and jerked a hand into the canvas bag for more food. He came away with a loaf of bread and tore it open. Conor would need to be prepared. Turning him in was right, but Ned would not do it without making Conor as comfortable and secure as possible. Their minutes in the cabin were numbered. Lissa had seen to that.

. . .

"Conor? Conor, wake up." He sat on the edge of the bed, jostling his brother. Conor groaned and opened one bleary eye. It was much like Conor's school days, when Ned had awakened him at seven fifteen every single morning, clowned with him to get him ready and onto the school bus. There, his responsibility ended until three twenty-five, when Conor would hop off the bus, with nary a schoolbook under his arm.

Except for those days when Ned had been summoned. He had spent years in the repair shop waiting for the phone to ring, never daring to travel too far from work. He'd noticed Conor wearing his cell today; well, let him. What harm could that do? The cell phone had become a blessing. Ned could pick up and deliver to customers without worrying so much what might be going on with Conor.

Hell, he never stopped worrying about what might be going on with Conor.

"Here, have some bread," Ned said now. "We'll be leaving pretty soon. I thought you might be hungry."

"Where's the girl?" Conor asked. He took a couple of slices and ate them hungrily. "I wasn't going to hurt her."

"She knows that," Ned said. "Don't worry about it."

"Where is she?"

"Getting help," Ned answered. "She's calling the police because all three of us know that's the best thing, right?"

"I guess so." Conor's glance darted around the room.

"They aren't here yet. But Lissa's getting them. Getting help for you. And for herself." Ned couldn't help the ragged catch in his voice. He hugged his brother tightly, and Conor accepted the gesture of affection. "It won't be too long, Conor," Ned said. "This is a big moment for her, the day she gets herself free of both of us."

Chapter 39

WELL, LISSA TOLD HERSELF, it was over, and it had been an interlude she would never forget, a bittersweet experience. She wished she could rid herself of the terrible churning in her stomach, the feeling that she had handled it all very badly indeed.

The driver of the plow had immediately contacted the police for her, and, with the roads freshly cleared, they had come quickly. She returned to the cabin to find both brothers sitting before the fire eating bread. It was nearly eleven o'clock at night. She sat near them in the overstuffed chair, wondering if Ned would hate her after all.

"The police should be here soon," she told them.

Ned nodded. "I guess this is the part where I thank you for letting me stay and eat your food and share your camp."

She smiled weakly. "I guess it is."

"And for the aspirin and the water and for cleaning up my injuries. And where I apologize for my brother and agree that we part amicably." He finished in a rush.

She nodded. There were no words to say.

"It's not a problem, Lissa. You're searching for independence; I want the opposite. You want the good life; I wouldn't even bother to hope for it. I have no goals; you're chock full of them. I'm sure you'll get exactly what you're seeking. And I'll have Conor for my whole life, to have and to hold. Right, Conor? So everybody wins."

Conor went on chewing bread. The loaf was half gone. Lissa didn't answer.

"We'll be okay, right Conor?" Ned patted his brother's arm affectionately. Lissa saw the younger man nod uncertainly. She hoped he would stay calm until he was safely with someone who could control him.

Well, Ned, she admitted, could control him. If Ned had been conscious, Conor wouldn't have had the opportunity to lure her into the bedroom. She knew that. When Ned said he wouldn't have allowed her to be hurt, she knew it was true. Looking at them now, seated together before the fire, she felt a surge in her throat. Ned was a good brother, a good man. He was all beat up, physically and emotionally, and still taking care of Conor. He would be a great guy for some girl up in Gorham, somebody who wanted to live in a backwoods community and ride around the countryside with appliances in the back seat of the car.

She felt ashamed of her snobbish thoughts, rose quickly from her chair and returned to the kitchen. She would wait here and let Ned spend this time with his brother.

When the police arrived, there were questions to answer, notes to be taken down. Lissa tried to respond as fairly and accurately as possible. No, Ned had not threatened her in any way. He had told her the truth from the beginning. Not the whole truth, her heart said, but she didn't tell them that. She did say that he had actually tried to protect her from his brother; she knew that now. And with his injury it had not been possible for him to leave. They had been captives of the unusually harsh winter storm.

And Conor had not intended to hurt her either, she was quick to tell them. Conor needed help.

Ned's car would have to be examined. The bruises on Ned's face and the injuries to his arm and leg interested them greatly. Ned was brief and matter-of-fact in explaining them, but his voice was tinged with the pain of explaining his brother.

Conor sat subdued in handcuffs, talking little, content that Ned was near.

Lissa was surprised that Ned was taken away as well as Conor, and she wondered how much blame for the fiasco he would have to share. She didn't have his street or email address or even a phone number, and she had wondered if Ned might ask for hers under the watchful eyes of the politely curious police sergeant. He didn't.

"Again, thanks," Ned said to her as he was led from her kitchen door. He gave her a small left handed wave as he slogged through the thicket of pines and hemlocks to the police car parked on the Arrowhead Lake Road. Lissa watched, her throat constricted, as the car drove away. She could see the brothers in the back, Conor leaning against Ned, slumped and childlike. Ned supported him, staring straight ahead, resolute and rigid. He didn't spare her a last glance.

She closed the door on the bitter cold night and locked the camp. She had given her statement, had signed her name to the truth, had declined their offer to help her make arrangements to stay elsewhere. It wasn't necessary, and she had nowhere else to go. She would stay in the camp until she could get her car out and return to Albany.

She wandered into the extra bedroom that Ned had used, folded and rehung his blankets on the wires overhead, straightened the mattress, stripped off his pillowcase, and repacked the pillow in the steamer trunk in her room. Her glance fell on the stack of framed photos she had removed from Ned's dresser. Scooping them up, she returned them to their rightful place. Steven, in a sailor cap even as a little boy, floating on the lake in a rubber dinghy. Margie and her husband Bo, arms entwined, smiling from a lawn swing, the trees a green backdrop. Her parents at the picnic table, Daniel brushing one of the dogs that had wandered through their lives, one of Lissa herself, her nose in a book, engrossed in the reading - so much that she never even looked up when the picture was snapped.

She picked up the photograph. Her hair was about the same, long, light, fine, hanging over her shoulders. She must have been seventeen or so in this picture. And it captured her well - always with her head in a book, or practicing the piano at school, or drawing.

Lissa set the picture down and hunted for another one of herself. Here she was, lying on the dock, eyes closed. Neal and Steven rough-housed nearby. Steven was about to go over into the lake; the expression on his face was priceless. And here was another one, Lissa, flipping through the pages of a magazine.

Did she ever look up at the world around her?

She sifted through the rest of the photographs: Uncle Jeff nailing boards in place when they had shored up the shed several summers before. Her father again, with cronies from work, everyone smiling and holding American flags. Sammy, her youngest brother, showing off the turtle he held, smiling a gap-toothed smile. Neal, Aunt Louise - everyone doing things, enjoying life, interacting. Even Katie, making a face from her wheelchair, learning to knit, the yarn cascading over her legs and trailing on the floor in a pool of fuzzy pink.

No, she told herself. I am the one who's doing things. I have a sense of purpose, ambitions. I am somebody.

Agitated, Lissa set up the rest of the photographs. There were too many people in her family, and they suffocated her. And how could she possibly expect them to welcome her back.

Her thoughts traveled to that last volatile argument with her mother. She had never had a chance to apologize, hadn't known until years later the monumental trust her mother had had in her. Her mother's bewildered face would be etched in her mind forever. She would make it up to her, though- to her and to Katie. She would try to become worthy of that trust.

Ned was right. She was too judgmental, had criticized her mother without bothering to know her. How could she have known how much it would hurt to lose her.

It was time to get some sleep, and Lissa turned off the lights in the camp, but instead of making her way to her bedroom, she stood in the dark kitchen for a moment. Her hand reached for the back of Ned's chair. How many times had he sat there in the past few days? For meals and to have his wound tended to, to drink tea with her and just to talk. That was the place she had first seen him, and she wondered how long it would be before she began to see it as just another chair.

She flicked one kitchen light back on and went to her bedroom. The poster across the window was doing a passable job of keeping the cold out, but she knew Daniel or Neal would come soon to do a better repair job. In the meantime, she felt safe enough.

Well, maybe one more light wouldn't hurt. She turned on the living room lamp just outside her bedroom, then went in and straightened her sleeping bag. He had sat right here, stroking his brother's back, gently convincing Conor that no one was going to abandon him. He'd shown the same consideration toward a mouse, of all things. And to her, as well, she realized. Gentle, compassionate, and kind.

And he had berated her selfishness, forced her to look at

herself and her life. She wasn't entirely pleased with what she saw there.

Lissa leaned against the window frame and gazed out at the moonlight draping ribbons over the undisturbed snow. Someday, she wondered, would she meet a man who had those same qualities? Exactly the right kind of man, who would be everything she hoped for and help her fulfill all her dreams? She knew now that William was not that man; he lacked the gentleness that she craved, the compassion to accept Katie without reservation. But there must be a different man, someone successful, someone she would be proud to know. Would he arrive one day, bringing her roses, and ask her to marry him in a most romantic way? She would say yes, and they would begin a lifetime of happiness together.

Right now, that man was studying, preparing, getting ready for life to start. Just as she was.

He would find her.

And then her heart would stop breaking over the loss of Ned Marchess.

Chapter 40

IT WAS TUESDAY, and half the day was gone.

The afternoon sun streamed into the camp kitchen as Lissa poked among the foods Ned had placed in her refrigerator. For breakfast, she had cooked two potatoes and eaten them hungrily, realizing how little she'd had the day before. They had frozen and thawed and tasted mealy, but she doctored them with a packet of pepper, carried them in paper towels and devoured them greedily, skin and all. To her surprise, they tasted as good right from her hand as they would have from the finest china.

Now, none of the food looked appetizing, but she finally settled on a can of soup with bread and set a saucepan of water boiling for tea.

She was sick of tea.

A thick blanket of white covered the lake and woods, but the road was plowed, with five foot scraper banks soaring on either side.

She sipped her tea, thinking of the weekend she had just spent. The cabin seemed strangely quiet, and she wasn't sure she liked it much. If she had made different decisions and investigated the Grand Marquis on Friday, she would have found Ned and saved them both a lot of torment. If she'd been a little braver. She had known it was right to check, but that was Lissa Tea, too afraid, too self-involved. What was best for her always came first. She banished the unsettling truth from her mind.

She looked forward to resuming her classes, getting back into the routine of homework and papers, trips to the library, dinners alone. She would study hard and make it through, and eventually send for Katie. They'd move somewhere - maybe out west or down south - wherever Lissa could land a job, and she'd find a daycare place for Katie. Katie, at least, would have friends.

The tea tasted hot and bitter, a good taste after all. Lissa caught herself sneaking looks out the side window and reprimanded herself. He wasn't coming. She'd made it very clear Ned wasn't the kind of man she wanted. Was she waiting for him to come groveling? He wasn't that kind of man either.

She squelched the picture that kept creeping into her mind. Ned and Conor, the evening before, led so unceremoniously from the cabin. But she was sure Ned was fine. He would explain his way out of it, probably already had, and he'd make sure Conor was cared for. She needn't worry about either of them.

This would be a good day to make some progress on that Aesthetics paper, and she promised herself to finish her lunch, gather up her books and notes, and accomplish some serious work right here at the kitchen table.

Ned had laughed at her for toting her assignment along on a winter weekend vacation. Well, wasn't it lucky she had? She could write the entire first draft today; that would save her so much time later for. . . . For what?

She couldn't help glancing out the window as she went to get her books. Snow - broad, white, and endless - tall pines and oaks, bare, gray maples, a pristine setting, undisturbed. Like Lissa Tea, she told herself, a young woman on the verge of life. Untouched, untried, unblemished. Waiting patiently for someone to appear who would touch her heart and mind, a man full of compassion and gentleness, one who might appreciate Thoreau or Robert Frost.

She jerked herself from the window, sat abruptly at the table, forced herself to read and take some notes, and made a few false starts on a first draft. Why was she having such trouble concentrating? They'd probably go easy on Conor, find him a safe place where he wouldn't hurt himself or anyone else, get him some counseling. And Ned, well, his only crime was believing his brother.

Lissa put down her pencil and read over the few lines she had written. *Through musical compositions, as with poems and paintings, the artist can express truths that are indefinable, in fact, inexpressible in any other way. While other mediums. . . .*

She sat and stared at the words and wondered why anyone would care. What was she even talking about?

It was growing dark outside, and she'd completed so little of her work. Sighing, she picked up her books and notebooks, pens and paper scraps, stuffed everything into her canvas sack and placed it next to her boots. There was no point in working on the paper here. It would go a lot faster if she used her computer back in the apartment.

A noise surprised her, and Lissa went to the window and peered out. A mist of snow floated by from the clump that had just slid from the steep, pitched roof.

She swallowed disappointment. Well, what had she thought it was?

She heard another sound and whirled quickly. Two tiny black beads stared at her. The mouse perched at the side of the sink, holding perfectly still. Lissa stared back, her heart thumping, and reminded herself that he was *much* more afraid of her than she was of him. Stay in the walls tonight, she begged him silently. Please don't come scampering across my bed. She glanced at the shelves near the kitchen stove and spotted the mousetrap there, but made no move to pick it up.

"Hey, little one," she crooned quietly. The mouse seemed to hear her. His head cocked delicately to one side. "No one is going to hurt you." Her heart was pounding. Ridiculous! Over a mouse!

"Go," she said. "Go!" She made a sudden movement and the mouse darted out of sight into a cupboard. She stood still, not sure if she trusted the animal to stay hidden. She knew she would not open the cupboards for the rest of her stay.

Tomorrow, she would leave. She had spent this whole day in the cabin, trying to write, waiting, hoping for something that wasn't going to happen.

She wandered into the bedroom Ned had used and slid her hand over the scarred wood of the mismatched furniture. The books in the bookcase were slightly askew. She knew Ned had looked through them, searching for something to help pass the time while he was stuck here with control freak Lissa Tea. He had reshelved the book of Frost's poetry and left another volume tented beside the bed. Curious, she picked it up. With all the cheap thrillers crammed into these shelves, he'd chosen a collection of Nathaniel Hawthorne's short stories and had gotten more than halfway through. Well, Ned was intelligent; that had never been the issue.

Her own finger-painting hung above the bed, *LISSA* printed in big, uneven letters. She wondered if he had noticed this proof of her childhood, if he'd been surprised to see she wasn't always this prudish, prissy girl with an inflated sense of her own importance.

She thought of some of the things she'd said to him. About Katie. About her parents' work, their lack of motivation, all their shortcomings. How could she have been so arrogant? Ned didn't look like a great success either, and she'd been blind enough to believe it was really a choice.

His devotion to Conor was touching, fatherly, and she realized suddenly how much she admired him; he had qualities she could learn from. She recalled her last glimpse of him, riding off in the police car, his upright posture, his capable handling of Conor. Ned was strong, smart, and moral. And she had judged him by the most frivolous of standards.

Two college degrees and another near completion. In some contexts they meant absolutely nothing.

Her eye passed over the photographs on the dresser, Steven, Margie, Katie, Uncle Jeff. Her mother and father, devoted, if flawed, parents. They had loved Katie so much that they'd arranged for her the best they knew how. Just as Ned had done for Conor. Could she muster up that kind of devotion, love Katie as she would her own child, without reservation?

Her eyes moved over the photographs. Margie and Bo. Daniel. Little Sammy. A sudden rush of affection for them surprised her tired heart.

And there was Lissa, reading, engrossed in the fictional life of some fictional character living out a fictional existence.

While the real world erupted around her.

What a stupid decision she had made.

He wanted to get to know her better, and she was too proud and too stuck within her narrow view to see him clearly.

She turned the picture over, laying it face down on the dresser top, and returned to the kitchen. There, she sat heavily and rested her arms on the table. Gently, she placed her forehead on her arm and closed her eyes. It didn't surprise her at all when the tears of regret began.

Chapter 41

WEDNESDAY DAWNED GRAY, with flurries of snow bouncing against the cabin window panes, but the roads were plowed, and Lissa was no longer a captive of the weather. She snuggled back into her sleeping bag and turned over, making herself more comfortable. She fell back to sleep, then awoke again and lay thinking for ten more minutes. She felt a great sense of calm, a confidence in the rightness of the decision she had reached last night. When she looked at her watch it was nearly ten o'clock, and she stretched luxuriously. Finally, she was catching up on the sleep she had lost since arriving on Friday.

If she were going to leave today, she should get organized. She ate a quick breakfast, then took stock of herself in the old-fashioned bathroom mirror. She hadn't washed her hair or worn any make-up in days; she hadn't showered since Friday morning and felt grubby and dirty. That was about to change.

She lugged the big pots outdoors, filled them with snow, and started it boiling. It was a very small amount of water for washing her hair and giving herself a welcome sponge bath, but she made it do. Over a dishpan on the kitchen table, she squeezed water and suds through her hair, painstakingly rinsing it until she could hear it squeak. She washed herself carefully in the bathroom, conserving water, and loved the heat and strength of the warm water as she cleansed her body.

She dried herself vigorously and put on her jeans and socks and the fleecy, oversized sweater she had worn on Friday. She had washed out the cuff where Ned's blood had stained it, and it felt warm and comfortable.

She wondered fleetingly if he was seeing a doctor. She hoped so. She had suggested it to him more than once. She had to trust that he would do so. He *would* do so; he wasn't stupid.

She wrapped her hair in a towel and found her hair dryer where she'd dropped it on Monday. Its noise and power refreshed her. This was more like it, the old Lissa, in control. She found her make-up kit and blushed as she recalled pulling it from the trunk of her car. She had been thinking of Ned, anticipating spending the evening with him. Opening her door to find Conor standing there had wiped from her mind all thoughts of impressing Ned. No, the idea had flown before that, the minute she had seen the air conditioner in the Grand Marquis.

Ned had been less than truthful with her. And she had been far from truthful with herself.

She opened her make-up bag and applied eye liner and a touch of lip gloss.

Her coat and scarf hung over the back of the chair where she had thrown them. Her boots stood in the dirty puddle made from her boots and Ned's in their long weekend of captivity. She put them on now, boots, jacket, gloves, hat, scarf. She grabbed her car keys, locked the door, rummaged in the shed for a shovel and, finding none, decided on a garden hoe. Armed for battle against the snow, she started the two mile trek back to her stranded car.

Walking was much easier now, almost a pleasure on the flat, cleared road. The temperature was still cold, but above zero, it seemed, and the sky remained gray as she walked. Stubborn snow flurries somersaulted lazily in big, soft flakes, and every now and then a big gust would chill her and force her to lower her head, butting her way forward into the wind.

When she reached her car, Lissa let out a groan of disappointment. It hadn't occurred to her, but of course she should have been prepared. The plows had been through all right, and they had piled even more snow onto her little compact. It was barely visible in the solidly packed snowbank. It would take her many hours to shovel out. Her plan to drive to Gorham would have to be postponed.

She walked a little further and rounded the bend. Ned's car was gone, its telltale impression a snowy cave by the side of the road. Lissa buried a glimmer of disappointment and returned to her car.

The hoe was better than nothing, but awkward at best. After

a half hour of hot, backbreaking work, she retrieved her snowbrush from the back seat, leaned wearily on the snowbank that still encased her car, and yanked off her hat, tossing it into the snow. It felt good to let the soft wind whip her long hair around, to welcome the snowflakes that fell on her head and shoulders. She was sweaty from the work, and unzipped her jacket, too.

She picked up her hoe and began to chop again.

When she caught a movement out of the corner of her eye, she turned and felt a sudden surge of happiness as she recognized him loping up the road. She watched him walk toward her and realized she had never seen him walk freely before. In the cabin, he was always limping or holding his arm in pain. He seemed better today.

She couldn't help smiling; she was glad to see him. And she would play this scene right. She knew how to go after the thing she wanted, the one thing.

"I didn't expect to see you," she said.

He was clean shaven and his hair was clean and tousled from the wind. He'd gone home, or somewhere, and looked freshly scrubbed. He wore jeans and a different jacket, some kind of woolly thing with a high collar that covered his neck, and the same rubber boots. Those boots had spent a lot of time sitting by her kitchen door.

He approached her. "I was hoping you'd still be around. You didn't think I'd run off with things that weren't even mine, did you?" He held out the plastic bag he carried and she recognized Uncle Jeff's shirt and the too-big pants she had given him. "They're clean and ready for your next guest."

"Oh, of course. I forgot about those."

"Well, I didn't." He put the bag down and grinned lazily at her. "You'll be happy to know I saw a doctor. He asked me to compliment the nurse who fixed me up."

"He did not."

"No, not really. But he said you didn't do any harm."

"Except that I wasted all that good wine. So are you all right? Any lasting injuries?"

"Good as new in no time. A few stitiches, a tetanus shot, plus some antibiotics. I can even look forward to a manly scar." Ned took the hoe from her and gave it a cursory look. "Up in Gorham, we have what we call shovels. They lift three times as much snow and make the job far easier."

"I couldn't find one in the shed," she said. "And you shouldn't help anyway."

"I'm fine. If we take turns, it shouldn't take us more than ten or twelve more hours."

Lissa laughed and he gazed at her. "How are you, Lissa?"

"I'm glad to see you. How is your brother?"

Ned leaned on the hoe and thought for a moment. "I think he's all right. He'll have to take responsibility for what he did, but they had a psychiatrist talking with him when I left him this morning. I'm hopeful they'll be easy on him." He dug in with the hoe and cut loose a big chunk of hard-packed snow. "You know where the money was? He stuck it in the air conditioner. He couldn't wait to tell them that, and sure enough, that's where they found it. Who would ever think to look there. He asked them very politely to make sure Cassie got some of it." Ned shoveled out a hoeful of snow and threw it. "I'd like Cassie to get what she deserves all right."

"So the money in your wallet really was yours?"

"My meager profits for a morning's work."

"It didn't look that meager to me."

Ned grinned. "Now and then I have a good day. But most of it will get eaten up by overhead. A pile of cash looks impressive until you start paying the bills. But the shop keeps floating. It might do better now that I don't have Conor helping."

"Do you think he'll go to prison?"

"I hope not, but it will be that or some other place." He looked at her frankly. "I didn't like to admit it, but he's pretty sick. But wherever he ends up, I'll be nearby. Even if I have to move."

"You'd do that for him? Give up your business and your home?"

He smiled slightly. "He's my brother."

He shoved the hoe into the snow and yanked it out again, pulling snow with it. With one arm, it was awkward. After a few more attempts, he stopped.

"My turn," Lissa said, taking over. He stood aside and watched her work. Soft snowflakes landed on her arms and shoulders. The lake created a pale backdrop behind her.

When a pick-up truck trundled toward them, Ned happily shelled out to a cluster of teenage boys trolling the countryside with shovels, just hoping for opportunities like this. He and Lissa stood aside and watched.

"How did you get here?" she asked him. "Where's your car?"

"It's been impounded. I hitched a ride to the intersection of the highway. It should be easy to hitch back to Gorham."

"I'll give you a ride to Gorham," Lissa said.

His gaze lingered on her face. "Maybe."

The boys finished their work and bounded off in their truck. Ned leaned on the car. "Are you headed back to camp?" he asked.

"Yes." Lissa's hands felt clammy suddenly. He was acting a little distant. She wouldn't blame him. She regretted her obstinacy, wished she could learn how to be a bit cooler in life.

"I'm headed there," he said. "Could I ride with you?"

"Of course." She got into the driver's seat.

Ned climbed in, too. It was hard to read her. She seemed glad to see him, but nervous, as well.

"Why there?" Lissa asked.

"I left my clothes there," he said simply. "My torn shirt? My jeans?"

"Oh!" Lissa felt herself blushing and moved the car forward. "Of course."

Ned peered over at her. "My clothes are dirty, and the shirt's not much good, but I'd just as soon have them back. Old times sake, you know. Besides, that shirt makes a darn good muffler on a cold day."

Lissa smiled in spite of herself. "Certainly you may have your clothes. I didn't intend to keep them."

He stole a glance at the prim young lady driving beside him and drew in a breath. "Lissa," he said finally, "I would like to talk to you about what happened the other night. Conor could have hurt you a lot worse, and that was my fault. You're absolutely right that I've protected him when I should have been getting him some serious help. When this is over, he won't be my responsibility anymore. At least not right away."

"I understand why you did it," she said. "He's your brother."

"Truthfully, I'm kind of relieved," he said. "He'll be away from Cassie, at least, in a controlled environment. She just never got it, even when I tried to talk to her about him."

"Where is he now?" Lissa asked.

"Right now, he's very safe. He's in a hospital, and he has a guard and a doctor. I'm going back to see him tonight."

"I can take you. Would that be all right?"

He grinned at her. "Yeah, that would be great. You know, the fact that Conor put the medal on you means he liked and trusted you, at least for that moment. You must have said all the right things to him, if you can believe me."

"I do believe you," she said. "I always believe you."

"The doctor said Conor's natural generosity makes him want to share that medal with everyone, but then he worries about losing it, losing Mom, so he wants it back and doesn't give anybody a chance to give it. People react negatively, so Conor panics. I feel good that he's got someone to talk to who can help him. I guess they'll help him understand himself, so no one will have to go through what you did. I wish I knew where he'll end up, though."

Chapter 42

LISSA PULLED THE CAR to the side of the road outside the camp. It was amazing how short the road had become now that it was clear and plowed. The miles that had seemed endless just days ago were nothing now.

She turned off the ignition and stepped out into the light snow that was falling again. The camp stood isolated on a gentle ridge; trees dotted the snow-covered property that swept down and away, merging with the rocky lake shore. Except for the white, rounded bumps of rocks, it was impossible to tell where the land ended and the lake surface began. It was a perfect melding, a seamless joining.

Ned climbed out, too, and stood beside her, following her gaze. A snow-frosted split-rail fence marked the invisible path to the water's edge, and he leaned against it, admiring the view. "It certainly is pretty here," he said. "You tend to forget that when the wind is screeching and the cold is making your bones ache." He smiled at her. "Are you going to invite me in? To get my clothes?"

She glanced at him and Ned was struck again by her eyes. Gray and clear. He wondered how many boyfriends she'd had in her short life. Not many, he ventured, but not because they hadn't been interested. He suspected Lissa had found ways to keep the admiring throng far, far away.

"Look," he said, and his voice was serious. "The way we left things- Now that we've both had time to think- I know what you're looking for in life, and you deserve all those things. I know I don't fit into your plans and it's just weird chance that threw us together. If we can stay friends, that would be good, but think about this: I'm thirty-two years old, and by now I know what I want, too."

The wind was playing with her long hair, blowing it across her face. He caught a strand and tucked it behind her ear.

"I'm not pretending to be anything other than what I am," he continued. "But I'm a good person, Lissa, and no one would take better care of you in the ways that matter." He shrugged a little, turned his head away and stared at the frosty scene before them. "I'm just saying we could give it a chance, that's all." He looked back at her. "Would you be willing just to go out a few times? See how it goes?"

A catch in her throat made it impossible to speak. Her breath was caught by the wind.

Ned nodded briefly and looked away again. "We better get moving then," he said. "I can help you load up your car, at least." He started for the cabin, relieved when she reached for his arm. Her gentle touch stopped him and hope flickered.

"What's it like living in Gorham?" she said. "I asked you that once, but you never really answered me."

He cocked his head, looking at her straight on. "It's a small town, dusty and simple."

She looked out over the frozen lake. Pellets of snow showered down from the trees around them. "You're not doing a very good job selling it." she said. She turned to look at him, her expression straightforward.

He tried to read her eyes. "It's a nice little place with the Hudson running right alongside. The river is pretty in the winter with the ice on it. Then in the spring, when it melts. . . . Well, you couldn't find a nicer place. Wildflowers, a little waterfall. How am I doing? I've never written a tour brochure before." He shrugged. "I could show you sometime. My house isn't much, but I might build a new one, depending on where Conor ends up, maybe buy some land along the river, build a nice new house."

"And Conor could come and stay."

"Yeah, and maybe Katie," he added.

She met his gaze. What a good man he was. He would never abandon Conor or anyone he felt responsible for. An image of Katie flashed into her mind. She missed Katie; she missed all of them, and Ned was right. She had been foolish to stay away so long.

"I suppose you could come, too, if you want," he said. "Katie might like that." He looked at her, one eyebrow arched.

Lissa laughed, a genuinely happy sound.

Ned grinned at her and tentatively put his hands on her shoulders. "I hope I'm reading this right," he said. "Old fashioned people like me need words, Lissa."

"Okay," she said breathlessly. "Yes."

He pulled her closer. "I knew you were just as smart as you seemed." He gently nuzzled his lips in her hair. "Mmmm; your hair smells good."

Her cheek felt the dampness of his jacket, and she could feel his heart beating, matching her own. She tilted her chin and he brushed his lips gently over hers.

"We can do this any way you want," he murmured. "If you want to finish up school and establish yourself in a career, I'll be there applauding, I'd never try to stop you from becoming whatever you want to be."

"You couldn't anyway," she said demurely.

He laughed and held her tighter. "Don't I know it."

When he kissed her again, she closed her eyes and kissed him back, pressing into him, clinging to him.

"Ned," she said softly, "I have just learned something new about myself."

He tilted his head to see her face better.

"That I like kissing you," she murmured. "Is that why you came back here? Because you knew I wouldn't be able to resist?"

He grinned, at a loss for words.

Lissa smiled softly and backed away from him. "So Gorham is pretty, even in the winter?"

"Especially in the winter," he said. "And in summer the guy down the road grows strawberries that people can pick. And in the fall people have been known to have hay rides."

"How hokey of them." Lissa put out her mittened hand, palm up. Fat snowflakes landed there, each one different, each one exquisite. "I can't believe it's starting to snow again," she murmured.

"If you decide you don't like Gorham," he offered, "I'll go wherever you want."

"You better stop making promises you might not want to keep," Lissa warned him. "Anyway, how will I know whether I like it until I see it?" The desolate vacationland she recalled from her childhood might not be the real Gorham at all, she told herself. Gorham might actually be quaint. It might be pretty and friendly. How could it be so terrible? Ned would be there. Or maybe not, depending on Conor. "Your brother is lucky," she said.

"Yep, he now has two people who care about him."

She smiled. "Just what I needed. Another troublesome sibling."

"He likes you," Ned said simply. "And I think we should go see your family soon, too. To patch things up and see how much they really despise you."

"You mean you want to go with me?"

"Let me, Lissa. I want to meet them all. I want to meet Katie. You know, your fear that they can't forgive you for the fight with your mother - I think that's just your perception. I think you can't forgive yourself."

"I feel very unsure about it, and I don't like the feeling." She grimaced. "It's new to me."

"That doesn't surprise me. But you also have courage. And I'm on your side, whatever happens."

"What an amazing thing to say," she murmured.

"So we'll go to Gorham," he said casually, "and I want you to meet my father and Jim, see the house I grew up in." He wondered if he had lost his mind. Once she saw the seamier side of Gorham, she'd run fleeing back to the city. "I don't want to start something up without us being completely up front," he said. "You agree, right?"

She became thoughtful. "You know what I'd like, Ned? I'd like to see Gorham in a snowstorm. With you there, throwing logs on the fire."

"I don't have a fireplace, ma'am."

"Or making strange little canapés with ground beef and crackers."

He laughed. "We don't eat many canapés up in Gorham."

"Maybe not. But you probably serve up a mean bowl of chili."

He cocked an eyebrow. "I've never made chili in my life. I can grill chicken, though, and I can mop floors. Since my mother passed away, I've learned to do it all. You'll be impressed."

She placed one hand gently on his cheek. "Do you think I'm looking for someone who can mop floors? Is that what you think

I've been holding out for?"

"I guess not," he said, "but whatever it is, I'll be that. I think I already am that." He grinned at her. "You just didn't know it."

She smiled at him and turned away suddenly, walking toward the camp, then paused and turned back. "Ned, we've known each other less than a week. Is this stupid?"

Her face looked so sincerely concerned that he laughed. "Sure," he said. "But let's risk it."

She laughed, too, and started toward the cabin again. Gray smoke from her earlier fire still hovered lazily above the chimney. The late afternoon sun was misted in flurries. Ned watched her go, a fullness in his chest, a catch in his breathing.

They entered the camp and hung their jackets over chair backs. She noticed that he no longer wore a sling on his right arm. He looked healthy; he looked perfect.

"Will your family like me?" he asked her. She noticed a tremor in his voice, and it seared her soul.

"I don't need their approval," she said. Then she grinned. "They will love you." She knew it was true. Ned was exactly the kind of man her parents would have chosen for her. How miraculous that she had gained the wisdom not to discount him just because of that.

He sat in his usual chair, and she brought him his clothes from the bedroom.

"Do I get to hear your songs, too?" he asked. "If we're going to get this career going, someone has to be your audience."

She gazed at him thoughtfully. Her dreams of fame had been a bit unrealistic, she knew. Maybe with Ned's help she could gain the confidence to share her music. "You can hear them, but they aren't that great," she confessed.

"Well, you're smart. You can make them great."

"I guess my plan to be world famous was a little silly."

He gave her a crooked smile. "Not silly. You're never that. We can start small, just see where things go."

"All this time I thought I was the realistic one," she mused. "You came along and turned everything upside down."

He laughed. "I'm used to seeing things as they are. And you know, Lissa, 'as they are' sometimes turns out to be better than you expect."

"I guess that's true," she smiled. "Do you want lunch? I have more options now."

He grinned disarmingly at her. "I've been dreaming of the frozen blueberries I found that last night. They were mostly thawed, so they really ought to be eaten, unless you've already had them."

She moved to the refrigerator and pulled out a damp package.

"Do you really want these?" she asked. "We could go to Marcy Falls for lunch, dinner really, but meantime. . . ."

"Lissa," he said quietly, "I didn't really come back just for my clothes, you know."

"I know," she said breathlessly.

He got up from the chair, sauntered to her, and took the sticky berry bag from her hand, setting it on the table. He pulled her gently to stand before him. "What did I come back for?"

"For this?" She reached up and tangled her hands in his hair, kissing him. He smelled the sweet berries on her fingers, pungent and mouth-watering. "And this?" she murmured. Her lips found his again and she laughed quietly against him.

"To tell you I love you," he said simply. "I mean, I know it's too soon. . . ."

She stared at him, completely still. Where was the successful, educated man she craved? Where was the prominence? She was trading it all in on Ned Marchess, a simple, kind-hearted man who loved his brother, who wanted her and would stand by her, no matter what.

It was humbling and astonishing.

She leaned into him and felt the strength of his body send a ripple through her. It was amazing how he could hold her so tightly with one arm injured, this captor of hers, this man who had held her hostage, who still held her hostage, while the brilliant sky turned to dusk and the snow swirled in little cyclones, and the wind whispered around the windows of the little cabin nestled in the deep, lovely woods.

A NOTE FROM THE AUTHOR

As a mother of three and a teacher of college, high school, and middle school students, I know how the media can influence the attitudes and actions of young people. Adults, too, often search for books that tell a good story without all the graphic sex, blatant profanity or gory violence. You won't find those in my books; other media certainly give us our fill if that's what we're looking for.

Rather, I try to write books that I might encourage my students to read, stories I would enjoy myself, with realistic characters who have lifelike problems to solve. I hope you have found here an entertaining tale that captured your imagination, with characters you might like to know and a setting that sparks your interest, perhaps a bit of suspense, some mystery, crises solved and relationships salvaged, and a world view that underscores the inherent goodness of people.

Thank you for taking the time to read CAPTIVE. If you enjoyed the book, I would encourage you to tell your friends and to leave a review on Amazon to guide other readers, and if you notice things in the book that you feel merit my attention, I invite you to contact me at janpresto@gmail.com. I love to hear from readers!

Happy reading!
Jan Prestopnik

THANK YOU

. . . to my excellent initial readers: Rosemarie Sheperd, Amy Sponenberg, Tom Prestopnik & Nate Prestopnik, whose suggestions and remarks were helpful, thoughtful, and almost always entertaining.

Also, a special thanks to Nate for lending me his Grand Marquis for this story and especially for his talent and professional expertise in designing the perfect cover. You may see further examples of Nate's work on his website, *imperialsolutions.com*.

Thanks to my husband Rich for helping me with the technical aspects of preparing this book for publication. No wonder everyone loves you!

Last, thanks to my friends and large extended family (all the branches) for years of love and encouragement and many laughs. If family & friends are the world's blessings, then I am blessed in abundance!

JAN PRESTOPNIK, a retired teacher of college, high school and middle school English and writing, is married and the mother of three grown children. Camping, traveling, teaching, performing, reading great books, and savoring the atmosphere of her beloved Adirondack Mountains are some of the things that have influenced her writing.

TITLES BY THIS AUTHOR

Available in Paperback, Large Print, and Kindle editions

Captive (2014)

Quarter Past Midnight (2015)

Made in the USA
Middletown, DE
22 June 2021